THE GAMEKEEPER'S RELUCTANT BRIDE

CHARLESTON BRIDES ~ BOOK 6

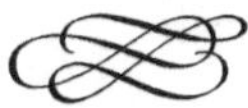

ELVA COBB MARTIN

WILD HEARt BOOKS

ISBN-13: 978-1-963212-10-5

"Nowhere else in the world has nature been kinder to her children than in those regions where the great plantations were formed out of the Eden-like wilderness of the Carolina Low Country. And that charm is an eternal one; though the civilization that it cradled and nourished has passed away, the charm survives."

— ARCHIBALD RUTLEDGE, OWNER OF HAMPTON PLANTATION, AUTHOR OF FIFTY BOOKS AND POEMS, AND SOUTH CAROLINA'S FIRST POET LAUREATE

"Jesus answered, 'Nicodemus, listen to this eternal truth: Before a person can perceive God's kingdom realm, they must first experience a rebirth...For this is how much God loved the world—He gave His one and only, unique, Son as a gift. So now everyone who believes in Him will never perish but will experience everlasting life.'"

— JOHN 3:3, 16, THE HOLY BIBLE, THE PASSION TRANSLATION

ACKNOWLEDGMENTS

I am forever grateful for my prayer partners who pray regularly for my writing. These include my husband, Dwayne; my two sisters, Sonya and Phyllis; my pastor, Rev. Phil Sears; Marilyn Krebs, Sandra Fowler, Evans and Sherry Massey, and Kay Maynard. In addition, we request and receive regular prayer for the writing from three ministry partners: Kenneth Copeland Ministries, Charles Capps Ministries, and Rick Renner Ministries.

Two wonderful writing partners who have been such a blessing to help proof the manuscript and respond to questions I often ran into are Colleen Hall and Libby Reed. Ladies, I thank you from the bottom of my heart, and please count on me to help with your projects any way I can.

I heartily thank my talented publisher, Misty Beller, and all her great editors and assistants at Wild Heart Books for taking my efforts and polishing them into something much finer.

And I thank God for you, all my readers who bless me by choosing to read my books and often send kind comments and post reviews. Thank you! Thank you!

Most of all, I thank my heavenly Father and Lord and Savior Jesus Christ and the Holy Spirit who continue to be with me, inspiring new stories and keeping me on task.

CHAPTER 1

CHARLESTON, SOUTH CAROLINA, 1815

In one swift motion, Helena Allston threw open the heavy damask drapes at her upstairs window to find the sight of her nightmares—George Beauregard on his white stallion, prancing up Allston Hall's front drive.

She would never marry the detested prig, no matter how hard her father pushed. And while John Allston was away on a merchant trip, this was the perfect opportunity to enact her escape plan to her aunt in England. She ran back into her luxurious boudoir and prepared.

Draping a simple green cloak over her riding frock, she pulled the hood over her pinned-up hair and glanced in the mirror. A servant girl with large blue eyes and a black curl escaping from the head cover stared back at her with determination—or was it fear? She patted the pouch of gold coins and the jewels hidden in her skirt that she would need for her escape and grabbed up her favorite riding crop.

At the door, she cast one last glance at her lavender silk and satin décor room, then hurried out and headed down the servants' entrance at the river side of the house. The jewels and pouch of coins bumped against her boots as she walked, and her heart raced as fast as her steps. The fresh, early-spring morning air filled her lungs as she stepped onto the expansive, grassy lawn with its patches of blooming daffodils and invitation to enjoy the lovely plantation. A pang of regret shot up her back. Could she really give all this up? A tingle of fear followed. Would her escape plan work? She lifted her chin and took a deep breath.

What could go wrong? With her cousin and best friend Rachel's help, she had put in place all the groundwork a week earlier, yet a sense of dread still tried to deflate her heart. She was leaving behind her home and family—the plantation that had been in her father's family for generations, their servants who acted like family to her, and most importantly, the memory and resting place of her sweet mother who had passed away from consumption when Helena was twelve.

Shaking sadness away, she hurried toward the stable. Stormy would take her the two miles down the Ashley River Road to the waiting rowboat. That, in turn, would take her to the English ship in the Charleston harbor. She'd hired a boy, the son of the rower, to ride Stormy back home.

The friendly, older British captain that Rachel had introduced her to had taken her trunk days ago. Thank God, he didn't know her planter and merchant father and didn't blink an eye at the name of Allston.

Another person flowed into Helena's thoughts and troubled her. Belle, her personal maid and friend, would be upset. Helena hadn't told her—or anyone in the household—about her plan to flee. But who knew what pressure her father would put on her or any slave for information once they found Helena was gone? But as everyone respected Belle's truthfulness, Helena's father and aunt would believe Belle when she said she didn't know about it.

She'd told Belle she would sleep late that day and not come to her until much later in the morning. She would write to Belle after she arrived in England. Perhaps she could even send for her. She snagged her lower lip with her teeth. Or would Aunt Aggie, her mother's sister, not welcome an extra servant to feed in her large household in Yorkshire?

As Helena entered the stables, the pleasant smell of hay and feed filled the crisp air. Horses peeked out from their stalls, nickering greetings. She patted a few soft noses goodbye as she hurried down the corridor to Stormy's stall. The dapple-gray Arabian mare lifted her head and whinnied when she saw Helena. Pressing a sugar cube to the mare's muzzle, she patted the strong neck and quickly pulled her into the corridor. She slid the bit in Stormy's mouth and fastened the English saddle on the silver back and mounted astride. Guiding the horse out the back entrance, she urged Stormy into a gallop toward the river on a little-used path.

With luck, no one from the house would see her leave. The servant who would answer George's knock on the front entrance would tell the man what she'd instructed Belle, that no one must disturb Miss Allston this morning. All other servants would be busy with their morning tasks. Aunt Sarah, at the breakfast table engrossed in the *Charleston Times,* could not see the path Helena took. The woman would have some choice words to spit out when she discovered the escape. A giggle escaped Helena. How nice to miss that tirade.

She followed the riverbank as fast as she dared until she came to the river road, then she urged Stormy into her fastest gallop.

Around the next bend, pounding hooves behind her shot a tremor up her spine. Glancing back, Helena stiffened in the saddle and tightened her knees. George Beauregard and his thoroughbred, bragged about as the fastest horse in Charleston, pursued her. How had he seen her leave the house?

Well, she'd show him. She knew these woods along the Ashley River a lot better than he did. She reined Stormy into the trees and raced through them, dodging limbs and jumping small gulleys, as she'd done since she was twelve. The tip of a limb snagged Helena's hood. Her hair sprang free from its pins, but she didn't slacken Stormy's pace. Behind, she saw the white stallion also turn off the road in pursuit. Drat George Beauregard. She'd give him the chase of his life.

At one point, she galloped back to the road and crossed to the other side, into a forest less familiar, but with the river always to her left, she'd be fine. Finally, when she no longer heard hoofbeats or saw flashes of white behind her, she crossed the road again and trotted back down near the river. She looked around. Where was the boat? Had she overshot the rallying point? Or not reached it yet?

She guided Stormy farther down the riverbank, thinking the meeting place was more distant. Passing through thick scrub trees, she galloped into a weeded area where the river turned away from her and flowed by a steep incline she didn't recognize. Stormy's sides heaved after the hard gallop, and Helena slowed her, then stopped to give the mare a chance to catch her breath. Had they entered the next parish during the wild gallop?

A sound behind her made her stiffen. She reined the mare around, and her heart stopped in her throat. How had he caught up with her? And he blocked her path back to the road. Grinding her teeth, she set her face in her sternest expression.

Smiling astride his sleek horse, George Beauregard broke through the scrub trees and laughed aloud when he met her glare. His stallion nickered at Stormy. "What a lovely sight you are, Helena, astride that gray streak with your gorgeous hair flying about your shoulders and anger tightening those lovely lips." His voice was a whiskey-infused croak, his laugh a bit too high-pitched and fake, like a drunkard trying to be merry with his friends. He stopped and dismounted, blocking her exit from the riverside. "I love an adventure like this, my girl. Why don't we just seal it with a kiss—or more? Then you'd be ready to marry me, no doubt."

He quickly twined the stallion's reins to a limb, never taking his eyes from her. His ridiculous figure in his blue satin morning suit, now ripped across the shoulders from passing through the trees in the chase, would've made her laugh except for the isolation pressing in on her.

Confidence lined his hard, sallow countenance, and his dark eyes gleamed like two pieces of coal in his bearded face. He had oiled dark hair combed straight back. The wild chase had not disturbed a single strand.

He swaggered down the narrow path between the thick riverside growth toward her. A seductive smile creased his thick lips. "Come now, Helena, you've nowhere to go with the river at your back and me blocking your way in front." He extended his soft jeweled hands and proceeded closer.

Panic welled in Helen's throat, and her heart pounded against her ribs. But she threw her head back and gave him her most disdainful challenge. "How dare you accost me like this, George Beauregard? My father will hear of this, and that will be the end of your suit. You're proving yourself no gentleman."

He folded his thin arms, his smirk widening. "Your father signed all the marriage papers with me last week, my little dear. And when I saw you out the back window riding away, I guessed your intention. Where can you go? Believe me, lovely Helena, you cannot escape me." He drew closer.

A whiff of his stale tobacco, alcohol, and heavy cologne sent shivers of revulsion through her. What could prevent him from having his way with her in this deserted place? Who would hear her loudest scream?

Stormy pawed the ground and tossed her head as the man approached.

Helena tried to swallow, but her mouth dried up like a potsherd. Taking a deep breath that ended with a sob, she gathered the reins tight and leaned down to whisper to the mare. "Forgive me, my friend. Jump high and wide. If we die, we die together." *Please, God, help us get over the embankment and into the deep part of the river.*

Stormy blew through her nose, arched her back, and sidestepped the approaching figure blocking the way back to the road.

"That's a good girl, Stormy." George extended his hand to reach for the mare's bridle.

With a gut-wrenching cry, Helena wheeled Stormy around and swung her riding crop down on the powerful rump. The mare reared with a high-pitched squeal and shot forward up the incline toward the river, flinging mud up behind her.

Curses burst out from George as Stormy leaped high over the ridge into the river. Helena's forehead banged against the hard, arched neck, and a scream exploded from her lips. The cold Ashley River closed over her and shut out sight, sound, and breath.

~

Just as Gideon Falconer emerged from the trees and scrub bushes along the rushing river, he heard a scream. A flying horse with a female aboard soared into the river almost overflowing from spring rains. Behind her, a foppish-dressed man stomped to the river's edge and cursed.

Gideon dropped the gun he'd been carrying across his shoulders. The large golden hound with him whimpered, but Gideon quieted him. "Sit, Bentley," he whispered.

When only the horse surfaced and swam to the far bank, the man hit his high boot with his riding crop and blackened the morning with louder curses. He walked down the river bank a few feet, returned to his horse, mounted, and galloped off.

Gideon shook his head in disbelief. The cur didn't even try to rescue the woman. Gideon ran to the river's edge, casting off his cloak and boots, and dove in. The icy water shocked his whole body, but he fought it and swam down deep. He searched underwater until he found the rider, her skirt caught on a rock. Jerking the fabric free, he rose to the surface with her in his arms. He strode from the river, laid her across his shoulder, and thumped her back as he'd once seen his father do in England when a child fell into the lake on their estate. Water spewed from her mouth and nose, and she gulped in air. He rejoiced. She would live. But then she fainted in his arms.

With gentle care, he laid her cold, shivering form on the mossy bank and covered her with his cloak. The hound came to sniff around her, and Gideon patted the large, soft head. "We've caught a very special fish today, Bentley."

The dog gave an excited bark as if he understood.

Gideon brushed long black strands of hair from the girl's face, beautiful even in deathly white and with a darkening bruise across her forehead. He tapped her thin, shivering shoulder. "Miss? Can you hear me?" She didn't respond, but short breaths continued to fan her full lips.

Quickly, he pulled on his boots and shouldered the gun. Then he wrapped her slender form in the cloak and lifted her in his arms. "Come, boy, we've got to see what we can do for this lassie."

After hiking several miles through a forest wilderness, he kicked open the door of his gamekeeper's cottage at Brighton Plantation and laid her on the single bed near the fireplace. He would not risk taking her up the stairs to a private bedroom. He needed to keep an eye on her. Stoking up the fire that he kept going in the chilly spring mornings, he busied himself about the place. Still, she didn't awaken. Concerned, he touched her icy hands, then her cold cheek. He paced across the floor, then ran his hand through his thick, dark hair. Right or not, he must get her out of her wet clothing and get her warm. For a fleeting moment, he thought of his dear mother in England. How he wished she were here to help with this. But she wasn't. And the plantation main house, awaiting its new owner, housed no servants either.

Closing the curtains to make the cottage dim for the young woman's modesty, Gideon removed her clothing. He tried to shield his eyes from her beauty. As he removed her skirt, he felt the heavy weight in the hem and a secret pocket sewed inside the garment, but he laid it aside. He dressed the girl in a set of his own clothes, which swallowed her from head to toe, then wrapped her in a warm blanket. He threw another log on the fire in the hearth and placed her clothing on chairs to dry. As he lifted the heavy riding skirt, a ruby necklace slid out onto his wooden floor, followed by a small pouch of coins.

Bentley came to sniff the objects, then padded to his bed near the fireplace and plopped down. He dropped his thick head onto his paws and rolled large, soulful eyes from his master to the still form on the bed.

Gideon replaced the pouch in the secret pocket of the girl's clothing but held up the necklace to a ray of sunlight entering through a slit in his curtains, and he whistled. "Bentley, do you see this shine?"

A movement on the bed drew his attention. He placed the necklace back in the concealed pocket and strode to her. "Hello, there. Are you awake?" He sat near her in a chair.

The girl's eyelids fluttered, and she stared up at him with eyes as blue as a summer sky but clouded with confusion. She didn't speak. The next moment, the dark lashes closed again.

He leaned down and touched her shoulder. "I'm Gideon Falconer. I fished you out of the Ashley River. What's your name?"

The delicate face creased into a frown, and a tear slipped down her cheek. Finally, a soft whisper came from dry, chapped lips. "I don't know." Then her chin dropped, and she fell back to sleep. Or had she lost consciousness again?

CHAPTER 2

Gideon frowned and leaned forward to examine the dark lump on his guest's forehead. Had this blow affected her memory? Soaking a cloth in cool water, he laid it on the injury. A doctor's visit would relieve his anxiety, but he dared not leave her alone to fetch the only one he knew miles away in another hamlet.

A silent prayer gushed from his heart. *Lord Jesus, You are the Great Physician. Please heal this young woman, cause the swelling to go down, and leave her remembrance intact.*

Gideon sat and stared at her as the light from the windows faded. Thunder rumbled over the cottage and lightning flashed. But that didn't awaken her. His heart stirred within him, and protectiveness washed over him for someone as weak and vulnerable as she appeared. But the girl also had courage and grit to jump into the river on horseback like she did to escape her pursuer. Admiration surged through him.

A wealth of black hair, loose and tangled from the river and shining like onyx, framed her shoulders. Full, dark lashes swept down over gently carved cheekbones and a perfect oval face. Lifting a small soft hand with long, sensitive fingers and neatly trimmed nails, he surmised the girl had never done manual labor. He thought of the expensive undergarments he'd removed earlier, still drying before the fire. Not a servant's clothing, like the outer garment. And the small fortune hidden in her inner pockets sealed it. The lovely young woman lying on his bed was no one's slave. So that marked runaway off his list. Could she be the daughter of a wealthy Ashley River planter?

But where was she going and why? And who was the overdressed gentleman pursuing her? His nostrils flared. That uncouth man cursed and didn't even try to rescue her from the river.

Gideon only left the cottage to get water and wood for the fire. He kept his vigil the rest of the day and fed the fire as rain pattered on the cottage shingles and sheeted off the porch roof. She did not awaken, but two or three times, she groaned, and he rushed to her side, as did Bentley. The dog licked her hand lying still on the blanket, then flopped back down on his little rug on the other side of the fireplace.

Late in the evening, Gideon lifted her head and got a few spoonsful of broth between her lips. He'd learned how to get a semiconscious person to drink liquid during the terrible years he spent as slaver ship captain before he had come to know Jesus Christ. He shook the terrible memories away as they tried to take over his mind. But God had forgiven him, hadn't He? He often battled doubt on that score and had determined to do everything in his power to help abolish slavery.

That night, he lay down on a pallet with his head turned toward the sleeping girl. He prayed it was sleep gripping her and not something worse.

Twice she awakened him with a terrible outcry. He went to her and fought the urge to take her into his arms to comfort her as he would a child. Instead, he patted her hand and spoke soothing words and whatever Scripture came to his mind until she quieted.

Bentley awakened him the next morning, licking his face. "Okay, boy. I know you want to go out and see if you can scare up a rabbit." He opened the cottage door to fresh spring air. The early rays of sunshine flowed in through the fir trees surrounding his gamekeeper's residence. Bentley flew across the porch and ran into the woods. The rain the day before made everything smell fresh, and a few daffodils, planted by an earlier resident, lifted their yellow heads just beyond the stoop. He took a deep breath and whispered a prayer of thanksgiving for the new day.

Gideon turned back into the cottage and swallowed his surprise and pleasure to see his patient leaning forward on an elbow, staring at him with wide, confused eyes. Her mass of dark hair flowed past her shoulders in lovely disarray.

He smiled and walked over to her, his heart skipping beats. She was even more lovely awake. "Well, hello. How do you feel?"

The porcelain forehead creased into a frown. She sat up, looked down at her clothing, and clutched the blanket closer. "Who are you and where am I?"

"I'm Gideon Falconer. You're in my gamekeeper's cottage on Brighton Plantation in the Princeton parish."

Her eyes widened. "How did I get here and where are my clothes?"

"I rescued you from the Ashley River yesterday morning. Do you remember jumping into the river on your horse?"

"There is no way I would've done something so foolish. Where are my clothes?"

Surprised at her response, he gestured to the chairs where her clothing had now dried.

She looked, then turned back to him, her face flaming, and her voice icy. "Who removed them?"

Gideon ducked his head and took a deep breath. "Look, young woman, I dragged you from the Ashley River and walked miles, carrying you in my arms, to this cottage. You were soaked through and through and unconscious."

She interrupted him. "I don't want to hear any more of your wild tale. Go from my presence and shut the door while I dress." She swung her feet from the bed and tried to stand but swayed and fell back. Her hands flew to her head. She cried out when she touched the lump on her forehead. "Why did you strike me, sir?" These words came out between gritted teeth.

Gideon's nostrils flared. "Miss or ma'am, whichever you are, I did not strike you. You must have hit your head on your horse's neck or a rock when you two jumped into the river." He took another deep breath. "For your information, all I did was save your life, if you'd like to thank me for that."

Bentley bounded up on the stoop and through the door. He went straight to the girl, sat, and lifted his head for a pat, panting from his morning run.

The girl removed her hand from her injury and looked at the dog. She reached out, patted the large head, and the animal walloped his tail on the cabin floor.

Gideon folded his arms. "Bentley was as concerned about you as I was."

She lifted her eyes to him without comment, then looked around the cabin and frowned.

"We're both glad you've gained consciousness. Are you hungry?"

She touched her middle. "Yes. But I ordered you to go away until I dress."

Gideon turned and went out the door, shaking his head. What a proud, unthankful young woman who had much to learn. He walked to the back of the house to a hen coop and gathered several eggs in a basket. He'd not even thought of gathering eggs the day before when he'd kept watch over his patient. His beautiful but ungrateful patient, it turned out.

He sat on the stoop until Bentley scratched at the door from inside. "Are you dressed, miss?" he called out and tried to keep his voice kind.

No answer.

Bentley barked.

"Miss, if you don't answer me, I'm coming in."

Silence.

He opened the door, ready to duck if she was the throwing kind. He entered and set the basket of eggs on the table.

She sat on the cot fully dressed but with a blanket across her shoulders, her full lips scrunched into a pout.

"Is there, uh, anything I can help with?"

She turned a stormy glance at him and exhaled an exasperated breath. "I need help with the back buttons on this blouse and on my wrists. I can't seem to do it. Where are your servants?"

Gideon walked toward her. So this girl had dressing help. Another proof she was no one's servant if he hadn't enough evidence already. "I don't have any servants, miss, except one freedman who's more a friend, and he's gone to visit his mother in the next parish. I'm all the help you have."

She grimaced and dropped the blanket. He reached behind her to button the garment. He had to push aside her hair hanging in riotous curls down her back to reach the buttons. Touching those thick, curly strands and her closeness did something to his breathing. Her womanly scent, still sweet after almost drowning in the river, wafted across his nose. When she lifted white slender hands for him to button the sleeves at her wrists, he dared not glance into her face. He finished the buttons and stepped back, then stooped to lift a locket on a lavender ribbon from the floor.

"This must have fallen from your clothing." He read the inscription. *Helena.*

She reached for it, turned it over in her hand, then thrust the item into her pocket. Leaning back against the cabin wall, she folded her hands. "I will take some eggs and bacon when you have them ready."

Dismissed by her proud gaze and words, Gideon frowned and turned toward the little kitchen. *And thanks for appreciating my first ever button-assist work, young lady, not to mention saving your life, Helena, or whoever you are.*

~

*H*elena swallowed a lump of fear and watched the man preparing breakfast. What had happened to her? Where was she? Who was she? The name on the locket seemed familiar, but that was all. She kept a stiff expression on her face, determined not to betray her confusion to her rescuer. Or was he her kidnapper? Was his name really Gideon Falconer?

She studied him as he prepared breakfast. He looked tough, lean, and sinewy. His massive shoulders filled the shirt he wore. He moved about the cabin with nonchalant grace and virility. His bearded face, bronzed by wind and sun, enhanced a rigid profile. Short, deep-brown curly hair covered his head, and some fell in a swath over his wide forehead above piercing gray eyes. The beard covered his face from his broad cheekbones to his chin. and a mustache lined his upper lip. Tall and strong, like a ship's main mast. She had to admit he was as handsome as any man she'd ever met. Then she cast that thought aside.

His large capable hands, maneuvering an iron skillet over the fire, had surprised her earlier by buttoning the tiny buttons on her clothing. A tingle went up her spine as she recalled the warm effect of his closeness as he bent to help her. His manly scent, reminiscent of pine forests, green moss, and sunshine, had flooded over her, making her breath hitch.

The smell of bacon frying filtered through the air, and her stomach growled. She patted her middle and continued her evaluation of Gideon. The conversation of the man, his movements, his demeanor, and his gentle treatment of her reflected something noble, aristocratic about him. But if that were true, where were his servants, and why did he live in a simple cabin?

He turned and caught her staring, and his lips parted in a dazzling display of straight white teeth.

Heat flowed into her cheeks, and she pretended to look at the fire as he finished the bacon and started on the eggs.

Bentley roamed around the room and barked, then flopped back down on his mat.

Gideon laughed. "Hungry, boy? I've got your name in this pan too." His confident voice filled the morning with good humor.

Breakfast proved a quiet affair, except for the large dog who snuffed his portion down, then sat on his haunches between them, begging for their scraps. Helena could not help noticing her host's good table manners and how, after seating her, he seemed happy to serve her, refilling her cup of tea, offering her more helpings of the delicious repast. Had he ever had servants to serve at table? The man was a mystery.

She finished her meal, touched her cloth napkin to her lips, and pushed her chair back.

Hoofbeats sounded in the yard, then heavy boots on the porch. She froze, and her eyes flew to her host.

Gideon threw down his napkin and stood. "It's my man and good friend returning from visiting his relatives in the Goose Creek parish." He strode to the door and swung it open, then hugged the man who entered. He could've been Gideon's twin in size and strength except for his dark skin and tight, springy black hair. They parted and patted each other on the back.

"My friend, how was your mother and family? I've missed you around here for the past two weeks."

The black man's eyes brightened, then they fell on Helena and widened an inch. His face stiffened and turned a shade lighter.

Gideon's lips thinned, and he turned his visitor back onto the porch and shut the door behind the two of them.

His strong voice echoed through the entrance. "I can explain."

Helena put her hand over her mouth. What had she fallen into? How could she ever escape from these two? If she only knew how to really, really pray.

~

Gideon clapped his hand on Samson's shoulder as they stepped off the porch. "It's not what you think, my man. I did not bring a woman to live here while you were gone." He smiled. "I rescued the almost-drowned young lady you just saw from the Ashley River yesterday morning."

Surprise faded from Samson's face, but his dark eyes sparked with interest. "The Ashley River?"

"Yes. She hit her head somehow and doesn't know who she is or where she's from, or I'd had her home long before now."

Samson folded his arms across his chest and rocked back on his heels and grinned. "Well, sir, you may be in some very hot water."

Gideon frowned. "For rescuing a drowning young woman?"

Samson's eyes flashed back toward the cabin. "For rescuing a rich planter's daughter and keeping her here alone overnight with no chaperone." He leaned forward. "We heard talk yesterday in my mother's parish about a rich planter by the name of Allston whose daughter disappeared riding near the Ashley. We understood the father was on some kind of merchant trip, but a great search did take place all day yesterday and up into the night, with no results."

Gideon expressed his thanksgiving. "Thank God we now have a last name. It's got to be the same young woman."

Samson raised his brows. "She's very pretty, boss. And you've been here all day yesterday and all night with her alone?"

Gideon balled his fist and swung at the man's shoulder. "Listen, you sly fox. You know I'd never take advantage of a woman."

"Oh, yes, I know. But what's that big papa gonna think?"

Gideon sucked in a breath. "I hope he'll be glad I saved her life, you mule. Go take care of your horse, and I'm going to see if the name of Allston will jolt back our guest's memory."

Samson, shaking his head, loosened his tethered horse and headed to the stable and his apartment above it.

Gideon strode up the steps and back into the cottage. Helena now sat on the edge of the cot, and she lifted angry eyes toward him. Or was it fear he saw in those flashing depths? He pulled a chair near and sat in front of her.

"Does the name Allston mean anything to you, young lady?"

CHAPTER 3

$\mathcal{H}$elena gasped and burst into sobs. Between bouts of tears, she answered him. "Yes, yes, I'm Helena Allston. It's all coming back. I live at Allston Hall." She swiped her cheeks with the back of her sleeve and reached out to touch Gideon's arm. "My horse, Stormy? What about my mare? Did she...?"

"Never fear, I saw your horse climb out on the other side of the river. I'm sure someone found her and returned her home, or she made her own way back."

Helena stood and paced across the room as the full impact of her situation dawned on her. She couldn't help wringing her hands. Home? She glanced around the simple cottage and at the man who called himself Gideon. Her father would be furious at what she'd done. A cold chill shook her. She'd spent the night here alone with her rescuer. She could hear Aunt Sarah's always proper voice that had chided and corrected her since her precious mother passed. The elderly woman's icy blue eyes would flash in anger. *Well, young lady, you've done it now. Your reputation will forever be in shreds when Charleston society hears of your stay overnight alone in the company of a man you say rescued you.*

Gideon stood. "I'll go saddle my horse. He can easily carry both of us. I think I know where Allston Hall is. It will be about a two-hour ride." He strode from the room.

After he left, Helena wiped her face and wished for a comb, pins, to do something, anything, with her tangled hair. She spied a small mirror over a cabinet on the opposite wall, a shaving glass. She glanced in it and stamped her foot. Her hair was a matted mess. She'd never get it in order even if she had a comb or brush. But Belle, dear Belle, would get the job done as soon as she got home. Her heart lifted.

She searched her skirt lining and confirmed her hidden pouch of gold coins and jewels had survived her ordeal. Pulling the purse of coins out, she walked over to the table, still laden with breakfast dishes, and laid it at Gideon's place.

He walked in the door behind her. His gaze fell on the small bag. "What are you doing, my lady?"

Warmth suffused her cheeks, but she met his eyes. "It's my payment for what you did for me. My father would insist."

He stepped forward, scooped up the purse, and returned it to her. "I want nothing for rescuing and sheltering you here. It's what any human would've done in my place."

"But there was another human who saw what happened. You haven't told me what the man did after I jumped into the river to escape him."

Gideon's face hardened. "Was he kin of yours?"

"No, absolutely not."

"He just cursed, looked up and down the river a few moments, then mounted his horse and galloped off."

"Sounds just like what George Beauregard would do. Not much humanity in his entire frame." She dropped her chin. "To avoid marriage to him, I planned my escape, but clearly, it didn't go well."

Gideon's lips twitched. Then he smiled. "Well, one good thing, you got to meet me, a lowly gamekeeper, and Bentley, a mighty fine dog."

She fixed her eyes on him. Was he serious? She'd be part of his humor. "Yes, of course, that's two good things. Goodbye, Bentley."

Gideon bent and patted the large blond head. "Boy, you guard the place while I'm gone. Samson will check on you soon."

The dog barked and wagged his tail.

Helena followed Gideon out of the cabin and admired the large black stallion saddled and waiting. His muscled form and strong legs impressed her, as did his fine wide forehead and well-shaped ears.

Gideon swung up into the saddle, then reached for her hand. She lifted her skirt and placed her foot in the stirrup beside his boot, then she gave him her hand. He pulled her up in front of him as though she weighed no more than a feather. The stallion didn't snort or bulge a muscle as her skirt spread across his shoulder. She tried to sit forward and not lean against Gideon.

"You can forget not leaning, Helena. Haven't you ever ridden double before?"

"Actually, not since I was about five and Papa would let me ride in front of him on days he checked on the plantation."

She leaned against his hard chest. He gathered strong arms around her and grasped the reins in his big square hands. His heartbeat rose in steady rhythm behind her, and his woodsy, fresh scent enveloped and tantalized her. Taking a quick breath of astonishment, she forced her mind away from the man so close his breath warmed the top of her head. How would she ever convince Aunt Sarah nothing had happened alone with this handsome man during a day and night in his cabin?

He made a clicking sound, and the horse started down the sandy road at a fast, smooth gait, one she'd never experienced before. It was neither a trot nor a gallop.

"What kind of horse is this, and what gait is he doing?"

"Hero is a Morgan, and this gait is called racking. How do you like it?"

"It's great. No bumping. And I'm amazed he isn't minding our riding double, nor my skirt flapping on his shoulder."

"Their easy temperament is another trait that makes Morgans special."

The sun, high in the afternoon sky, beamed down on them when the horse brought them to the large wrought-iron gate to Allston Hall. A young black boy about ten or eleven jumped down from his perch as they arrived.

His eyes bulged as he stared at them. "Miz Allston, ma'am, is that you?"

"Yes, Jimmy, open the gate."

He scrambled around and drew the gate wide. They entered the long, oak-lined drive, and the boy shut the gate behind them, then took off at a fast run past them across the field and through the trees toward the house.

She sighed. He'd have the entire Hall alerted before they arrived.

Helena snagged her lip between her teeth at the thought of confronting stiff, unforgiving Aunt Sarah. Thank God her father would not be back until the end of the week, but she must face her aunt today.

As they approached the front entrance with its large, columned porch, her heart lurched. Not only did her aunt stand there with her austere face and haughty manner, but every house servant lined the perimeter.

"Looks as though they might be glad to see you, Helena—back from the dead, as it were." Gideon's strong, confident voice with a smile behind her did nothing to still the dread gripping her.

~

*G*ideon reined Hero to a halt in front of the steps, and Helena slid down. She turned toward him. "Please, you must dismount...and tell my aunt what happened."

Gideon observed the only white face amid black countenances— an older lady in a regal day dress standing stiffly near the door with her arms folded. She made no effort to come and hug her niece, now returned alive and well. Right. A battle-axe in a skirt. He dismounted.

A servant appeared at his side, and he handed him the reins and followed Helena up the steps.

A squeal emerged from the gathered servants, and a young black woman a few years older than Helena pushed her way toward them. She grabbed Helena and hugged her with tears streaming down her face. "Thank the Lord, thank the Lord, you are safe."

Helena accepted the happy greeting of the person she called Belle, but her eyes never left her aunt. The woman watched the hug, heard the words, but without a trace of her own emotion.

"Hello, Aunt Sarah. May I present Gideon Falconer? He saved my life."

The woman sniffed and looked Gideon up and down. "I'm glad you're home safe, Helena, but I want to talk to you and your Mr. Falconer in the front parlor."

"He's not my Mr. Falconer, Aunt Sarah. He rescued me when I was drowning."

"Come along." Before entering the house, she turned to the gathered servants. "Run along now, all of you, and get back to your posts. This is not a holiday."

Her stern voice made them scatter like chickens before a thunderstorm.

Gideon pulled his hat from his head and followed the woman and Helena into a lovely parlor decorated in shades of blue and yellow.

"You two sit there." The aunt gestured to a sofa and large stuffed chair. Gideon chose the chair. Helena sat on the edge of the brocade sofa.

"Now, first, Helena, why did you leave Allston Hall as you did?"

"Surely, you've guessed, Auntie. I do not intend to marry George Beauregard. Ever. I was attempting to run away to England to my mother's sister in Yorkshire."

"You need have no fear of a marriage with George, young lady. I doubt he's still interested."

Helena's eyes flashed at her aunt. "But you haven't even heard what he did. Who cares if he's not interested anymore?"

"What did he do?" Her aunt crossed her hands in her lap.

"He followed me when I left on Stormy. In fact, he chased me so far down the Ashley River that I lost my way. He confronted me, threatened to...pull me from Stormy in that deserted place. And my only recourse was to jump into the river to escape him." Helena swiped tears starting down her face.

Gideon sat forward, surprised at the aunt's brittle stare. "And that's where my part of the story begins. I am custodian and game-keeper at Brighton Plantation, which is awaiting its new owner. That morning, I'd been checking the estate's outlying acreage and doing a little hunting with my dog. I saw the whole thing Helena is telling you. The man had no good intentions. I understand exactly why she forced her horse to jump in the Ashley. After she did, her mount surfaced and pulled itself out on the opposite riverbank. Beauregard just cursed a blue streak, looked up and down the river for a few moments, then jumped on his horse and galloped away without a single effort to rescue Helena. I dove in and found her skirt caught on a rock and rescued her."

The woman sniffed and pointed a bony finger at Gideon. "And why didn't you bring my niece home yesterday, young man?"

Helena twisted her hands in her lap and dropped her chin.

"Because she hit her head after she jumped, and it affected her memory. You can see the bruise. She was unconscious. Not knowing who she was, my only choice was to take her to my cottage at Brighton until she recovered and could tell me who she was. That occurred this morning. And here we are."

"How many servants did you have in your house yesterday and last night to assist with Helena's care, Mr. Falconer?"

Gideon took a deep breath and remained silent for a moment. "None. My one man was away visiting relatives."

The aunt stood, her face a tight mask. She walked over to the mantel and looked at both of them, but she spoke to her niece. "Helena, you know as well as I do what Charleston society will say about your spending a day and night alone with..." She glanced at Gideon but didn't use his name. "Alone with any man. Your reputation will be in shreds in a matter of days. Our servants who saw your disheveled arrival today will tell other servants. You know how stories travel fast, my girl." She balled a tight fist and tapped the mantel. "I can't imagine how your father can hope to deal with this and it come out in any good way, as he's done in the past with your lapses."

Gideon swallowed ire rising in his throat. "Ma'am, am I to assume you're not happy your niece is alive and not at the bottom of the Ashley River?"

She turned steely blue eyes on him. "Of course, I'm glad, Mr. Falconer, but you obviously have no concept of what's expected of a lady like our Helena and how this episode can ruin her life." The woman took a deep breath. "Helena, go upstairs and get presentable. I've never seen you look so disheveled."

Helena rose to leave, as pale as Gideon had ever seen her. He wanted to reach out to her. Assure her. Do something, but the aunt's voice stopped any idea of doing so as he stood up.

"And, young man, you may go. I'm sure Helena's father will want to talk to you at length when he returns from the islands. He's due back Friday. You'll hear from him. Good day, sir."

He walked out of the house without being able to say goodbye to Helena. As he exited, he saw her going up the staircase, swiping tears, with a maid behind her—the one who'd shown real happiness to see her back safe.

God, bless Helena Allston and protect her.

～

*H*elena trudged up the stairs feeling as though a hundred-pound weight pressed on her back. Her aunt would undoubtedly make things worse with her father when he returned.

"Miss Helena, I've alerted the kitchen for hot water and the tub. We'll have you put to rights very soon." Her dear Belle's voice shook some of the despair away.

Yes, a bath, shampoo and clean clothing would be wonderful. "I can't wait to get out of these garments." As soon as she reached her room, she peeled off everything with Belle's help and slipped into a silk robe to wait for the tub and buckets of hot water.

Belle insisted she start working on some of the knots in Helena's hair before bathing, so Helena sat at her dresser as her maid's sure hands went to work.

"What's this bruise on your forehead, my lady?"

"I promise I'll tell you the whole story, just tell me what happened here after you discovered I was gone."

Words flowed from her friend. "Yesterday, after the midday meal, a boy and his father came up the drive leading Stormy and shocked all of us. I burst into tears knowing you'd never willingly leave that fine mare of yours."

Helena looked at Belle in the mirror. "So Stormy is safe and well?"

"Yes, I'm happy to say, but the whole household here assumed you'd..." Belle swallowed and swiped at her eyes. "Drowned, because the boy told us he'd found your horse on the Ashley riverbank, soaking wet. *Allston Hall* was stamped on the saddle." She stopped her work on Helena's hair to wipe her own face with a handkerchief.

"Well, George Beauregard is responsible for this whole situation." Helena told Belle the entire story.

Belle listened, then folded her arms and smiled. "The man Gideon, he is most handsome. He hardly took his eyes off you in the yard. You spent the night...alone?"

Helena stamped her foot. "Stop that kind of thinking right now, Belle. Nothing happened between me and Gideon Falconer. He's a perfect gentleman. My virtue is intact, if you must know. He rescued me, saved my life, and brought me home as soon as my memory returned. End of story."

If only the story would end there. Despair clogged her throat.

~

Gideon rode back to Brighton Plantation at a leisurely pace, his mind filled with Helena. The cool reception of her aunt disturbed him. She might have been happier if he'd come to report her niece's death. And would her father still insist she marry George Beauregard? His nostrils flared. He prayed not.

On Friday, he and Samson were cleaning out the stables when a rider galloped into the yard on a fine bay stallion, his good bloodlines evident. "Message for Mr. Gideon Falconer," the young, breathless man announced as they stood in the barn door.

"I'm Gideon. What's the message?"

"The Honorable John Allston demands your presence at Allston Hall."

Gideon stood his tallest and crossed his thick arms. "Demands?"

The man blinked. "Those were his exact words...sir." He added the last word with an apologetic air, after looking Gideon up and down.

Samson exhaled, clapped Gideon on the shoulder, and whispered aside, "What did I tell you, man? Big Papa will have his say, and should I add, his way?"

Gideon shrugged and addressed the young man in his most noble voice. "You may return and tell your master it will be my pleasure to answer his summons in the morning before noon." He frowned at the lathered horse. "Meanwhile, why don't you cool, then water your mount, and give him a break? And don't ride him so hard back home. Understand?"

The messenger ducked his head and walked the stallion around the yard for several minutes under Gideon's watchful eye, then headed to the well and watering trough. After he relieved his own thirst and that of the horse, he remounted and started back at a more leisurely pace. He cast one last glance at Gideon still watching.

"Remember, your master will be angry if you run that fine horse into the ground, young man." Who knew what the youngster would do when he got out of sight?

Midmorning of the next day, Gideon arrived at Allston Hall. He'd made some effort to look his best to face Helena's father. The man must see Gideon as a gentleman whose word he could trust. He'd do anything to help Helena. Wouldn't he? He couldn't think of her without his heart tripping but didn't take time to analyze that feeling as a servant escorted him into John Allston's study and left.

A gray-headed man of medium height, thick about the girth, rose from behind a wide, shiny desk and dumped his pipe. His blue eyes, so like Helena's, brightened as they took in Gideon.

He came from behind the desk and held out his hand. "I'm John Allston. Thank you for coming."

Gideon shook his hand. "Gideon Falconer, sir, at your service."

"Please have a seat." Allston gestured to a red leather chair in front of the desk.

Gideon removed his hat and sat, breathing in the smell of tobacco, books, and leather.

Allston returned behind the desk and sat. He leaned back in his chair and steepled his fingers. He looked like a man in the habit of giving orders and receiving immediate obedience. "Mr. Falconer, thank you for rescuing my daughter. She's the only light in my life since her mother passed. I've heard Helena's story. Now let me hear yours, sir."

Gideon met the man's blue eyes without flinching. He told of his rescue and his care of her until her memory returned and he brought her home.

When he finished, John Allston sat silent for a few moments. Was the man ruminating on the story or was he evaluating Gideon?

"You'll be pleased to know, I've torn up Helena's marriage contract with Beauregard. I've guessed he didn't attempt to rescue her after his dastardly chasing her into the river. Thank you for saving her life. You have my eternal thanks."

"You and she are most welcome, sir." Gideon smiled. Relief flooded him that she would not marry the pompous coward.

Allston refilled and relit his pipe. "I know Brighton's former owner who hired you to work for him. We were in the same club. He spoke about you. I understand you emigrated from England a few years back, and that you not only have estate management experience, but once even sailed as captain of a ship. Is this so?" He took a draw from the pipe and exhaled, and the pungent smell of tobacco floated over the room.

Gideon rubbed his beard. "Actually, sir, the truth is, I didn't emigrate from England. I fled arrest for allowing starving cottagers to take small game from my employer's large estate where I worked as a gamekeeper. Before that, I did once sail a ship, to my shame now, to the African coast where we took on slaves for the islands. But when I became a believer in Jesus Christ, I totally forsook the slave trade and now stand for abolition with people like John Newton, who led me to Christ, and his great friend, William Wilberforce."

"I've heard of those two." Allston didn't smile. "What slave owner hasn't? But tell me, how did you connect to the owner of Brighton Hall?"

"My aunt, Sophia Rutledge, helped me obtain the position as estate manager."

The man's eyes brightened. "You're related to the Rutledges?"

"Yes, Sophia's husband was my mother's brother. Mother married a Falconer."

"So, just as your employer told me, you're really a gentleman, a noble's son who fell on hard times due to mismanagement of the estate by a relative after your father passed." It was a statement, not a query. He dumped his pipe again and leaned forward. "Now I need to ask you a question, sir." The man's eyes blazed into Gideon's. "Did you violate my daughter when she was in your care? She says not, but what do you say on your honor as a gentleman?"

Gideon stiffened and stood. "I assure you, sir, I did not. Honor or no honor."

"All right, I believe you, as well as my daughter. Please sit down. I have one more question."

Gideon sat on the edge of the chair, his muscles still rigid.

"Again, I thank you for saving my daughter's life. She's all I have." The man leaned closer across the desk, his eyes softened. "Now I need you to save her again."

Gideon's breath caught in his throat, and his eyes widened.

"Save her reputation. No one in Charleston will believe she's not lost her virtue since spending a day and night alone with you in your cottage. My sister, Sarah, is right on that score."

Licking his dry lips, Gideon swallowed and croaked out a query of his own. "What exactly are you asking me, John Allston?" Samson's earlier warning splashed over him in force.

"I am asking you, sir, to marry my daughter."

CHAPTER 4

Gideon sat speechless, his heart threatening to pound out of his chest. Marry Helena Allston, the most beautiful young woman he'd ever seen? And the most spoiled, he had to admit. But the thought of marriage to her stirred him in the deepest part of his being and with an excitement he'd never felt before. He swallowed and blinked. Had he already made an emotional tie with Helena Allston that could grow into love? But what John Allston was suggesting was preposterous. He took a deep breath. "Sir, surely, you don't want your daughter to flee another marriage you've planned."

"She won't flee. Helena's willing. You only need to ask her. And I need to tell you a cotton plantation comes with her, and she will one day inherit my entire estate."

Heat flooded up Gideon's neck, and he stood, stiff as a board. He plopped his hat on his head. "Mr. Allston, I would never marry Helena or any other woman to receive even ten plantations or estates." He stomped toward the door.

But John Allston jumped up, hurried around his desk, and blocked Gideon's exit. The effort cost him. His face paled, and his breathing became labored. With his back to the door, he looked up into Gideon's face. His words came fast. "Forget the plantation. Think only of Helena." The man loosened his collar and sucked in a deep breath. "I tell you she needs rescuing now more than the day you dove into the Ashley River."

His voice held a pleading tone that wrapped around Gideon's heart. He backed up, removed his hat, and ran a hand through his hair. Helena's young, lovely face and bright eyes floated before him. She often intervened in his daylight hours now and quite a few of his dreams. If he weren't already, how hard could it be to fall in love with such a woman? *Lord, what do I do?*

Several questions bombarded Gideon's mind. One he threw at Allston, who still stood as if guarding the door. "You don't understand. Besides neither of us being in love with the other, I'm a Christian, and of the Moravian faith. I could never marry a nonbeliever."

John Allston threw out his chest. "My good sir, Helena is a believer. Maybe not as strong as some of you Moravians. Since a babe, she's been part of the church and received confirmation when she came of age."

"But we hardly know each other...and there's the age difference."

"How old are you?"

"Twenty-nine."

The man leaned toward him and smiled. He laid a hand on Gideon's shoulder and pressed him toward the chair he'd occupied. "Helena is seventeen, almost eighteen, but the age difference matters not one whit, sir. And perform your courtship after you marry. As her mother and I did. We need the marriage to take place as soon as possible to stop the tongues wagging that will ruin Helena's life and relegate her to social ostracism and spinsterhood."

Gideon sank into his chair. "I need to think, sir." *Pray.* Social ostracism and spinsterhood? Who could knowingly wish that kind of life on the young woman he saved from the Ashley River? But marriage?

Allston patted his shoulder. "Certainly, take your time, Gideon. But not too long. I'll leave you for now." He left and pulled the door closed behind him.

The swoosh of the heavy door seemed an omen to Gideon. Was life as he'd known it somehow embedded in that closing sound?

Gideon tried to pray. He closed his eyes and leaned his head against the back of the chair, hardly able to put a prayer into words but calling out to God, anyway. He did not know how long he sat thus...until he became aware of another presence and a fragrance in the room.

"Is the thought of marrying me causing you that much pain, Gideon?"

He bounded out of the chair, and his breath stopped in his throat at the vision of Helena standing before him. He'd never seen such a poised, lovely young woman as the one clothed in a sky-blue silk dress that magnified her eyes. Nothing of the water sprite he'd rescued remained. Roses blossomed in her cheeks, and gems blazed at her throat and on her earlobes. The black tresses he'd only seen damp and matted by river water now fell in long, silky curls that framed her face and made her look more mature than her seventeen years.

He blinked and swallowed. Then a deep excitement sparked through him. His sanity and male enchantment of beauty came into full play. He smiled and gave Helena a courtly bow. "Causing me pain? Not in the least, Miss Allston." He would make light of the serious situation and give her a chance to back out if her heart chose. Surely, her father had misjudged her mind. "I'm simply dumbfounded that you might even consider marriage to a simple gamekeeper such as myself."

"We both know that's not all you are, Mr. Falconer. As far as consider a proposal, I don't have one from you to consider." Her skirt swished as she moved a step closer. Her rose scent enveloped him, and her blue eyes challenged him and looked as though they held a secret.

His heart thundered, and something like warm oil flowed over him. She was inviting him to propose. How could it be? Was this God's answer? What should he say? Should he get down on one knee? Instead, he reached for her small hand and lifted it to his lips.

Then he cleared his throat. "Miss Helena Allston, will you do me the honor of becoming my wife?"

"Yes, Mr. Falconer. I will." Then she pulled her hand away and turned and left the room, her silk skirts whispering behind her.

Gideon stood stunned, hardly believing what had just transpired. He'd proposed. The beautiful Helena Allston had accepted. But was that a tear he saw in the corner of her eye? His lips tightened. This would never do. How could any Christian gentleman marry a reluctant bride that her father and aunt had unduly influenced?

He strode from the room to follow her, but the hall proved empty. Then the sound of a door sliding into place sounded up the way. He walked to that entrance and pushed it open. It led into a parlor, elegant in mauve and gray fabrics and window treatments.

Helena stood at a long window, looking out over the front lawn, weeping. The sound of her grief clutched his heart. He strode to her and put his hands on her trembling shoulders, and she turned to face him. With his thumb, he gently wiped the tears from her soft cheeks.

"Listen to me, Helena. You do not have to marry me, or anyone you don't want to, as far as your reputation is concerned. You can weather whatever the Charleston old biddies might dish out. And my aunt Sophia will be happy to help you do it."

Helena sniffed and tried to smile. "Yes, I know of her, and she probably could and would." She looked into Gideon's eyes, and his heart melted. "I want to marry you. It's the best way to solve...everything, including making Papa happy. He's not well, you know."

"No, I didn't know that. He looks strong and capable to me. So what is the real problem?" His heart lurched. Was marriage to him so distasteful? He could understand her reaction to the dandy Beauregard, but surely, she didn't think of him as the same type. The idea curled his lip.

She turned from him to gaze out the window. "It's just that this was...never the way I dreamed of receiving a proposal. We scarcely know each other." She swallowed and glanced back into his face. "But I know you'll treat me...well."

A shock rolled up Gideon's spine. Was she concerned, nervous about the intimate marriage relationship? Well, he could put her mind to rest on that score. He spun her around to face him. "Helena, if we marry, I will never ask you to fulfil certain wifely duties, such as consummate our marriage, until you're ready. Does that ease your mind?"

Her eyes widened. "You'd do that?"

"Yes, you have my word. Your father even suggested we go through the courtship period we missed...after the wedding."

She breathed what sounded like a sigh of relief. Her tantalizing, soft lips were inches from his face, and her rose scent delighted him. "But there's one thing we will do, the normal thing to seal a marriage proposal."

He drew her close into his arms, then lifted her chin with his thumb. He gently touched her lips with his own, and a jolt gripped him from head to toe. He pressed her into the curve of his chest and kissed her again, a more telling, passionate kiss. When he raised his head, he started to release her, but her knees gave way. He chuckled, swept her into his arms, and carried her to a nearby chair. As he sat her down, she looked up at him with awe, or was it fear in those cloudy eyes?

A movement near the door, which he'd not heard open, drew Gideon's attention. Helena's father strode toward them, grinning. "I'm happy to see the courtship is progressing in leaps and bounds."

At the sight of him, the blood drained from Gideon's face. From the corner of his eye, he saw the roses deepen in Helena's cheeks. He addressed the man. "Sir, I..."

Allston shook his head. "No explanation needed, Gideon. It's wise to get your mark on these Southern belles as soon as possible, and she does look marked." He grinned and patted Helena's shoulder, then rubbed his hands together. "Now, we've a wedding to plan."

Riding back to Brighton Plantation, Gideon couldn't calm his shocked senses at what had transpired at Allston Hall. He'd proposed, the beautiful Helena Allston had accepted, and the wedding would take place next Friday in their church chapel for family only. He would be able to invite Aunt Sophia. But all these thoughts only floated on the perimeter of his mind. The blazing memory of Helena's soft lips responding to his own displaced all other thoughts and kept his heart beating faster than Hero's racking gait all the way back home.

~

*B*efore sleeping that night, Helena gave in to the pressing need to relive Gideon's kiss. Her heart raced, and she touched her lips in wonder. All day, she'd kept that kiss pushed away to focus on plans for the small wedding. Tomorrow Charleston's finest seamstress would arrive to begin the wedding dress. She'd never dreamed of a kiss such as Gideon pressed upon her. Only his strong arms kept her from fainting. And then to discover her father may have witnessed it all made her cringe again.

Surely, it was a kiss of love.

But could Gideon Falconer really be falling in love with her? Doubts plagued her until her common sense and an overheard conversation emerged like a ghostly shadow, and her heart sagged. The man was hardly falling in love. Her father had told her aunt that he would promise Gideon a plantation and confirm that she would inherit the entire estate when he passed. Her lips tightened, and the wonder of the kiss evaporated into the darkness. Money was always the greatest motivator. Why else did the man acquiesce so fast?

Nevertheless, when she fell asleep, she still dreamed of being in Gideon's strong arms.

The following days passed in a whirl of dress-fitting, trousseau planning, chapel decorating, and wedding breakfast plans. Aunt Sarah and their housekeeper took charge of most of the arrangements.

One morning as Belle worked with Helena's hair, she smiled at Helena in the dresser mirror. "Have you told me everything that occurred between you and that handsome Mr. Falconer you must've fallen in love with? I mean, with this hurry-up wedding and all."

Helena frowned at her maid. "Belle, I've told you, Papa, and Aunt

Sarah everything that truly happened. And, no, I'm not in love with him. I'm marrying him to stop the gossip. And I forbid you to bring up the subject again."

Belle's face fell, and she quickly went back to work on Helena's hair. "Well, I can say one thing for sure. That Samson who rode over with him the past two days is sure one hunk of a man. I hope to get to know him better during the wedding." Her voice faded into a whisper as Helena glared at her in the mirror.

Why did her maid's chatter about Gideon Falconer and his man grate on her nerves so much? She swallowed and blinked back moisture. Would she forever regret marrying a man she didn't love?

Gideon discovered John Allston had plans for him while Helena spent hours with the dressmaker. So he left Samson in charge of closing their Brighton Plantation cottage and moving their personal items to Allston Hall. He instructed the man to take their chickens to his mother's family but be back at the plantation the day the new owner arrived.

Meanwhile, Gideon sat beside Allston in his carriage as they drove toward the harbor.

The man cleared his throat. "First, I want to show you our merchant's office, Gideon. It's just across from Gadsden Wharf. Years ago, I decided it'd be more profitable to take my rice or cotton to market myself. I bought one ship to start. Now Allston Shipping has three ships, and we trade in much more than rice." He turned to face Gideon. "Of course, that doesn't include slave trading even before our country passed the 1808 law prohibiting the importing, buying, and selling of slaves. Never cared for that business at all, to tell you the truth."

Gideon nodded. "I was glad that law passed here, following Britain's example. But it'll take more legislation to free the already enslaved masses."

Allston's brow rose. "And war, my man. The Southern planters I know will never give up their slaves without a fight."

The carriage pulled up at the row of two-story buildings facing Gadsden Wharf. Harbor sounds and smells permeated the morning as they disembarked. Shouts of sellers and buyers, bleats of sheep, and squawking fowl competed. The rich aroma of pork barbecuing somewhere down the busy harbor filled the air.

Allston led Gideon up a flight of stairs at the back of the buildings to a door with *Allston Shipping* painted on it in gold lettering.

When they entered, a thin, middle-aged man with spectacles arose from the desk strewn with charts, ink, and paper. "Good morning, Mr. Allston." His dark eyes then moved to Gideon.

"Morning. James Cooper, this is Gideon Falconer. He's marrying Helena on Friday, and I want him to get a feel for our merchant business. Can you enlighten him on the basics? Shouldn't be difficult as he's captained a ship or two of his own in the past." He slapped Gideon on the shoulder. "Meanwhile, I'll go down to the wharf and check out the *Maribelle*. Want to make sure she's tidy and ready for a wedding trip to Savannah."

"Most certainly, Mr. Allston. And that is the only one of our ships in port right now. The *Lucinda* headed to the Mediterranean this morning, and the *Victoria* returns from the islands tomorrow."

Allston pulled his pipe from his pocket, lit it, and left the office.

Gideon glanced around the interesting room, but a large bay window facing the harbor with its varied vessels docked drew his attention. Sloops, frigates, and cargo ships, their sails wrapped tight, bobbed with the tide. He walked over to look closer until he saw John Allston stride into view heading down the wharf.

"Mr. Falconer, is it?" Behind him, James Cooper's voice held a smile.

"Yes." Gideon gave the man his attention as he proceeded to show him pictures of the three vessels, sailing charts, and shipping lists. The man answered every question Gideon asked without hesitation. He knew the shipping business well. Allston was lucky to have a good shipping clerk.

By the time his future father-in-law returned, Gideon had a basic knowledge of the shipping company—a very profitable business, no doubt, with the ships leaving Charleston with rice, cotton, leather, and indigo for Europe and the islands and returning with manufactured goods from Britain and sugar from the Caribbean.

They climbed back into the carriage and headed out of Charleston. "I want to show you Windemere Plantation where you two will be setting up housekeeping, Gideon," John said. "It's my only cotton plantation, and we've built a lovely manor house with stables. Helena loves it. I have a factor in charge there for now, but don't think he's doing the best job. I've given him notice to leave at the end of the month. I'd like you to take that position since you have a background in estate management. But let's look at the property and see what you think."

Was this the plantation the man had offered him upon the marriage? Good thing he'd set Helena's father straight about that. But managing the plantation would be acceptable.

Gideon's stomach was rumbling by the time their carriage entered a lovely oak-lined drive with green meadows and a stand of cedar trees flowing out beyond the drive as far as the eye could see. The house, when it came into view, caused Gideon's breath to lodge in his throat. It rivaled Allston Hall. How many such estates did the man own?

A flock of servants in green livery met their carriage and ushered them into a formal dining room set for the midday meal.

Gideon ate heartily of baked fowl, butterbeans, squash, sweet potatoes, and plump apple dumplings served by servants in green-and-black attire. It was good he did, for a long tour of the cotton plantation and outbuildings filled the rest of the day. He met the factor, a swarthy middle-aged man, and smelled alcohol on him. He also met his muscle-bound young assistant, a cocoa-skinned teenager named Kunta, whose startling blue eyes shocked Gideon. Kunta only grunted and never gave the slightest indication of a smile or welcome when introduced to Gideon.

As they walked back to the buggy, Allston shook his head and frowned. "I freed Kunta a few months ago." His voice was low, strained.

Gideon stopped midstride and faced the man. "Sir, do you lean toward...abolition?"

Allston pushed his hands into his pockets, and his lips tightened. Somehow, he looked tired and older. "No. It's a long, sad story from my not very honorable past. Kunta is my son from a slave woman. That's why I've freed him and let him learn to read and write. He earns a small salary to assist the factor with the slave women, as his mother used to do before she passed of fever two years ago." He took a deep, labored breath. "But freeing him may have been a mistake. Besides his general sour attitude he's developed, I've discovered he spends his Saturdays with unsavory characters, even pirates, in the Charleston Harbor taverns."

Gideon sucked in a breath, swallowed, and tried to digest all this surprising information. "Does Helena know Kunta is your son?"

"No, and I don't want her to know. Can you keep a secret, Gideon?"

Withholding information from his new wife sat uneasy on his conscience, but truly, the secret was not his to tell.

CHAPTER 5

The wedding day dawned cloudy and humid. Helena, dressed in her lovely ivory satin gown, stood looking out the window in her room. How she missed Rachel being a part of her wedding, but her cousin had gone to Europe with her family for the spring and summer and knew nothing of what had transpired in Helena's life the past week. She sighed. Perhaps a real downpour would come in time to cancel her father's smaller sloop that was supposed to take her and her new husband on a wedding trip to Savannah. How could she stand to be alone with the man all those hours and days, knowing his real reason for marrying her? If her father chose to believe it was for the noble reason to save her reputation, let him believe it. But the man who owned no land of his own, gentleman or not, would have to be happy to come into the good fortune that would come with marriage to her. A tear fell down her cheek. She swiped it away as Belle moved into the room with tea and a buttered scone.

"Come, Miss Helena, you must eat something before we leave for the church. The wedding breakfast is a long way off." She set the food on the small side table.

The smell of it made Helena's stomach twist, so she made no move toward the tray.

Belle put her hands on her hips. "Come now, do you want rumbling sounds coming out of your middle in front of the minister?"

Helena groaned and moved to the table. She took two bites of the scone and a sip of tea. Somehow, she would make it through this day...and night. Would Gideon keep his promise to her about...intimacy? She shook away that disturbing thought and set her teacup back on the tray.

~

In his spacious bedroom on the other side of the house, Gideon, who'd already sampled breakfast, dressed for the wedding with Samson's help in front of a chifforobe mirror. He donned black silk trousers, a white silk ruffled shirt and black waistcoat, then pulled on shining black boots—all purchased by his considerable savings from his work at Brighton Plantation. Allston had offered to buy the clothing, but Gideon would not consider it.

With skilled hands, Samson looped the snowy white cravat around Gideon's neck. "Now you know exactly what I meant about big papa would have his say and his way. Look at you, marrying a woman you've only known this brief time." But a grin accompanied his words. "I do have to say, she's a beauty for sure and a real lady." He turned back to pick up a brush to stroke any dust or hair from the waistcoat. "And that maid of hers has caught my eye. I'm making it my express purpose to get to know Belle better."

Gideon glanced at him but didn't reply. His mind hung on the marriage that would take place within the hour, then the wedding breakfast, and off to the harbor and waiting ship to Savannah. With the lovely Helena Allston as his bride. Was he dreaming?

A knock sounded at the door.

Now fully dressed, Gideon moved from the mirror. "Enter."

John Allston strode into the room, clad in an elegant blue silk waistcoat and white trousers. He cast one cool glance toward Samson, and the man vacated the room and shut the connecting door between them without a sound.

Gideon's future father-in-law pulled a legal document from his waistcoat pocket.

"This is the deed to the Windemere Plantation."

Gideon frowned. "What are you saying, sir? We had this settled."

The man looked straight into his eyes. "I've not been untruthful with you, Gideon. This plantation does come with Helena because it was her mother's family estate when I met and married my deceased wife. It will become yours when you marry under our coverture laws for married women."

Gideon exhaled a deep breath and crossed his arms.

The man continued. "But it's in no way a reward for your marrying Helena. In fact, I never meant it to ever sound as though it was a bribe to get you to marry her." He smiled. "I believe you'll agree, she's much too beautiful for that ever to be necessary. And you have in no way accepted it as such."

"Sir, I haven't accepted the plantation whatsoever." Gideon's tight voice broke the peace of the morning.

"Come now, of course you will. I'll give the deed to your man to store in a safe place until you and Helena return after your trip. Or would you prefer I keep it in my personal safe for you? It already has your name on the deed with hers. But as her husband, you will have the full ownership responsibility as outlined in our South Carolina coverture law."

"It's an unfair law, sir."

"Of course, it is, but it's still the law until it's changed." He waved the folded document. "To your man or to my safe?"

Gideon unfolded his arms and cracked his knuckles. Did Helena know about this? Did her father even tell her he'd put the estate in her name when her mother passed? Probably not. Would she think he married her for the plantation?

Allston clicked his tongue. "Come, we must leave for the church. I've your carriage and mine and Helena's ready for our separate drives out front. My safe or give it to your man to store in your papers?"

Allston's hurried words stopped Gideon from mulling over the deed. The thought of the lovely Helena becoming his bride within the hour forced away his frustration. "Put it in your safe."

The man nodded, walked to the door, then glanced back. "I'll give you about fifteen minutes to get to the chapel ahead of us. Then I'll follow with Helena. You mustn't see her until she comes down the aisle, you know." John smiled and hurried away.

Gideon took one last glance in the mirror. He looked and felt stiff in the formal black silk waistcoat and white lacy cravat his man had tied with expertise. He much preferred simpler clothing, but Helena would be pleased, wouldn't she? His lips tightened. He'd seen very little pleasure on her lovely face since she agreed to marry him. He slammed a fist into his open palm. Was he making the biggest mistake of his life? He whispered a prayer and strode from the room.

~

The vision of Helena floating down the church aisle on her father's arm in her ivory silk gown and gossamer veil crowned with snowy gardenias took Gideon's breath away. His heart overflowed with joy. Was falling in love possible in the brief time he'd known her? She drew close to stand beside him in a cloud of sweet fragrance. Her presence set his heart ablaze. The luster of the wedding dress magnified the shine in her blue eyes. Then he did a double take. Were those tears, almost overflowing, making that extra shine? And she didn't look directly at him. She kept her face trained on the minister before them once her father spoke his part and moved to the front pew.

His heart lurched in pain for her and for himself. How could he, Gideon Falconer, be standing before a minister with a reluctant, tearful bride? Yet he'd felt God's confirmation to marry Helena. What would their future hold? Thank God he'd sent his mother traveling funds to emigrate. She would know how to advise him.

Lord, I am trusting You and believe You are going to work good out of this marriage.

He took Helena's gloved hand in his, then gave the minister his attention. Merle Falconer Rhett, as much as anyone he knew, would know how to help him win the heart of his reluctant bride.

~

*H*elena blinked back moisture and forced herself to concentrate on the words of the minister. She must respond at the appropriate times. But Gideon's presence beside her, more handsome in his wedding garments than she'd ever seen him, kept her heart hammering and her voice breathy.

When the minister finally pronounced them man and wife, she turned and lifted her face toward him but was not ready for the warm, loving look he bestowed on her. He pulled her into his arms, and his spicy male scent enveloped her. He touched her lips with his, the blood roared in her ears, and she felt faint. He lifted his head and steadied her with a firm grip on her shoulders. Then he placed her hand on his arm and turned the two of them toward the small group of attendees smiling in the pews. She succeeded, she hoped, in wiping her dazed expression away before facing them.

Later, at the entrance of the church, she stood by Gideon's side, and greeted guests, still trying to recover from that kiss. She hardly heard the kind remarks as people passed, then she gasped. George Beauregard, dressed to the hilt in a light blue satin waistcoat, thick lace cravat, white silk trousers, and shining black boots sidled up to her. He made quite a picture of arrogant wealth and confidence. His dark, secretive eyes mocked Gideon instead of portraying jealousy.

"So...coming where you're not invited is also one of your vices, George?" Helena set her face in stone.

Beaureguard leaned toward her and whispered in her ear. "Don't assume it's all over between us."

She tightened her lips and pushed him away with a sharp jab of her elbow.

He left, flashing a confident grin to include Gideon.

~

Seeing his aunt, Sophia Rutledge, coming toward them next, Gideon leaned toward Helena. "What did the man say to you?"

Helena just shook her head and whispered, "Something as crazy as he is. He said, 'Don't assume it's all over between us.'"

Gideon ached to follow the man and knock the silly grin off his face. But greeting his aunt and Hannah White erased all thought of Geoge Beauregard and his foolish boast. Hannah was still a pretty young woman, but she no longer made his heart jump into his throat. That honor now belonged to Helena Allston Falconer. His insides jolted just thinking of her standing beside him as his wife.

He opened his arms to Aunt Sophia, and she drew close to him and gave him a kiss on the cheek, her remembered lavender scent baptizing him. "Gideon, I'm happy to see you settling down. Where will you two lovely people be making your home? Surely, not Brighton." She smiled at Helena and gave her a hug.

"No, as you know, Brighton has been sold." He cast a sideways glance at Helena. "We'll be making our home at Windemere Plantation. Mr. Allston has asked me to manage the estate."

Hannah White moved forward and smiled. "Gideon, I just knew all things would work out well for you. I'm so glad it has. Adam hated to miss your wedding, but something urgent at the Becket Law Firm kept him in town." She turned to Helena. "My husband and I got to know Gideon well after he emigrated from England, and we're so happy for both of you. Are you going on a wedding trip somewhere?"

"Yes, Savannah, Georgia." Helena's voice sounded flat. Would dear Hannah or his aunt notice?

Mrs. White continued in a cheerful voice. "Oh, that's where Adam and I spent our honeymoon. You'll love the place. The garden squares, the lovely old homes and atmosphere. It's a well-planned city. And thank you so much for the invitation to the wedding breakfast, but we must decline. We now have four little ones. Two are suffering from a spring cold, and our governess may be at her wits' end if we don't return soon."

After the women excused themselves, Gideon attempted to catch Helena's eye to share a smile, but she would not meet his gaze. Because of what he had said about Windemere or due to the mention of their honeymoon? Either way, it did not bode well for Gideon.

~

By four o'clock, Helena stood beside Gideon on deck of the *Maribelle* headed out to sea while Belle unpacked for them in their separate staterooms. Her maid had lifted her brows when Helena chose two cabins, but she said nothing.

Keeping at least two feet between her and her new husband, Helena remembered Belle's words as she had helped Helena change into her traveling clothes after the wedding. It was uncanny how the woman guessed the truth of situations that Helena wanted to keep hidden.

Belle had sent their baggage down to the carriage and finished the last buttons on Helena's teal traveling dress. Then she'd faced Helena with hands on her ample hips. "So now you are Mrs. Gideon Falconer?"

Helena had glanced in her mirror and placed the matching bonnet over her coiled hair, then tied the silk bow under her chin. "Apparently, I am."

Belle sighed. "I've never seen such a disinterested new bride, and I have one piece of advice for you. Gideon Falconer is a fine man as well as the most handsome beau who has ever graced your door, young lady. You'd do well to do your best to make him happy, or some other woman will. Mark my words."

Helena stared across the Charleston Harbor. Some other woman? Had Gideon any other romantic interest? He'd have mentioned it, wouldn't he? The lovely, friendly face of Hannah White and Gideon's lingering glance at her snapped into focus. Had there been something between the two of them in the past? But whatever had transpired then, the vivacious woman was now married and the mother of four. No threat to anyone. Besides, jealousy related to Gideon was nonexistent as far as Helena was concerned.

She glanced at him leaning on the railing. He seemed completely at home on the ship and had perfect balance like an experienced sailor would have on board a sailing vessel. And, she had to admit, he was every bit as handsome as Belle had declared.

~

As their ship left the harbor, Gideon turned from scanning the choppy blue Atlantic and met his new wife's glance. Just looking in her face sent a spiral of warmth up his back. "Would you care for some tea, Helena?"

"Yes, I think so."

He led her to a small table and two chairs firmly planted against the outside of their cabins, then strode across the deck and called down the hatch which led to the kitchen and the crew's lodging. "Tea appreciated up here."

In a few minutes, Belle came with tea, cakes, and small sandwiches. "I guessed you two would be ready for tea." She smiled and deposited the tray, then found a chair in the bow and pulled some sewing from her pocket.

Gideon wolfed down two sandwich wedges. Too many people had demanded his attention for him to properly enjoy the wedding breakfast. "Have you been to Savannah before, Helena?"

Helena sipped her tea. "Once when a child with my mother on a shopping trip. I don't remember much about it."

"Well, it's grown since then and has quite a few sights to see."

She gave him a level look. "Gideon, I need to tell you, I'm not much for seeing sights. I prefer a comfortable hotel room and restful days. Do you mind?"

Gideon fought down a swell of disappointment and instead offered a smile. "Whatever makes you most comfortable, my dear."

But did his wife have any inclination to make theirs a true marriage at all?

~

Gideon found Helena had meant exactly what she said, and her words sat in his heart like a stone after their arrival in Savannah. He spent the short days of their honeymoon taking lonely walks along the shady streets of Savannah and bringing flowers back to Helena from the female street vendors. He also spent time at the harbor checking out the many ships arriving daily. He had no idea how Helena spent her daytime hours after their joint breakfast in her room. Helena had insisted on, and Gideon permitted, separate suites, but he insisted on a connecting door—which, he noticed, she kept locked at night.

Good-natured Belle spent time with her during the day and ran her errands. The maid had a room in the servants' quarters on the third floor. "A lady like Helena can never travel without a servant to help her dress," Belle had told him with a bright smile when he'd first discovered she would be going on the honeymoon with them.

One thing Gideon had looked forward to on his daily outings was having dinner with Helena. Their first evening, she'd begged off with a headache and did the same the following night, informing Gideon she and Belle would dine in the room.

The third afternoon, with plenty of time for her to prepare, he came through the connecting door, unlocked for the day, and confronted her in her room with a firm request, more of a demand. She sat on a sofa with Belle doing needlework. "Helena, I need you to dress and come down to the dining room and have dinner with me this evening. I do not like dining alone."

She looked up from her needlework and frowned. Even with a scowl, her porcelain face and bright blue eyes still caused his heart to skip a beat. "Oh, haven't you met anyone you know?"

Beside her, Belle expelled a long breath, plopped her sewing into her bag, and headed for the hall.

Gideon took a deep breath and stepped closer, his back ramrod straight. "No, I haven't, and it's my wife I want to dine with, not anyone else."

Color flooded Helena's face. She stood and threw her needlework on the sofa. Her eyes flashed. It was obvious she seldom had anything asked of her again after she'd tried to refuse. "If nothing else will make you happy, dear husband, then catch Belle in the hall to help me dress." She strode to her wardrobe and wrenched open the door. It banged on the outer wall.

At the dinner hour, she entered the dining room in a lovely pink silk gown with lace ruffles around the neck, cuffs, and hem, albeit with a stiff, haughty face. But even with that attitude, heads turned to stare, and men glanced at Gideon with envy.

If they only knew. He squelched those words as soon as they arose in his spirit since they didn't agree with what he was praying for Helena. The many things he kept bringing to God's attention helped him keep faith that a breakthrough would come. Would she ever fall in love with him as he now loved her? Would she grow up and overcome the spoiled, rich-girl image that still clung to her?

He stood and pulled a satin-lined chair out for her and helped her sit. The dinner began without further incident. Helena smiled at him once and pleased him with conversation while they dined on tender roast beef, steamed cabbage, rice and gravy, and strawberry pudding. He enjoyed watching her eat. There was nothing wrong with the lady's appetite.

Back in their adjoining rooms, Gideon heard the lock click on the connecting door. At first, the locked connecting door aggravated Gideon. He was a man of his word. He'd assured her he would never press intimate attentions on her until she was ready to receive them. Did she trust him at all? He knelt beside his bed. "Lord, please show me how to win my wife's heart and trust." He exhaled a heavy breath and started to stand up. But then he added, "And please help me have patience until that happens."

Late that night, a scream from Helena's room ripped Gideon from a deep sleep. He bounded to the floor, barefoot, in his nightshirt, and strode to the connecting door. Another cry exploded. He grasped the doorknob and bit back an ugly exclamation. Of course, she had the door locked. But this inner chamber door was no match for Gideon's strong shoulder. He thrust against it, and the lightweight wood frame gave way and separated with a cracking, popping sound.

In three steps, he reached her bedside. Moonlight filtered through the tall window. His heart slammed against his ribs at the sight of Helena lying in the bed with tears streaming down her face, soaking her dark hair spread in disarray over her pillow. He sat on the edge of the bed and drew her into his arms. She shook like a leaf. Muffled words came from her, pressed against his chest. "The river. I was plunging, falling, deep into the frigid river again. Stormy disappeared from under me." She sobbed, and he pressed her closer, breathed in her sweet, womanly scent, and pushed strands of damp hair from her forehead.

"I pray you never have nightmares about that again. I'm so sorry you ever went through it." He kept murmuring sweet nothings, patting her shaking shoulders, comforting her as one would a child.

The tears finally stopped. She pulled away from his embrace and hiccupped, then gazed into his face. "I want to go home, Gideon. Will you take me home?"

His heart swelled as though it would burst. She did need him. Gone was the stiff, sophisticated, needing-no-one young woman he'd married. He hugged her against him again. "Of course, I'll take you home, dear Helena. We'll set sail first thing in the morning." He lifted her chin and gently touched her lips with his own, reveling in the salty but infinitely sweet kiss.

She pushed away from him and pulled the coverlet to her chin. "Will you go now?" Her voice trembled, and he fought a strong temptation to pull her back into his arms. "Please?"

Her tear-stained face closed like a clam under attack. And the warmth in the room disappeared as if a cold breeze had blown in from the sea.

He stood, forced his senses under some semblance of control, and moved to the shattered door. He stepped through and pulled the frame back into the opening. Before climbing into his bed, he shook his head and flexed his fist. *One step forward, two backward.* But he wasn't about to give up.

~

After Gideon left, Helena touched her burning lips with her finger. What kind of man had she married? He'd saved her from the river, comforted her like a child from the nightmare, and threw all her senses into confusion and excitement with the gentlest kiss she'd ever imagined. This was not the same kind of kiss as the one he'd given her after she accepted his proposal. That one was fire, ice, and a near faint. This one was chaste, sweet, and yet manly and strong at the same time. But how could she trust a man who surely married her for her fortune he now possessed under South Carolina coverture laws?

How she wished she could believe he simply married her to save her reputation. Never mind if he fell in love with her as well. Could there ever be a true love between them? She bit her lower lip and set her mind on something else—home. She missed home.

Windemere flowed into her heart. Helena had passed many of her growing up years there with her mother while her father spent much time at sea with his merchant business. She loved the large white-painted cypress plantation house with its many rooms in which she'd played hide-and-seek with her friend and cousin Rachel. The place had been her mother's ancestral home, and her mother preferred it to Allston Hall even after she married her father.

Helena enjoyed the huge back lawn, covered with springy grass that stretched down to the Ashley River dock where slaves loaded the harvest for Charleston. She often inspected the many outbuildings surrounding the estate, wonderful places to explore and watch the slaves at work. All sorts of tasks by skilled servants took place daily. The men built furniture and shipping barrels, shod horses, and made knives and swords in the blacksmith shop. Women spun yarn from the herd of sheep, washed clothes over a firepit, and milked cows and churned butter. When company came, Helena loved the barbecue aromas from the smokehouse.

But the detached kitchen of Marm Esther became one of her favorite places to spend time, especially when the smell of freshly baked bread and cinnamon rolls drew her from her play.

Stormy dominated Helena's concluding thoughts as drowsiness crept over her. She couldn't wait to gallop across the estate on her Arabian mare.

Home. All would be well again. She fluffed her pillow, turned on her side, and fell asleep.

Gideon breathed in the fresh breeze when they set sail the next morning for Charleston. He tried to forget the wonder of Helena needing him for that special moment in the night, then her instant and chilly change.

She sat in the doorway of her stateroom, seemingly oblivious to the jovial small crew's activities on deck and the lovely sunshine and weather. He marveled at the disappearance of the little girl of last night who seemed so grown up and distant today. Still lovely in her green traveling dress and bonnet tied against the sea breeze, she tripped his heart. Belle sat beside her, but Helena sat silent.

He cast thoughts of her and her moods aside and began to think of Windemere, its people, and the varied plantation work he'd be overseeing. Enjoying a lot of ease had never been part of his life, and he looked forward to having meaningful work to do—and less time for thinking or worrying about Helena. His mother—praise God for her wisdom and practical outlook—had often impressed upon him the value of work. Was she already on the way to America? He'd sent her traveling funds before his wedding to Helena. And he'd sent a second letter announcing his marriage. He prayed for his mother a safe journey from England. Counting on her wisdom and help to win Helena's heart, his mood lightened.

They arrived at the Charleston Harbor in the late afternoon, and

John Allston gave them a hearty welcome. "Glad you decided to come back early, daughter," he told Helena. "Did you get a little homesick as your mother used to do?"

"I just wanted to come home." She smiled at him. "Maybe I did miss you."

His face lit up, and he gave her another hug.

Gideon oversaw the crew as they removed the baggage from the sloop and repacked it into the Allston carriage for the drive to Windemere. He'd already helped Helena and Belle into their seats.

Allston pulled him aside. "Gideon, I want to thank you again for rescuing my family. You'll never know what seeing you two married and your taking over Windemere means to me. I have more peace than I've had in years, and I believe everything is going to be fine. Simply fine."

Gideon blinked and took a deep breath. "Do you think Helena is happy?"

"Of course, she is."

"She has a strange way of showing it most days." He dared not mention *nights*.

"You watch and stay patient, my man. Helena will come around. She's still got some growing up to do. She's always had her own way, and we never asked much of her." He chuckled. "I have an idea you're going to enjoy helping her grow up."

Gideon climbed into the carriage beside Helena, and Allston came alongside just before they left. "Now, I'll be looking for a dinner invite soon, and so will your aunt Sarah. You hear, Helena?"

"Yes, Father. But give us a few days to settle in."

And they were off.

When the carriage crunched onto the shell drive of Windemere Plantation, the heady scent of flowers filled the air, and the horses increased their pace. Gideon caught sight of the majestic white-columned house at the end of the drive, amid its avenue of oaks, spacious green lawns, and the blooming shrubs lining the landscape, and a new peace and anticipation flowed over him. Was Windemere truly now his home and where he and Helena would spend their days? He turned to face her. Her eyes sparkled like sapphires as she caught sight of the plantation house.

"Are you happy to be home, Helena?"

"Oh, yes." She smiled at him, and he took her small soft hand. Warmth flowed between their palms, and he rejoiced. She didn't pull away until the carriage stopped in front of the steps.

Were they making progress? The days and the nights in Savannah had proven a hard temptation for him not to shower affection on his lovely wife, especially during her nightmare. He doubted she had any idea of his deepened feelings for her. Would she ever reciprocate?

He helped Helena exit the carriage and then Belle. The maid slipped from them, then up the steps and through the entrance.

Next to the front door, Bentley, barking joyfully, broke away from Samson's hand on his collar and bounded toward Gideon. The large dog almost knocked Gideon down with his lively leap toward him.

"Good boy. I know you're glad to see me, but let's hold it down a bit." Gideon rubbed the blond head and accepted wet licks on his hands.

"Sho' is good to see you back, sir." Samson's smile reminded Gideon of how much he'd missed his freed servant and friend. He grabbed the man's large extended palm.

All the house servants stood lined across the porch, and they gave Helena happy greetings and bows as she moved up the steps. A stout, middle-aged black woman with moisture shining in her dark eyes threw her arms wide and pressed Helena to her ample bosom.

"Marm Esther, I've missed your good cooking." Helena smiled into the warm face.

A movement beyond the corner of the wide porch caught Gideon's attention. Kunta—John Allston's son by the slave woman and Helena's half brother—stood with stiff face, flared nostrils, and strong brown arms folded against his thick chest. He turned his brittle blue glance from Helena to Gideon, then shrank into the shadows.

Gideon exhaled a heavy breath. He had more to worry about than courting his wife. How would he handle Kunta in the days ahead?

CHAPTER 6

The next morning, Gideon left by the back entrance and strode toward the outbuildings to join Samson. Today he wanted to ride over the estate, meet more of the people, and check on the cotton crop planted earlier. He had much to learn.

Most plantations had many slaves with various skills and training, such as Brighton once had. Besides the larger number of field workers and the well-trained house servants, there would be carpenters, tanners, coopers, gardeners, spinners, stable hands, and other helpers that met every need of planter families. He refused to see enslaved people as commodities, as he once had as a slave ship captain. He pushed that horrid memory back and hoped once again God had truly forgiven him. The Africans were competent, hardworking people whom God loved, with their own customs, beliefs, and practices. He'd found those at Brighton gifted in imagery and harmony. Enslavement had horribly wronged the African nations. Could he do something to correct that wrong?

With that thought, the dream deep in his soul flowed over him again. What would it be like to free all slaves? That great desire in his heart, planted years ago by John Newton and nurtured by William Wilberforce, must have come from God. How often had Gideon read and meditated on the very words Christ proclaimed in the beginning of His earthly ministry? *The Spirit of the Lord is upon me, because he hath anointed me to preach the gospel to the poor; he hath sent me to heal the brokenhearted, to preach deliverance to the captives, and recovering of sight to the blind, to set at liberty them that are bruised.*

John Allston had freed his son, Kunta, but confirmed he was not of the abolitionist mind. Would he agree with Gideon freeing the Windemere slaves? The man had forced him to take ownership of Windemere. Was it all part of God's plan so he could help the slaves? He whispered a prayer that the Lord would show him what to do and the right timing.

A door opened in a white-washed cottage near the stables, and Bentley came bounding toward him barking with joy. Samson strode behind him with his traditional wide grin.

Purpose flowed through Gideon. Time to get to work.

~

From her bedroom window, Helena watched Gideon and Samson emerge from the stables on horseback. They galloped toward the farm road with Bentley easily loping with them.

She pulled the servant cord next to the large brick fireplace. A morning ride in the early summer air and sunshine was exactly what she needed herself.

When Belle appeared with a bucket of fresh water for bathing, Helena made a quick toilette and donned her brown riding habit with its split skirt she'd designed herself to ride astride while at the plantation. As she sailed down the stairs, then out the back door toward the separate kitchen, the delicious smell of cinnamon drifting in the morning air filled her nose and made her mouth water. Marm Esther knew her favorite breakfast and hadn't failed to supply it her first day back home from her wedding trip.

As she dashed up the three steps and into the warm kitchen, the servant pulled fresh rolls from the large brick oven next to the fire-place. Her kind eyes flickered over Helena before she drizzled thin white icing across the rolls. "Is you off on that dangerous horse of yours first thing, Miss Helena? No telling how that one will behave after no one riding her all last week."

"Yes, I'm going riding, but Stormy is not dangerous, just spirited." Helena grabbed a hot roll, bounced it in her hand and blew on it, then sat down, and bit into its sweet, cinnamon warmth.

"Want a cuppa tea to wash that down? I'se already poured it, so it'll be cool 'nuff." Marm Esther set a blue porcelain cup and saucer before her.

"Thank you." Helena took two sips, grabbed an apple from the bowl on the sideboard, and headed out the kitchen door.

As she strode to the barn, the sun beamed warm on her face, and birds twittered in the large, towering oaks as she passed under their shady limbs. The loud screech of their two elderly peacocks disrupted the morning peace and surely awakened any sleepy head left on the place. Thick green grass crunched under her boots until she entered the packed dirt of the stable entrance.

A shrill neigh from a stall greeted her as Helena proceeded down the hard-packed corridor smelling of animals, hay, and feed. Helena recognized the sharp tone of Stormy's welcome. The animal was letting her know she'd missed her mistress.

Tom, the hired stable hand, clunked down the steps from his apartment above, looking disheveled and unsteady. Helena's lips tightened. Had the man been drinking this early, or was this part of the hangover from the night before? Her father, who had hired the former soldier three months earlier at the request of a friend at his club, had talked of dismissing the man. She wished he had. What had Gideon thought of him earlier? Or did he and Samson saddle their horses themselves?

She patted Stormy's nose and held the apple for her to munch off great bites, then she threw the core away.

"Miss, you wanting Stormy saddled? I hav'to tell you, she's been purty hard to handle since you been gone. Don't know what's got into her."

"Saddle her. Might just need a good run." The horse's too-shrill welcome neigh meant something. Had the man not been properly caring for her, including the daily run of the big corral?

Helena climbed astride the plantation saddle, and Stormy pranced out of the barn entrance, tossing her head. "Settle down, girl. We're going to have a great ride this morning and get all the kinks out."

Stormy nickered as if she understood.

Helena reined her toward the wide, open fields beyond the driveway, then pressed her knees to the horse's side and bent forward. Stormy took off like a cannon shot, and Helena clenched her flying mane in one hand to stay astride. But it felt wonderful to run with the wind without a care in the world.

Stormy's gallop slowed to a walk as she entered a barely marked path in the woods. She knew where they were going. "Yes, girl, I've missed my secret place. Have you too?"

She allowed the mare to pick her way through the thick stand of cypress and pine. As a child with her first pony, she'd discovered the place close to the Ashley River, a deserted area with only deer tracks around it. The wild animals smelled water ahead and made the trail.

When Helena came to a clearing near the river, she gasped in happiness. Wisteria hung in cascades from several of the trees and filled the air with their fragrance. She dismounted, tied Stormy's reins to a low tree branch, then walked around the clearing and took deep breaths of the moist, perfumed air. She brushed off her favorite rock protruding toward the river, then sat and watched the ripples caused by a flock of fowl far out in the middle searching for breakfast. Thank God no gunshots came from the secluded riverbank against them. The warm sunshine wrapped her in its golden rays streaming through the trees, and she closed her eyes for a moment to think. She'd done some of her best mulling over things in her life right here, especially after her mother passed. It was here she had decided to flee to England.

As the disturbing thoughts of what happened tried to intrude into her peace, she opened her eyes and stood. She never made it to her aunt in England. Now she was a married woman. Gideon's handsome face made her heart drum faster, but did he genuinely love her? Or had her father and aunt talked him into marrying her to save her reputation and with the promise of Windemere? She shook her head in frustration, the dilemma pressing her. Was this how her life was supposed to turn out? Surely, there was more to life and to marriage. Gideon seemed a kind, strong, and wise man. But could she trust him with her heart and future? She sighed, untied Stormy, and mounted.

She guided the mare back through the trees, then urged her into a gallop as if flying across the fields as fast as possible would help her escape the questions, find peace.

Before coming to a forest which marked the border of their plantation, she slowed Stormy to help the horse catch her breath, then reined her onto a narrow, marked path through the tall green trees filled with bird chatter. She welcomed the shade and breathed in the woodsy scents of pine, sweet cedar, and birch laced with the damp, earthy smell of last year's decomposing leaves. Was the old woman who lived in a hut in the woods still there?

Years earlier, Helena had visited on her pony with her last governess, Miss Hanks, who wanted to learn whether what the slaves whispered concerning the woman was true. Was she a root doctor who could give them a healing herb or a witch who would give them a talisman to protect them from evil spirits or help them put a curse on their enemy? As a child playing with the African children, Helena heard about the evil beings that inhabited the forest, and later, she had nightmares about them—the hags, haints, plat-eyes, boo-daddies, and ghosts.

They claimed a hag was a disembodied spirit of an old woman who had practiced witchcraft.

A haint could change from the body of a person to a ghost at will. Believers in the supernatural being prevented a haint from coming into their houses by placing a brush or flour sifter inside the front door overnight. The evil being would stop to count the hairs in the brush or the holes in the sifter, and by the time the creature finished, the sun would be up and the haint would have to disappear. For a year, Helena had placed her hairbrush on the floor inside her bedroom door.

A plat-eye had the distinct characteristic of being able to change from one creature to another. Folks said they led people away from buried treasures. Not knowing of any buried treasure on the plantation, Helena had marked plat-eyes off her list.

Boo-daddies were spirits of conjure-doctors that escaped the physical bodies of the conjurers at night but kept their physical shape, and they could cast or remove jinxes and spells. The slave children assured her some of their parents cast jinxes on their enemies, and the old woman in the cottage in the wood helped them.

Helena's mother always assured her there were no such beings as they described, and she pointed out how most of the same slaves who believed in these stories were just as zealous regarding their religion and seldom missed Sunday church service.

Shaking aside her thoughts, Helena trotted Stormy into the rutted front yard of a shack and stopped near the porch where an elderly black woman sat smoking a corncob pipe. A large brown hound rose from the front step and barked but quieted and flopped back down at a word from its owner. The smell of tobacco floated in the air.

Helena smiled at the thin African woman sitting in a rocking chair. A blue scarf covered her springy gray hair. She wore a faded, once-blue skirt, which had several sachets and herbs pinned to it. A strange necklace caught Helena's eye. It was part of a snakeskin, and she shivered.

The woman drew the pipe out of her mouth with a work-worn hand. "Hullo there, Miz. You need something from me today? I've got a fresh harvest from my garden of chamomile tea leaves for rest, mint for flavoring, horehound for cough, ginseng for long life, and lavender for sachets." She touched some of the bags on her skirt as she spoke.

"No, I just wondered if you still lived here. I was much younger the one time I came before. I am Helena Allston Fal—"

"I knows 'zackly who you is and where you from, Miz Allston Falconer." The woman pushed the pipe back into her mouth and took a deep draw, then exhaled the pungent smoke. She looked straight into Helena's eyes.

"You do?" Helena sat back in her saddle, surprised, but then relaxed. Their slaves who visited the woman undoubtedly brought her the latest news and gossip which they delighted in sharing.

The woman removed the pipe. "Yep. I've suffered something relating to you and your plantation this week. That's why you was drawn here. You needs to be on watch. I've been seeing some disturbance in the sky over that place. Might mean something, might mean nothing."

Helena wanted to smile but suppressed it. The woman must believe she possessed special powers, whether she did or not. "What sort of disturbance do you think?"

"It's people disturbance. People who don't like other people."

Helena did smile. It was general enough to mean anything or nothing. She looked with pity on the frail woman. Did she have needs Helena could help meet? "You seem to know me, but I don't know your name."

"All your slaves do. It's Granny M."

"Well, Granny M, do you need anything? You live a distance from any place to purchase things. Can I send you something?"

"I have all I need." She pushed the pipe back into her mouth. "On second thought, you can send that brother of yours to see me."

Helena cocked her chin. "Oh, I'm sorry. But I have no brother. I'm the only child of my parents."

The woman gave her a long look, and shutters came over her dark eyes. "No brother? My mistake."

"Do you mind my asking if you have enough food?"

"I got plenty whenever I needs it. Thank ye." With that remark, she stood, dumped her pipe across the porch railing, and shuffled into her house. The dog followed.

Helena reined Stormy back the way they had come through the trees at a trot. The way home was a good ride away, but Helena looked forward to every minute of it. Stormy was a great mount and strong. When they reached the large open field through which they'd come, Helena clicked her tongue and tightened her knees, and Stormy lunged forward and was soon at her fastest gallop over the terrain, her hooves barely touching earth.

As they made it to the middle of the field, the saddle lurched and flew out from under Helena. She screamed in horror as her body sailed through the air and hit the packed dirt hard. The breath swooshed out of her lungs. A sharp pain shot up her leg, and her head slammed onto the unforgiving ground which opened into a deep, dark pit.

The sun warm on her body woke her sometime later. When she groaned, she heard movement in the grass nearby, then a low nicker, and a damp muzzle nudged her shoulder.

"Oh, Stormy, what happened to us?" She tried to lift her head, but faintness caused her to give up that effort. She lifted a bruised, scratched hand and touched Stormy's warm nose. Then she tried to lift her head again and partially succeeded, peering at the horse to check if the animal had suffered any injury. But that effort brought back the dizziness and such pain in her right leg, she fell back in the grass and passed out.

When she came to, she tried to sit up, but the effort caused intense waves of pain to shoot down her leg and up her back. She couldn't rise. Tears flowed down her cheeks as helplessness flooded over her. What would she do if couldn't get up? She gritted her teeth and swallowed to relieve her fear and dry throat. How far away were they from the house and help? How soon would anyone at the plantation miss her? And how long would it take anyone to find her?

Windemere spread over five hundred acres. They'd galloped several miles, and she noted the passage of time by how high the sun hung in the sky. Its merciless heat blanketed her and made her head hurt more. She managed to probe the back of her skull to where it hurt the most. She touched the wetness and brought her hand back to check. Blood. She blinked and moaned, then called the horse who was cropping grass nearby. The animal came closer and nudged her cheek. The mare's nearness somehow brought comfort.

With super effort, she rose enough to grasp the two trailing reins, then she pulled the great head close. The animal's warm breath feathered Helena's cheek. "Stormy, you must go home. *Home!* Do you understand me, dear girl? I'm depending on you to bring help." Then she pushed the muzzle away and slapped the thick neck smartly. "*Home!* Stormy, go home!" Helena screamed the command, then fell back drained, biting her lip at the pain in her leg that shot up through her whole body.

The horse tossed her head, snorted, then wheeled and galloped away.

Helena threw her arm across her face to block the sunlight and fell into a strange, delirious dream in which she was no longer hot, but cold. Her mother came to her and bent over her. "Don't give up, Helena. You have much more life to live." She reached out for her mother's face, wishing with all her heart to go with her.

Then she thought she saw Gideon's face, heard his deep voice. Was he listening to her cries for help? Where was he? But he couldn't help her. He was only interested in Windemere. Wasn't he? But his kind gray eyes told her a different story. Tears streamed down her face, and she shivered and fell back into the dark pit, calling his name.

~

Gideon took off his hat and swiped the sweat from his brow with his handkerchief. He reined Hero toward a shady area near a creek bordering one of the cotton fields where the slaves had stashed water jugs. Two women stood nearby, and two small children played around their skirts. He and Samson dismounted, watered their horses in the creek, and Bentley lapped his fill, then trotted toward the children.

The younger woman moved to block the huge dog's path. Fear paled her tense brown face and widened her eyes.

"Bentley, come here." Gideon's firm, deep voice reverberated in the small area. The dog looked back at him, then returned and plopped down at his feet. Gideon stooped down and laid his hand on the large head, then he smiled at the petite, protecting woman. The children still held their hands out toward the dog. "Bentley's big, but he's very gentle, especially with children. He'd never harm them. I assure you, ma'am."

Both the women's faces registered surprise at the word *ma'am*. The younger woman moved a step aside and allowed the two boys to amble slowly toward Bentley still at Gideon's feet. The dog slapped his tail on the leaves and inched toward them as they drew near and reached out their small hands to pat him. Bentley sniffed, then licked the boys' hands. Soon both were sitting on the leaves beside the dog, patting and chattering.

The older servant woman lowered a large dipper into one of the jugs and brought it to Gideon as he stood. The other younger woman did the same for Samson, but she kept glancing back at the dog and the children.

Gideon drank the water and spoke to the elder woman. "Thank you. That was just what I needed. Are these your children?"

She gestured to the younger woman. "They's hers, and I'm her mother. I'm Sadie and she's May."

Samson thanked the nervous May, who gave him a dipper full of water, then hurried back toward the children. But she didn't attempt to touch the dog.

Gideon noted the ragged clothing of the women and the children. Was this Kunta's idea of helping take care of the women slaves? "Can you make yourselves new clothing? What kind of cloth would you two women like to have?" He ducked his head. "But first, let me explain." He pointed to Samson. "He's Samson Johnson, my right-hand man and best friend. I'm Gideon Falconer, the new owner of Windemere. I've married Miss Helena, and we intend to do some things differently here if you'll let us." What would Helena think of his including her in his projects?

The older woman's dark eyes brightened several degrees. "Yes, suh, we knows who you are, and we'd sho love to have some decent cloth, whatever you can get for us, to make new clothes. We can make 'em. Yes, suh."

Gideon plopped his hat on and remounted. "I'll see about it. You can depend on it, Sadie, and May." The two women thanked him with hope lifting their faces.

Samson mounted and they left the clearing.

Bentley licked the faces of the boys, who chortled in glee.

Gideon called the dog, and he dashed after the horses.

A mile or two later, with the sun high overhead, Gideon glanced at his partner. "You about to get hungry, Samson? I am. Let's head back to the plantation. I bet Marm Esther has something good cooking in that kitchen of hers about now."

"Yes, sir. By all means. Let's do it." Samson grinned and clucked to his horse to keep up with Gideon's stallion heading home at a good clip.

The sun stood high overhead as they rode into the stable yard and dismounted. The groom came out to take the reins. Gideon took stock of him. He'd smelled liquor on his breath that morning when he came to saddle up for them, and he still looked unstable. He would hate to let a man go on his own first week managing Windemere, but he'd never keep him on when he was drinking on the job. Apparently, the firing of the factor because of his alcohol problem had no warning effect on the stableman.

He opened his mouth to give that warning, but the sound of hooves coming fast down the plantation road distracted him. All three of them looked up. A barebacked horse galloped up to them at the stable entrance and stopped, tossing its head. The loose reins flew in the air.

"Why, it's Stormy!" The stable foreman's face blanched, and his eyes widened. He grabbed the dangling straps.

"Did Helena go out this morning on Stormy?" Gideon's voice was far from gentle.

"Yes, sir. I done tol' her the horse might be hard to handle since no one rode her the whole past week." His voice trembled.

Gideon swung back up on Hero. "Let's follow the tracks, if we can."

Samson jumped back into his saddle, and they galloped down the road with Bentley loping beside them.

An hour or so later, they came across Helena's expensive saddle tossed onto the ground, its silver stirrups flashing in the sunlight. Samson swung off his horse and strode to it.

Bentley bounded toward something yards beyond lying almost hidden in the grass, and he barked.

Helena! Gideon jumped off Hero and ran forward. He found her lying still and silent on the ground like a broken doll. His breath lodged in his throat, and a cold sweat popped out on his forehead. Bentley licked her face, but she made no response.

Gideon dropped to his knees beside her. *Dear God, don't let her be...!*

CHAPTER 7

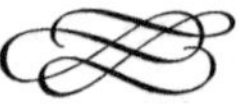

Gideon shooed the dog away from Helena. The sight of her face and lips, pale as porcelain, struck his heart like a sledgehammer, and anguish seared him. He touched her shoulder. "Helena! Helena!"

No response.

He swept his hand over his sweaty forehead and moistened his dry lips. *Get a hold, man.* The fall knocked her unconscious. He gritted his teeth and prayed. The memory of a similar scene, when a young boy on his slaver ship had died in his arms, taunted him. He shook away that dreadful recollection and focused on how the tragedy had led him to consider giving up the abhorrent slave trading business. With gentle fingers, he began to examine Helena, while still calling her name.

Samson walked up with the discarded saddle in tow. He dropped down beside Gideon. "I know what happened. The girth on Stormy's saddle was cut or eaten half through. By rats or...a human kind of rat. It finally gave way, and Helena flew off with it." His voice was hard.

Gideon looked up at him. White-hot anger blazed through him and tightened his jaw. "How could our groom miss seeing a damaged girth, except he was drunk?"

Helena groaned.

Gideon's shoulders sagged. "Thank God. She lives."

Samson pointed. "Yes, thank God, but look at that right leg, sir. It ain't turned exactly right. Must be broken."

"You're right. But what can we do to get her home without injuring it further?"

Samson smiled. "During my time long ago assisting my first master, a doctor in the upcountry settlements, I learned all sorts of makeshift ways to help the injured. We've got to stabilize that bone before we can move her. You wait right here. I'll be back in a shake." He stood, mounted his horse, and rode toward the tree line.

When Gideon pushed back the loose strands of dark hair on Helena's cheek, she turned her face into his palm and groaned. That's when he saw the clotted blood at the back of her head. Could she have a concussion too? They'd have to be most careful moving her. He took her hand in his and held it. *Dear Lord Jesus, please heal and comfort her. Help us get her home without further injury.*

A word issued from her, little more than a whisper. Had he not been leaning forward, he'd have missed it.

Gideon.

He rocked back on his heels, and joy flooded him. Unconscious, but she'd called his name. That meant something, didn't it? He pressed her hand, his heart hammering. "I'm here, Helena, and we will get you home."

But she didn't respond.

Samson returned, carrying two stout limbs he'd whittled into rough poles. He pulled a rope from his saddlebag, and Gideon helped him tie the two rods on either side of Helena's injured limb to give it stability. Her moans during their efforts clutched Gideon's heart, and he ground his teeth.

Samson glanced at him. "Now you don't go worrying none, sir. You know we must get it stabilized if we're going to move her."

Gideon nodded, a muscle working in his jaw.

Finally, they were ready to leave. Gideon mounted Hero, then

Samson slid his thick arms under Helena and her bound leg, lifted her from the grass, and handed her into Gideon's arms.

The slow ride back to the plantation with the sun sinking into the west and Helena in his arms filled Gideon with an unexpected peace. Three times, she whispered his name and baptized his heart with hope. Could God work good out of this accident and bring them together as true husband and wife?

～

"*I* will not drink any more of that horrid broth!" Helena knocked the tray from Belle's hand. The cup smashed against the wall, and the brown liquid streamed down onto the polished pine floor and ran toward the bedroom rug. How dare Belle ignore her instructions.

Belle's nostrils flared. "Well, Mrs. Falconer, what do you want to eat? We're just following the doctor's orders."

Helena glared at her injured leg, propped up on a pillow. The doctor had plastered it with a dried mixture of egg white and flour. Beneath the clumsy cast, her leg ached, and a spot behind her knee itched. She tried to lift her leg to a more comfortable position, but her limb refused to move. Flopping back onto the bed, she glowered at the carved cherubs on the ceiling. "I don't care what Dr. Thomas said. Two days of broth is long enough. I want some real food."

She reached for her hand mirror on the bedside table and glanced at her face. She forced the angry lines to relax. Who wanted to get wrinkles like that? Belle had plaited her thick hair into two braids and tied the ends with pink ribbon that matched the lovely gown her father and aunt had sent her just after her accident. She wanted to look beautiful, even with her plunky, stiff leg, but she felt ugly and useless. And she was downright hungry.

A knock sounded at the door.

"Enter," Helena called. Anger still laced her voice, but she didn't care.

Gideon strode in and up to her bed. "What was that I heard

coming down the hall?" He glanced at Belle busy cleaning up the spilled broth and broken cup with her lips in a tight line.

Helena cast her eyes up to his and said as calmly as she could manage, "Gideon, I need some real food."

He smiled and sent his hat spinning onto her bed. His gray eyes shone as he drew near. "And you will have it. In fact, how would you like to get out of this room for a bit?"

Had she heard right? "Oh, Gideon. Could I? But how...?" She glanced down at her immobile limb and shook her head.

"Like this." He stepped close, bent, and slipped his arms beneath her, including her plastered leg. "Now, put your arms around my neck."

"Oh-h. I will." She placed her arms around his shoulders and clasped them behind his neck. His fresh outdoor smell of sunshine, horses, and hay made her frustration melt. But when he lifted her into his arms, she expelled a fast breath, expecting pain in her injured leg. But none came. She laid her head against his chest and smiled. His heartbeat drummed against her cheek. No other man had ever made her feel so safe and cared for.

"Belle, bring that pillow and Helena's robe." Gideon eased her through the portal and down the hall. At the door that led onto the second-story veranda at the back of the house, he stepped outside. A view of the river beyond a wide sweep of green lawn met Helena's gaze. Her husband strolled across the porch with her in his arms and, with tender care, settled her in a cushioned wicker chaise lounge. She released her arms from around his neck, exhaled a happy breath, and relaxed against the chaise. Looking up in his face, she smiled.

The maid arrived with the pillow and robe. She placed the robe over Helena's shoulders.

With a careful touch, Gideon lifted her injured leg and propped it on the pillow.

Helena looked around and inhaled a deep breath of fresh, sunshine-laced air. Birds twittered in the tops of oak and pine trees towering beyond the porch railing. Thick green grass carpeted the lawn. Beyond the outbuildings and stable, the Ashley River gleamed in the bright sunlight. She grabbed Gideon's hand. "Thank you so much, Gideon. How tired I was of my room."

He grinned and squeezed her fingers. "There's no reason you can't be out here most days if you'd like to be. Now, my lady, what would you like for a starter of real food?"

Visions of bacon and eggs, grits, and biscuits floated across her mind. "Tell Marm Esther to send all my favorites. She'll know."

Belle sidled closer. "*All* your favorites, ma'am?"

Helena cast her servant a fleeting glance before she directed her smile at Gideon. "Well, some now and others later."

Belle left, clicking her tongue.

Gideon folded his arms. "I'm glad you have an appetite, Helena. It's a good sign you're healing. Now I'll head out to the farm. I'll be back in a few hours to see if you're ready to go inside."

He retreated into the house, and the screened door clanged behind him.

Helena snagged her lower lip between her teeth. Without his presence, the veranda became lonely, and the sunshine lost some of its luster. The memory of his arms carrying her still caused a hitch in her breath. And she loved being out of her room in the pine-laced air.

Why was Gideon so good to her? She stared out across the veranda railing to the greenery and flowers, past the sundial, and down the path to the boat dock. The Ashley River gleamed in the sun and reminded her why he was good to her. Windemere—the rich jewel her father had promised him if he married her. She forced her pleasant thoughts of Gideon back into the cage of make-believe where they belonged. Her leg ached more. The root doctor's words came back. Trouble over Windemere. People not liking other people, the woman had said. She shivered. In no way could that have anything to do with her feelings about Gideon. She adjusted the position of her leg with her hands for a little relief from the new ache starting up her limb. One thing was sure. Her broken leg spelled nothing but trouble.

～

*G*ideon retrieved his hat from Helena's bed, then stood a moment breathing in the room's lavender fragrance. Lavender, the scent his wife loved to wear. Carrying her in his arms had made his heart ache with longing for the loving relationship they should be enjoying. Why had this accident happened and put a hindrance on that possibility? But would it be a hindrance or rather some help? Helena would need him to carry her to the veranda for several weeks. Having her arms around his neck and her head resting in the curve of his shoulder had been pure bliss.

By the time he had Hero saddled, he was whistling. He galloped to the slave village where Samson was to help Kunta distribute the promised cloth to the women. The day before, when Gideon had instructed Kunta to provide the women with cloth, the young man's blue eyes had flashed. He'd declared that Gideon was coddling them and would regret it.

When he rode into the slave village, the happy chattering of women greeted him. Groups of women gathered about the delivery wagon, where the final bolts of cloth and sewing notions were being distributed. He dismounted, tied his horse's reins to the wagon seat, and hailed Samson as he handed out the last bolt of cloth, thread, and needles to Sadie and May, whom they'd met earlier.

Sadie smiled as he came up. "Sir, we alls really 'preciate this cloth. We wuz in sore need, but now we'll be fine. Just give us time to make it up into dresses and shirts, and you'll be proud of us."

Humbled at her gratitude, Gideon ducked his head. "You're most welcome—all of you are."

After Sadie and May left, Gideon turned to Samson. "Where is Kunta? He was supposed to help do this." He kept his voice low so the slaves couldn't hear it.

Samson nodded. "Yes, sir, I know he was, but he had such a stinking attitude. Said you'd be real sorry for petting the slaves. Hope you don't mind, but I tol' him to just go on about his business with the cotton hoeing if he couldn't be happy to help the women, and he stomped off."

Gideon's lips tightened. "This was a chance for him to show his respect for my orders, Samson. And he's failed the test. I'm glad you didn't let him come and spoil this for the women. I will have to take that young man in hand, soon. But first, I want to deal with our stable hand. Did you put Helena's saddle up somewhere?"

"Yes, sir. I did. I knowed you would want to show it to him one day. He had to be drunk or plain careless to saddle her horse up with that cinch bitten halfway through."

"When you get back to the stable, I want you to bring that saddle to my office and leave it."

"Yes, sir."

Samson climbed into the wagon and headed back to the plantation. Gideon spoke to the other slaves standing in their doorways, then mounted Hero and arrived back at the stable just after Samson left the wagon.

Tom came out to take care of the horses and wagon. Gideon spoke to him. "Tom, go ahead and put up the horses and wagon, then come to my study. We need to talk."

Tom's eyes widened and his hand shook as he took the reins of the horses. "Yes, sir. In the house, Mr. Allston's office he used to have?"

"Yes, that's right." Gideon turned his back on the stable hand and stalked into the house, turning his steps to the study. Pushing open the door, he tossed his hat onto a chair and sat behind the desk. Samson had placed Helena's saddle on his desktop, the damaged girth plainly visible. Angry heat rose up his neck as he looked at it. Minutes later, a knock sounded at the door.

"Enter."

Tom entered, hat in hand, and the smell of old tobacco floated around him. His eyes lit on the saddle, then on Gideon.

"This is the saddle you placed on Mrs. Falconer's horse the day she had her accident." Gideon pointed to the cinch.

The man's dark eyes widened. "Why, that cinch done been eaten through, maybe by rats." Then his eyes blazed, and he folded his arms. "Or somebody done cut it, but it wasn't me. No sirree. You can't blame that on me."

"However it happened, Tom, how could you miss seeing it when you put this saddle on Stormy?"

The man gulped. "Sir, I...don't know about that." His deeply tanned face turned red. Then his tobacco-stained lips tightened. "You sure this is the same saddle?"

"Yes, I'm sure. Tom, I'm sorry but you can no longer work here. Drinking while on the job is never a good thing. You had to be drinking to miss seeing this. I hope you can get your life together. If you do, come back to see me and we'll talk." He pulled open a drawer and withdrew a small bag of coins. "Here is a month's pay and a little more."

Tom ignored the offer. His whole body stiffened, and his lips drew into a snarl. "You think you can fire me over this? We'll see what Mr. Allston has to say about it."

"I know Mr. Allston hired you because his friend recommended you. But I now own the plantation." He worked hard to give the man a nonthreatening look. "If I show this saddle that resulted in his daughter's accident to John, do you think he'll still back you?"

Tom grabbed the money, then turned and stalked out of the room, muttering angry words.

Gideon listened to his retreating steps, then sank back into his chair for a moment. Firing a person was never a happy task.

He rose and headed up the stairs and to the veranda where Helena awaited his return, hopefully.

Halting in the doorway, Gideon gazed at the woman he loved. His heart raced, and his breathing hitched. Would the sight of her always do this to him? She reclined on the chaise lounge with her leg propped on the pillow. The deep pink color of her gown complemented her fair complexion and accented the blush on her cheeks. A book lay gripped in her hands as she gazed over the railing, a thoughtful expression on her face. This was not the childlike girl he'd comforted that night in Savannah. This was a woman with all sorts of possibilities blossoming within her.

As he stepped onto the balcony, she swung her head in his direction. Her face brightened as she saw him, and it pleased him more than he wanted to admit. Was she missing him and welcoming his presence? He stopped in front of her and noted the glow on her cheeks, her shining eyes and relaxed attitude. "I believe this outdoor time has been good for you, Helena, and you'll be up and about in no time."

"I'm glad you're back, Gideon. I'm ready to go in." She held up her arms.

Did her voice carry a welcome, or was he imagining it? He bent and scooped her up, clutching her book in her hand. When her other wrist circled his neck, he inhaled her sweet lavender scent and held her close. She surprised him by not resisting. Surely, they were making progress.

In her room, he tightened his arms around her before he laid her on her bed. She looked up at him with a question in her eyes, and unable to help himself, he leaned closer and kissed her lips. At first, she stiffened, but when he deepened the kiss, her lips responded and set his heart on fire. The next instant, she pushed away.

"Put me down, Gideon."

With great reluctance, he released her onto the bed and tried to control his breathing. He propped pillows behind her head and under her leg, then he took her hand in his and looked deep into her eyes.

"Helena, surely you've guessed that I've fallen in love with you. Do you have any feelings for me? I know you do from that kiss just now."

She pulled her hand from his. "Kisses can mean a lot of things." Averting her face, she picked at the embroidered flowers on the bedspread. Finally, she looked up at him and met his intense look. "I don't know what I feel for you, Gideon. You are a...good man, and I appreciate all you've done for me. But I still need more time for...our relationship to grow." She opened her book.

Gideon frowned, turned, and strode out the door. Better to leave than to say something he'd regret later. He wanted to remind her she was his wife, and it'd been several weeks, though it seemed like months, since they'd married. And hadn't he done everything he knew to show her love and win her affection?

He clenched his eyes shut for a moment, then popped them back open. His mother would know what to do to help him win Helena's heart. Surely, she would arrive soon. Or had her ship met disaster between England and Charleston?

A pang struck his heart. He'd neglected some of his diligent praying the past few days. And where was the nearest house of worship to assist in his spiritual walk? He needed to find a church, like the small one he'd once seen through the trees on Charleston Road. The little chapel at Brighton Plantation he'd attended closed when the property was sold. Would he be able to interest Helena in attending service once she was out of her cast? Surely, if they grew together spiritually...

He strode to his room and fell on his knees by his bed and prayed a fervent prayer for his mother's safe arrival.

~

As the door closed behind Gideon, Helena sighed. That kiss of his had almost undone her. What was she thinking to allow it? Not to mention, respond to it and his magnetic presence? Yet, even now, his handsome, sad face as he left the room managed to tug at her heart. Yes, she was beginning to have feelings for him. But she must keep reminding herself why she should not give in to those emotions—until she knew the truth. Did he really love her, or did he agree to marry her for the gift of Windemere? Or was it simply to save her reputation? That was definitely why she'd married him. She shook her head and sighed, hating to mull over the same old thoughts. Perhaps she was as guilty as he in marrying for the wrong reason. Could God build anything good out of their union? There had to be a way to find real happiness such as her father and mother had enjoyed. She snagged her lower lip between her teeth. *Hadn't* they enjoyed a good marriage? Her father had been gone a lot, but her mother hadn't seemed to mind it so much.

Helena picked up her book. Meanwhile, perhaps she should make more of an effort to get to know the man she'd married, for right reasons or not. She smiled. He'd really been attentive to her needs during her recovery.

~

The following Sunday, Gideon invited Samson to visit the small church he'd found on Charleston Road. They must have passed it each time they came to Windemere, but he'd hardly noticed it hidden among the Spanish moss–covered trees towering around it like sentinels. As they reined their horses into the narrow drive and approached the modest brick structure, a fenceless ceme-tery emerged around one side and stretched around the back of the building. Old sun-bleached headstones rose from the ground like actors in a suddenly ceased drama. Flowers bloomed along a seashell path among the tombstones. The rest of the yard surrounding the church was also neat. Someone had thought of making the place more pleasant to the eye.

Samson turned to Gideon. "What kind of church is it, sir?"

Gideon gestured to the small brick sign just ahead. An engraved metal plate read, *St. John's Parish Church–Founded in 1740.*

"But notice the newer sign closer to the entrance." Gideon read it aloud. "'First Baptist Missionary Church, 1805, Reverend Thomas Wingard.'"

He reined his stallion to a hitching post where other horses stood nearby and dismounted as Samson did the same. "The war may have changed the church's identity, especially if it was built by loyal British." Gideon eyed the few carriages parked under the shade of trees, their servant drivers with them. Not a large congregation, most likely.

Samson hesitated and turned to Gideon with his brows raised. "You think a black man'll be welcome in this church, sir?"

Before Gideon could answer, a small cart drawn by a mule came up the drive and stopped under a shade tree near them. To the surprise of them both, Belle, Helena's maid, disembarked and rustled toward them in a red dress and headpiece, leaving her boy driver with the cart. She carried tan gloves and a reticule.

Samson whistled under his breath, and Gideon smiled.

"Good morning, sir." She nodded at Gideon and turned to Samson. "You wondering if you can go in?" She turned a bright smile on him, and her amber eyes beamed in merriment.

He ducked his head, then grinned. "You got that right, Miz Belle."

"Come with me. We sit in the balcony."

"Yes, ma'am." Samson's face glowed with pleasure as he threw a glance at Gideon, then followed Belle into the church.

Gideon strolled through the heavy wooden doors into the sanctuary's cooler interior. The building's thick walls shut out the muggy heat that lay like a smothering blanket outside. An organ pealed forth "A Mighty Fortress Is Our God." He found an empty boxed pew made of bright reddish-brown mahogany and smelling of lemon oil. A low titter of women's voices sprung up around him from nearby pews as he took his seat. He discerned the words of one voice. "Why, it's the new owner of Windemere who married Allston's daughter."

The minister, holding a Bible and notebook, emerged from an interior door and walked onto the platform. Unlike the thin, studious clergy Gideon had often seen, this thickset man exuded strength. He stepped to the lectern, laid his Bible and notes there, then beamed a pleasant smile and welcome over his congregation. Gideon gave the clergyman a respectful nod when the man's bright eyes hesitated on him. Silver streaked the man's short, dark hair, and his face evidenced a tan as if he spent time outdoors. He engaged Gideon's full attention.

When the man prayed the opening prayer and began his message, his robust voice rolled over the sanctuary with anointing and confidence like the voice of Gideon's English minister friend, John Newton. The speaker easily held the congregation's attention with his text and exposition of the prodigal son in Luke 15.

At the door after the service, the minister offered a surprisingly strong, roughened hand to Gideon. "Thomas Wingard, sir. We were delighted to have you visit our service."

Gideon shook his hand. "Gideon Falconer."

"From Windemere Plantation, I believe?"

"Yes, I married Helena Allston."

"How is she? We've only recently returned from an extended upcountry mission trip, but we've heard about her riding accident." A quick smile creased the minister's face. "The slaves' chatter line is alive and well over the parish. Never doubt it."

Gideon smiled. "Doing well. She'll be rid of her leg cast in another couple of weeks."

The woman who had played the organ drew near and hesitated. The minister touched her arm. "May I present my wife, Mary? Dear, this is Gideon Falconer, from Windemere, Helena Allston's husband."

The petite woman, dressed simply in a lavender dress, had the same pleasant expression and smile wrinkles as her husband. The hair that peeked from her bonnet was mostly silver. "Happy to make your acquaintance, Mr. Falconer. Do you think Mrs. Falconer would appreciate a visit from us? We would have come before had we been in the parish. Her mother once attended here, but more often, the two of them attended a church in Charleston nearer their town house and other plantation."

"I'm sure Helena would welcome a visit, ma'am. Her leg in a cast prevents her from making visits herself. Why don't you plan to come for tea? Most any day would be fine."

"We'll do that one day this week. How about Tuesday, about four p.m.?"

"That will be fine."

Mary Wingard moved away toward other groups gathered to talk on the front lawn.

Several greeted Gideon as he walked to his horse. Samson appeared and mounted his own horse for the ride back to Windemere.

"Seem like some fine people, that minister and his wife. Belle told me they not only care for their members, but they also keep the property in attractive shape."

"I agree, they seem like good salt of the earth people, and they said they'll visit Helena." He grinned at Samson. "And how was your time with the attractive Belle in the balcony? Did you hear any kind of bells ringing?"

Samson shook his head. "Don't go there, sir. She's a fine woman, but what man can keep up with what goes on in that clever mind?"

~

After church, Gideon found Helena already on the veranda. She'd been sleeping when he left that morning. The crutches he'd made for her leaned against the wall nearby. So she'd learned to use them when she'd been refusing to even try. Good girl. Hoping she'd attend church with him when out of her cast, he took a chair next to her and shared his experience with her, including his invitation to the minister and his wife for tea.

"You invited *who* to come have tea with me?" Helena's voice verged on shrillness, and pink flooded her frowning face.

"Pastor Thomas Wingard and his wife, Mary. Fine people. Have you met them?"

"From that little Baptist church which they stole from the Anglicans after the Revolution?" Her lips thinned into a tight line. "Oh yes, I visited once, and I don't like them. He doesn't even wear a robe when he preaches, and his hands are like a field worker's. And she doesn't dress like a minister's wife should—she has no idea of current fashion." Helena bent and adjusted the pillow under her leg and then turned back to glare at him.

Gideon folded his arms and frowned. "Helena, you sound like a spoiled child."

Her eyes flashed. "It's not spoiled to want to choose your guests for tea, Gideon."

Her hard voice struck something deep inside him. Was she that coldhearted and careless about showing kindness and hospitality to others? He'd seen enough of that before he'd left England.

Biting back a retort, he stood and strode into the upstairs hall. A muscle quivered in his neck, and he took a deep, exasperated breath. Helena would receive the Wingards, even if he had to bring her down to the parlor himself when they came. He made a mental note to tell Belle to alert him when the minister and his wife came.

Two days later, on Tuesday, Gideon was directing the work on a new fence past the back corral when Belle came to tell him the Wingards had arrived promptly at four o'clock. He dismissed his helpers, washed off at the watering trough, and headed upstairs to the veranda.

Helena sat propped up on her lounge in a yellow day dress, reading a book.

"The Wingards are here, and I expect you to receive them. I'll carry you down to the parlor."

She lifted her stiff face to his. "I know they've come, but I have a headache and will not be able to receive them."

He gritted his teeth and bent to pick her up, anyway, but she held up her hands to resist.

"Gideon, I will not accept this kind of treatment. I told you I did not want to entertain them, and I won't." Her lips hardened into a pout.

He straightened and crossed his arms over his chest. Heat shimmied up his back and into his face. White-hot anger rose in his throat, but he bit it back and forced his voice to calmness. "All right. But let me tell you what that will force me to do. As my wife, you have certain responsibilities, and receiving our guests is one of them. If you won't come down with me and be the hostess you should be to these good people, I'll make your excuses. But tomorrow, I will have Belle pack your clothes, and I'll send you back to your father's house to stay until you decide you want to be a decent wife and mistress at Windemere."

Her hand flew to her chest, and her eyes widened.

He turned and strode through the door. Perhaps she had finally heard him.

CHAPTER 8

$\mathcal{H}$elena squeezed her eyes shut and gulped. How would she ever live it down if Gideon carried out his threat to send her packing to her father? All her Charleston friends would pity her. Even Rachel, due back from Europe at the end of summer. Her enemies would gloat over her fall from marital bliss. And her father might have a heart attack. In short, it would be a disaster.

She took a deep breath. "Gideon!" Her voice cracked with the effort to make herself heard.

His heavy steps soon sounded on the landing. When he pushed through the door, she held up her arms. "I've changed my mind. Take me down to the parlor and the Wingards. Even those two will be a welcome change from this upstairs existence."

His gray eyes brightened, and a smile played at his lips. "Good." He bent and lifted her.

She placed her arms around his neck and savored the outdoor smell of him laced with a familiar spice. Would it be such a bad thing...to please him?

week later, Gideon walked to the stable, relishing Dr. Burton's good news. He would remove Helena's cast at the end of the week, but he advised her to continue using her crutches for a few days. But how long would Gideon be able to keep her off Stormy? She was already talking of galloping again over her favorite trails on the plantation. Showing her the saddle with its new cinch might have been a mistake. He frowned, then remembered how well the visit went with the minister and wife after he insisted Helena receive them. She carried on a good conversation, put them at ease, and made friends. A perfect hostess. Perhaps she was growing up, and their relationship had moved to a new level. At least he could hope.

He threw the tack on Hero and went for a long ride. With Bentley loping beside him, he inspected the growth of the cotton and mulled over the meeting he'd called for Kunta later that day. He would not allow the young man to undermine the helpful things Gideon intended to do for the Windemere slaves. Samson's report of how Kunta responded when asked to help distribute the fabrics to the women annoyed Gideon. One would think the man would be happy to make the lives of his own people easier. If his response to Samson was an example of his attitude, how would he respond to Gideon freeing all the plantation slaves one day?

Back at the house while he sat at his desk awaiting Kunta's arrival, he groaned as a flashback to his slaver ship days possessed him. If God had forgiven him, why did the memories still taunt him? Would his freeing the slaves at Windemere finally bring his own release? He took a deep breath and clenched his eyes for a moment. Had Father God sent the memory to make sure he wasn't too hard on the young man? Kunta resented his mixed parentage and place in life as a result. Had he been the firstborn son of John Allston in a legal marriage, he would have inherited the Allston estate, but he had been born of a slave woman instead. Did Kunta resent him and Helena, the new owners of Windemere Plantation?

A sudden change in the room's atmosphere caused Gideon to open his eyes and sit forward. Kunta stood inside the doorway, clutching his sweat-stained hat in his hands and staring at him with a stiff, rebellious face. He wasn't as tall as Gideon, but he made up for it in a stocky build with thick broad shoulders and muscled arms that strained the seams of the blue shirt he wore. Was it the color of the garment he wore that made his eyes look so blue and reminiscent of John Allston?

"Come in and sit, Kunta." Gideon gestured to the chairs in front of the desk.

The boy eased into the room and slid into one of the seats. But he sat forward on its edge. "What you wanna to talk to me about, Mr. Gideon?" His nervous voice rumbled from deep in his chest.

"Kunta, are you happy here at Windemere?"

The young man's eyes flashed. "Why shouldn't I be? It's always been my home, and Massa Allston done give me my freedom papers."

"Yes, I know." Gideon hesitated but a moment, then decided to place all the cards on the table. "I also know you are John Allston's son, but your mother was a slave."

Kunta's nostrils flared. "Old news. What else is on your mind?"

Gideon sat forward and steepled his hands on the desk. Could he figure out how to break through the tough shell of this sixteen-year-old? Would Gideon's own story open a door? "I'm going to share something of my history, Kunta, that no one else knows yet at Windemere, but first, let me tell you what prompted me to call you here today."

"That's what I'm waiting for."

Gideon heard the mumbled words and decided to ignore the disrespect that laced them. "Samson alerted me to your attitude when we distributed fabric to the slave women. I'm simply curious. Why wouldn't you want to help some of your own people?"

"Give 'em an inch, and they'll want more, that's why."

"Well, I'm telling you today, Kunta, that I have other plans, a lot bigger things I may do for the enslaved people at Windemere. If you would like to stay here—you're a freedman and can go anywhere you choose—but I need you to flow with the plans if you want to stay."

Surprise flooded Kunta's face. His full lips thinned. "But...Massa Allston would never 'low you make me leave."

Gideon looked him straight in the eye. "Kunta, I'm now master here, and John Allston has given me full authority to do whatever I feel best." He leaned back in his chair and said in a more pleasant voice, "But I hope you'll become a willing part of my efforts to better the lives of the slaves and be a good helper. But that's your choice. Now back to the personal history that I mentioned, so you'll understand where I'm coming from."

"I heard you come from England."

"Yes, I did. When in England, I became good friends with two men who are to this day working to stop the slave trade and then free every slave in the British Empire. Their names are John Newton and William Wilberforce."

Kunta's eyes widened, and he sat back in his chair and gave his full attention. "All the slaves?"

Gideon moistened his lips and exhaled his breath. "Yes, all the slaves, and I happen to believe like they do. You, of all people, having been born a slave, ought to understand how good freedom is."

"You call yo'self one of them 'bolitionists?" Kunta's voice rose with disbelief.

Hopefully, he'd not made a mistake sharing this with Kunta. He needed to reach the man's heart. Had he?

"I don't call myself anything but a man who loves God and his fellow man, no matter the color of his skin."

Kunta shook his head as if he didn't believe what he was hearing or couldn't process it.

Gideon stood. "Think about it, Kunta. What do you say? Do you want to stay here and help me help your people, or would you prefer to find another place to work? In fact, I'll even give you a parcel of land you can farm on your own, if you want to leave."

Kunta stood, holding his hat, frowning. "No, suh. I ain't wantin to leave. No, suh. This here is my home."

"Then can I count on your cooperation? Because if I can't, we can still arrange your finding a new place to live." Gideon gave him his most serious look.

Kunta's fists tightened on the brim of his hat, and his eyes blazed before he lowered them. "Yes, suh. You can count on Kunta." His voice was flat and low. He moved to the door, plopped the hat on his head, and left.

Gideon sighed. Had he made any progress with the young man at all? Had he made a mistake telling him his thoughts on abolition? Time would tell. He sat in his chair and pulled out the plantation books to check the accounts and the harvest schedule.

~

On the first day without her crutches, Helena leaned over the balcony railing and spied the new stable manager's—Joseph Laurens's—twelve-year-old son, Daniel, leading Stormy from the lower pasture to the barn for the evening. The boy's mother was also their new housekeeper.

Stormy looked to be in excellent shape. Her heart skipped a beat. Tomorrow she would ride the mare again for the first time since the accident. Gideon made her promise to wait this one extra day after dispensing with the crutches.

She whistled, and both horse and boy looked up at her. "Tomorrow, Daniel, tomorrow, I will be able to ride Stormy again. Will you have her ready early in the morning?"

"Yes, ma'am. How early? I'll be happy to have her ready."

Helena liked the respectful attitude of the boy. The Laurens family came as indentured servants from Ireland and had already endeared themselves at Windemere with their positive outlook, diligent work, and Christian faith.

"As soon as it's daylight." Helena almost sang the refrain—*as soon as it's daylight*—and she chuckled. How she had missed riding Stormy, exploring the acres and woodlands of Windemere and spending time in her secret place.

Galloping hooves and the bumping and squeaking of a coach and four sounded from the front of the house. Startled, Helena checked the small watch pinned to the top of her day dress. Visitors? Who could be coming in a coach to Windemere at five o'clock in the afternoon? She hurried to her room to freshen up.

CHAPTER 9

Gideon rode into the stable yard and flung himself from the saddle. He handed the reins to Joseph Laurens and strode toward the house. From a distance. he'd seen the large coach and four horses headed down the long Windemere drive. Hope rose in his breast. It had to be her—his mother from England.

He entered the back door and hurried through the house to the front entrance as the heavily laden conveyance pulled up to the steps. One of the two drivers jumped down to hold the lead horse's bridle. The other climbed down to open the passenger door. The man bowed and said, "We're here at Windemere Plantation, ma'am."

Gideon grinned as his mother, Merle Falconer Rhett, leaned forward to stare at the house and remark to a fellow passenger Gideon couldn't see, "Thank God. We've made it, dear, and isn't it a beautiful place?" To whom could she be talking?

Gideon flew down the steps and extended his hand to his mother. She alighted, and he drew her into his arms for a warm hug and kiss on her cheek. "Mother, I've been looking for you and praying all was going well."

Another face emerged, framed in the coach door, a face he knew as well as his mother's. "Lydia?" His voice had turned hoarse.

He released his mother and held out his hand to help his former fiancée disembark. His head whirled, and for a moment, his brain refused to process what his eyes saw.

Lydia Lewis leaned over and gave him a brief hug. "Yes, it's me, Gideon. Had you forgotten me? I got tired of waiting for a letter from you, and when your mother announced she would be coming to America and needed a traveling companion, of course, she thought of me." She shook wrinkles out of her mauve gown and removed her bonnet.

Heat filled Gideon's face, and the breath strangled in his throat. "Of course, I haven't forgotten you, Lydia. Welcome to Windemere...both of you." He ducked his head, and with a lady on each arm, led them through the group of curious servants who'd gathered on the veranda, then into the parlor.

"Son, I thought you lived at a place called Brighton Plantation. But a man at the harbor who met one of our fellow passengers at the dock told us you'd be here. He was so kind to hire this coach for us." His mother smiled and eyed the spacious parlor. "How did you come to be at this lovely place called Windemere?"

Gideon's mind grappled with surprise and not a little unease about the passenger accompanying his mother. But thank God, John Allston's clerk had assisted them to Windemere. "I will explain, Mother."

The new housekeeper, Nell Laurens, appeared at his elbow. "Tea for your guests, Mr. Falconer?"

He turned to her, trying to wipe the perplexity from his mind, and spoke in a low voice. "Yes, Mrs. Laurens, the very thing. And please prepare two rooms for our guests and have the footmen take up their luggage."

Lydia walked about the area, admiring the drapes and new fabrics on the furniture, reminding Gideon of her sewing and design skills. She was still an attractive woman with her slender form clad in a fashionable green dress and cloak she'd probably made herself. Her brown hair gathered in soft coils on her head complemented her graceful form. What would Helena think of her? How would he ever explain himself to either of them—his wife or his former fiancé?

He tore his gaze from Lydia to seat his mother on the best chair in the room, then asked in a lower voice, "Did you not get a second letter from me after I sent you the traveling funds? I explained everything."

Her pale gray eyes widened. "A second letter? No, only the one you sent with the traveling funds. Did you send another letter?" Her countenance took on a troubled look. She surely discerned, as she'd always been able to, that something disturbed him.

Lydia approached them. "Gideon, this is a lovely room. Whoever chose the colors and patterns really has excellent taste." She started to say something else but hesitated and looked from one of them to the other. "Is anything wrong? You two look concerned about something."

Gideon tried to smile but failed. "Come, Lydia, sit near Mother. I have something...surprising to tell you both." *And it's not going to be easy*, his mind screamed, *for either of you*. Especially his former fiancée. Although he'd never actually proposed to Lydia, they'd been close long enough for people to assume their engagement. And his mother had been one of those. How could he make the news of his marriage less upsetting?

He sat across from them and addressed his mother. "I did send you a second letter about a week after the first one I sent with the traveling funds." He took a deep breath and made himself meet Lydia's expressive brown eyes. "The second letter announced...my marriage."

Lydia clasped her hands together, and a shadow dropped over her face like a curtain.

His mother's mouth fell open, and she reached over and patted Lydia's clutched hands. "Married? Why, Gideon, I've never been so surprised." She turned a kind glance on the younger woman. "Maybe not as much as Lydia, but you never mentioned in any earlier letters about a...a courtship here."

Gideon sucked in a hard breath. "I know... It's a long story."

"What's a long story?" Helena appeared in the parlor doorway. The housekeeper followed, clutching a tea tray. "Gideon, who are our guests? I heard the coach arrive, and I came down as quick as I could to meet our visitors." Her eyes flowed from his mother to his former fiancée, then back to him.

Gideon rose and came to her side. "Dear, come join us. This is my mother, Merle Falconer Rhett, who has arrived from England, and Lydia Lewis...her traveling companion." He stumbled over the last introduction, but Helena didn't appear to notice. "This is my wife, Helena."

Lydia's face turned to alabaster beneath her smile of acknowledgement.

His mother's eyes widened, then softened. "Why, how delightful. So happy to meet you, Helena."

"Your mother?" He almost missed Helena's soft voice as she stared at his mother, then took a seat.

"Yes, my mother decided to emigrate from England."

Helena smiled at Mother, then cast a look at Lydia. "Happy to meet both of you."

His former fiancée nodded, returned Helena's glance, then lowered her eyes.

Gideon swallowed. What was going on in Lydia's mind or his wife's? How would he ever be able to explain without angering or disappointing one or both? The fact that he'd never actually proposed to Lydia didn't seem to be much of an explanation or excuse—and one he'd never mention.

After setting the tea tray on the small table in front of the sofa, Mrs. Laurens curtsied to the ladies and left.

Helena's voice broke the silence. "Mrs. Rhett, would you be so kind as to serve the tea? My head's in a bit of a whirl, and I don't trust myself to do the best job. Then we will continue our conversation." Her voice lacked its usual bold confidence.

"Certainly, my dear."

His mother's calm manner as she poured the tea into gilt-rimmed cups restored Gideon's composure. She would handle the situation with her usual wisdom and finesse. He only needed to sit back and listen. He expelled a breath, not knowing he'd been holding it, and reached for a cucumber sandwich.

Helena stirred three teaspoons of sugar into her tea and took a sip. "Gideon, what's the long story you were mentioning as I arrived?" She cast her blue eyes at him, then toward his mother.

Lydia studied her tea plate.

Gideon swiped the napkin across his mouth and searched for the best reply. His mother intervened with the plain truth. Her nature never tolerated sidestepping or fabricating. She leaned back in her chair with her cup in hand. "Oh, I had just expressed surprise upon learning he was married and told him I didn't recall his mentioning a...courtship in any of his letters. That's when he said it was a long story."

Gideon cleared his throat. "Yes, well, we've only been married a few months. It was sort of a—"

"Whirlwind romance?" Lydia's soft voice floated on the air. He'd forgotten what a sweet, feminine tone and intuition she had. "I've heard of such. And, Gideon, seeing you here at this beautiful plantation with your lovely bride, I'm happy for you both." She turned a smile toward Helena.

The grace in the woman's heart astonished Gideon, and he fought the guilt that tried to oppress him. Unquestionably, she'd agreed to come to Charleston thinking the two of them could continue their courtship. Then to find him married without so much as a word to her beforehand. The back of his neck grew warm.

Helena set her cup and plate on the tray and glanced at the two women. "Actually, it's a very short story." Something akin to fire ignited her blue eyes when she turned them back to Gideon.

His breath caught in his throat, and he hastily took a swallow of tea. Would she share all the facts of their hasty marriage?

"I was in the process of running away from an undesired marriage offer from a hated suitor, and I drove my horse into the Ashley River you passed coming here. I would've drowned had Gideon not arrived and rescued me."

His mother's face relaxed. "So that's how you met. Sounds just like my son. From a boy, he was forever rescuing someone or some furry creature."

Mrs. Laurens arrived in the doorway. "Please excuse me, sir, but we have the two rooms ready for your guests." The housekeeper looked from him to Helena, then to the new arrivals.

Gideon wiped a bead of sweat from his upper lip and stood. "Mother, Lydia, we can continue our conversation at dinner tonight. I'm sure you're both tired and would love to get unpacked. Our servants have moved your luggage into your rooms. What do you say?"

"Oh, son, you're exactly right. I would so love to freshen up and rest a while before the evening meal. I'm sure Lydia will agree." She stood, and Lydia nodded and rose beside her.

Helena stood as well.

Mother reached for Helena's hand and pressed it. "It's been wonderful to meet you, my dear." Then she gave Gideon a peck on his cheek. "See you, later, son."

After his mother and Lydia followed Mrs. Laurens from the parlor and their steps echoed on the stairs, Gideon turned to Helena. "Thank you for bailing me out with your simple account of our meeting, Helena. I wasn't sure how much you might want to share...about our marriage. Do you think we'll need to give more detail at dinner tonight?"

She looked at him and folded her arms. "No, let me handle it. I look forward to getting to know your mother better. Kindness fairly oozes from her." She cocked her chin, then added, "And her traveling companion seems nice as well, but not the dowdy companion type one usually sees."

Was that a question mark at the end of Helena's last statement?

~

The next morning, Helena sat at her dresser as Belle brushed and set her hair in a sophisticated hairdo. "I know you want to look your best for Mr. Gideon's mother...and her friend." Her dark eyes sought Helena's in the mirror.

"Belle, what do you think of our two guests?" The disappointment of having to put off her morning ride in honor of their guests still rankled Helena. She'd sent word to Daniel after dinner the night before.

Their evening meal had answered the questions Helena might have wanted to ask as Mrs. Rhett led the conversation in a confident voice and told of her life in England and her late husband's death of a heart attack. Then Gideon's letter came with the invitation to America.

The quiet Lydia had inserted, "And I, too, had nothing to keep me in England, so I was happy to accompany her."

There was never a need to give more detail about Helena's marriage to Gideon.

She couldn't help but notice how Gideon looked at Lydia when she spoke and how the conversation between them flowed so naturally. Had Gideon and Lydia been friends when he lived in England? Or...

Belle cleared her throat and brought Helena back to the present. "What do I think? Gideon's mother and Miss Lewis are special and nice folks. But..."

"What?"

Belle bit her lip as if not sure she ought to say what was on her mind. "Nothing. It's nothing."

Helena knew her maid and friend too well to let it go. "Yes, it is. What were you going to say?"

Belle took a deep breath. "That Miss Lewis is a lovely, kind person, and...I just wonder if...she and Mr. Gideon might have been good friends back in England. That's all. They seem to know each other well, the way they talk."

The same idea had come to her at dinner. Was Lydia more than

Mrs. Rhett's traveling companion? She sighed and pushed Belle's hands away. "That's enough on the hair. Please go ask my husband to come to me." She'd question him outright about any former relationship with the attractive Lydia.

Belle soon returned. "I can't seem to find Mr. Gideon. At least he's not in the dining room. Shall I go out to the barn?"

Helena's lips tightened. "No, I'm sure he'll show up for breakfast." She dismissed Belle and headed down herself.

Midway down the stairs, she heard voices in the study. When she stepped off the last tread, she turned in that direction, then halted as the words became clear.

"Gideon, please don't worry about me. I would've left England, anyway. I need a new beginning. It's why I came to America." Lydia.

What did she mean? Wasn't she returning to England? And why should Gideon be worried about her?

"Will you let us help you settle here?" Gideon asked. "Your sewing and nursing skills should open opportunities for you. And I repeat my invitation. You're welcome to stay here as long as you like."

"Thank you, sir. I will be praying for God to open whichever door He has for me to obtain work. I will need to find employment."

When they emerged into the hall, they didn't see Helena at first. Lydia Lewis was as tall as Gideon. She wore her thick brown hair pulled back into a net-covered chignon at the back of her neck. Though not beautiful, her face was arresting and lively. Her smooth skin glowed with pale gold undertones as if she spent time in the sunshine. Gideon had his hand on her arm, and the way she looked at him made Helena falter. But Gideon's expression as he returned her glance—something that spoke of honor or respect—amazed her more. Obviously, they had known each other before. Maybe quite well.

Helena cleared her throat, and both turned toward her.

Gideon strode toward her. "Helena, Lydia says she wants to stay in Charleston and find some kind of work, have a new beginning. I've pledged our support. Will you help?"

She looked at the woman whose countenance held a strange

peace. "Yes, of course, Lydia. Let's find time to sit down and talk after breakfast. And let's invite Gideon's mother."

"That would be nice, Mrs. Falconer. Thank you."

"But only if you'll call me Helena." She smiled at the woman and proceeded toward the dining room with Gideon at her side. He turned and invited Lydia to follow.

After the meal, Helena led the two women into the parlor while Gideon went out on the plantation. Lydia's skills and talents amazed her. Gideon's mother was the one to share about them as Lydia proved too modest. "She is an excellent seamstress and hat maker, who took orders for quite a few of the nobility in our city. She also has practiced midwifery and nursing, can grow many of the healing herbs, and is also a passable cook."

Helena gave Lydia a thorough perusal, and for the first time, she noticed the other woman's capable hands. Those hands, unadorned by flashy jewelry, had designed beautiful clothing and delivered babies. She dropped her gaze to her own small hands. Their manicured nails attested to the fact that she did no manual labor. Rings glittered on her fingers. The valuable jewels sparkled in the sunlight and proclaimed her privileged status.

Pain stabbed through her middle. Could that be jealousy? Certainly not! She had no reason to be jealous of Lydia. She who had had everything her whole life had never been envious of anyone. She'd had to battle that from others. Besides, she didn't need to make her own clothing, or, God forbid, deliver anyone's baby. Was all this why Gideon seemed impressed with the woman?

With a sideways glance at her husband's friend, Helena noted the subtle signs that betrayed Lydia's age. Though she still possessed a slender figure and rich brown hair, the fine lines at the corners of her eyes placed her age closer to Gideon's than Helena's. The woman probably approached thirty.

Helena offered a smile. "Lydia, with all your skills, I'm sure you will find much you can do here and in Charleston. I will contact my friends." She glanced at Mrs. Rhett. "And, as Gideon said, you're welcome to stay at Windemere as long as you like."

Gideon's mother patted Lydia's hand. "There, not to worry. God has a plan."

Lydia's face glowed. "Thank you very much, Mrs. Falcon —Helena."

The following morning, Helena rose early for her delayed ride on Stormy. She galloped to her secret place without any other meandering, tied Stormy's reins to a branch, and sat on her special rock overlooking the Ashley River. She would have at least two hours before she needed to be home. One of her friends, whom she'd contacted about Lydia's sewing skills, was coming to discuss the possibility of employing the English woman to create a new wardrobe. Good seamstresses being rare, Jane Pringle, who was preparing for a trip to Europe, made an appointment right away.

With her arms curled about her updrawn knees, Helena lifted her face to the sun. The birds' chatter and the bees' humming provided soothing music. The scent of the wildflowers scattered around the clearing perfumed the air, yet an unfamiliar restlessness filled her. Today nature's beauty didn't lift her spirits. The talented Lydia Lewis filled her mind. Who was she, really? And how important a place had she had—did she still have—in Gideon's heart?

Something about the woman made Helena feel young, inexperienced, even useless. Taking a serious look at her own main skills— playing the pianoforte and embroidering—Helena shook her head. She couldn't dispel a feeling of lacking in something important, a new emotion to her. But if so, who had to stay that way? She would learn all she could from Lydia and surprise Gideon. And she could always just ask Gideon about any former relationship he had with the woman. She leaned back on the warm rock and closed her eyes. The heavy thinking made her drowsy, and she slept.

Sometime later, she awoke with a start. The sunshine had disappeared, replaced by dark clouds, and thunder rumbled in the west. Stormy nickered as if to warn her they needed to get home. She jumped up, untied his reins from the limb, and mounted. "Gracious, Stormy, we've got to get home fast." And would she make it in time to introduce Lydia to Jane—hopefully, her first client? Stormy seemed to understand and flew out of the woods and across the fields, but the rain still caught them.

She made it in time to change from her wet clothing and head down to the parlor.

Gideon met her on the stairs. "Thank you for calling your friends for Lydia, Helena. They won't regret letting her make clothing for them. My mother has used her many times."

Helena cocked her chin and smiled. "It's the least I could do. She...seems to deserve our help." She swallowed and looked straight into his eyes. "Would you have time to meet me in your study after the midday meal? I...want to know more about Miss Lewis. To be the best help I can be."

Gideon's face tightened, but he smiled and nodded.

CHAPTER 10

All through the meal, Gideon grappled with what to tell Helena about his former relationship with Lydia without compromising her and the help she needed. Truth was the only way to go. But could he prevent any misunderstanding? Had he been wise to offer Lydia shelter if she needed it, given that she very probably came with his mother with the hope they would continue their courtship?

He walked to the study, whispering a prayer for wisdom, then sat in front of his desk to wait.

Helena swished into the room a few minutes later and closed the door. Taking a seat across from him, she folded her hands in her lap. "You obviously knew our guest Lydia well in the past, Gideon." Her eyes met his with questions in their depth. "Am I right?"

Taking a deep breath, Gideon leaned forward. "Yes, you're right. I've known Lydia for quite some time. And I'm glad we're talking about this." He raked his fingers through his hair, then cast an imploring look at his wife. "Lydia is a fine woman. We courted before I left England, but I never formally proposed. She did emigrate with my mother, not only for a new beginning, but probably assuming we might continue our courtship." He paused, then took another breath and plunged on. "I wrote my mother the day you and I agreed to marry, but she never received that letter, as I think you know."

Helena nodded. "Yes, that came out the day they arrived. But at the time, I didn't connect it having anything to do with Lydia."

"Well, it did. But you need to understand I assumed Lydia had forgotten all about me after I fled England and settled here, especially since I had never proposed. We were never officially engaged." He cocked his chin. "In fact, though I highly respected her and still do, I never...fell in love with her."

Helena bit her lower lip. "But you never contacted her after you came to Charleston to let her know you were not interested anymore? Here, if a courtship continues for some time, we assume an engagement whether formally expressed or not, whether in love or not."

He ducked his head for a moment, then met her eyes. "Yes, that's where I failed in this, Helena. No doubt about it. But you don't know what I went through in England and how distracted I became. I'm not proud of some things in my past and where Lydia is concerned, but I want to tell you my story. Not as an excuse for my failures but because you need to hear it as my wife. I want no secrets between us. Do you understand?"

She gave a brief smile. "I think so, Gideon. Please tell me your story. The noble and the not so noble part you're hinting about."

He leaned toward her, relieved at her invitation and its tone. "It's true I was born the son of a nobleman, but my father died when I was ten years old, and his brother took over our estate. Mother disliked him very much, but she had no say in the matter. Uncle Henry was a hard gambler, and by the time I was fifteen, he had gambled away our entire estate and declared bankruptcy. He ended up committing suicide." He took a deep breath and flexed his hands. "The new owner of our estate offered Mother marriage. I begged her not to marry Julius Rhett, but she did, and I ran away to sea. I realize now she really had no other option, and Rhett was not so bad a man, not as bad as others I would soon come to know."

Leaning back, he lowered his eyes from hers for a moment and cleared his throat. "To make a long story short, I fell in with a very evil sea captain, a slaver, who brought slaves from Africa and sold them in whatever port he could find. The man was the devil incarnate, and I soon hated him and everything connected to him, but he forced me to become a strong seaman. Three years later, when he died and most of the crew perished in battle with our captain's archenemy, three men and I managed to escape, and I took over the ship."

The shocked expression on Helena's face stabbed his heart. He shoved to his feet and paced to the window. She was to be further shocked.

"I'd like to tell you I then gave up the slaver business and returned to a decent life, but I didn't, not for three more years. Though more miserable than I can describe, something drove me to keep at it, hoping to make enough money to start a new life back in England."

Gideon pivoted and met her tragic gaze across the room. He thrust his fingers in his hair again and took one step forward. "But in port one day, I met up with an elderly former slave ship captain, the abolitionist Reverend John Newton and later, his friend William Wilberforce. Newton, who has now gone on to glory, took me under his wing, led me to the Lord Jesus Christ, and drew me out of slave trafficking. That was the happiest day of my life." He walked closer to her, looked down in her face. "I need to tell you I now feel the same way those two men do about slavery."

She swiped a tear from her cheek. "You were young to go through so much, Gideon." But then she sat up straighter, and her face tightened. "But how can you even think like those men about slavery? I've heard of them. What Southerner hasn't? Southerners hate to hear their names. My father has always said slaves are not persons like us, and they are simply fulfilling their God-given destiny to be slaves, and our destiny is to be their masters and take care of them."

Surprise and aversion rolled over Gideon, but this was not the time to debate the slavery issue. Lydia was the topic for now. He needed to continue his story. Ignoring her last remarks, he continued. "When back in England, I tried to live with my mother, but her new husband would have none of me. So Reverend Newton helped me obtain a job and a cottage as a gamekeeper for a neighboring estate.

That was about the time I met Lydia. She came to the manor regularly with sewing appointments. She knew my mother already, and they were friends. We became friends." He hesitated.

Helena leaned forward. "But what prompted you to emigrate to America?"

"That's another part of my sad story. The owner of the estate charged me to keep all poachers off the grounds. He instructed me to shoot to maim, then turn them over to the sheriff. I tried to do what the owner wanted, but I could not shoot the hungry poor who could keep starvation from their doors with a rabbit or wild fowl so plentiful on the estate. In the end, the owner fired me and sent the sheriff to arrest me for helping poachers. I fled England and came to Charleston where I knew my father's sister lived."

"Your aunt Sophia Rutledge I met at our wedding?" She smiled at him.

"Yes. She helped me get the position at Brighton, and you know the rest." He strode back from the window and sat beside Helena. He reached out and took her hand in his. She didn't resist. He looked into her azure eyes, his heartbeat increasing. "Remember, Helena, I started this story telling you I never fell in love with Lydia, but I would like to assist her if I can. She has no family to go back to in England. I believe she can carve a new beginning here with our help."

Helena took a deep breath. "Thank you for sharing your story, Gideon. And I don't mind helping Lydia." She turned her face aside. "But I have to wonder how she feels about you."

Gideon quirked an eyebrow at his wife. Was it possible she battled jealousy? He pressed her hand and leaned forward. "Helena, there is no one I'm in love with but you. Can't you believe it? I think I fell in love with you the same day I rescued you from the river. You were so helpless and lovely...and stubborn and proud like a hurt child."

Helena stiffened and pulled her hand away. "Your mother said you were always rescuing someone or something. And so, Lydia needs rescuing now. Is that all there is to it?"

"Yes, and will you help me, dear wife? You said you wouldn't mind."

She nodded, then smiled. "I will help, Gideon. After all, it's the Christian thing to do. Help someone coming to America for a new beginning."

Gideon's heart expanded in gratitude and love. Helena did have some real kindness beneath her crusty exterior.

A knock sounded at the door.

"Enter," Gideon called, and his mother opened the door, then looked from him to Helena. "Am I interrupting something? Please forgive me if I am. But you have visitors."

"No, Mother, you're not interrupting." He glanced at Helena and stood. "We've just finished our conversation."

Helena rose beside him. "Please come in, Mrs. Rhett. You're family and always welcome. But will you excuse me? I will see about our visitors." She swished out the door.

Gideon hugged his mother. "Thanks for alerting us. Our elderly butler must be poorly again, and Mrs. Laurens must have been busy."

"It's a distinguished man and aristocratic older woman calling. I seated them in the front parlor. Sorry, I only caught the last name. Allston, I think."

Gideon grinned. "It's my father-in-law and his sister. Come and meet them."

He strode into the parlor and witnessed John give Helena a hug. Walking up to his father-in-law, Gideon extended his hand. "So good to see you, sir. And you, Miss Sarah."

Allston shook his hand firmly. Sarah gave a stiff nod.

With a proud smile, Gideon turned to his mother and curled an arm around her shoulders. "And you must be wondering who this is. John, Miss Sarah, please meet my mother, Merle Falconer Rhett. She's emigrating from England."

Both their faces registered amazement, but Sarah recovered first. "Pleased, I'm sure."

"Why, I think I see a resemblance, Gideon—those gray eyes."

John took his mother's hand. "Glad you've chosen to come to Charleston and to Windemere, Mrs. Rhett."

Miss Sarah looked Gideon's mother up and down, then sniffed.

Helena gestured to the sofa and chairs grouped around the blue-tiled fireplace. "Won't you be seated?"

Miss Sarah and his mother sat, and Helena followed.

But Gideon clapped John on the shoulder. "Sir, would you like to see the improvements we're making on the plantation?" Gideon hoped he'd think of them as such.

"By all means, son." His eyes sparked. "And I have something important to ask you."

Leaving the women alone in the parlor, the men strolled from the room.

∼

Soon after Gideon and her father departed the house, Helena looked up as the housekeeper appeared in the parlor doorway. A spotless white apron covered her gray dress. "Ma'am, would you like tea served, and may I assume we will have guests for the evening meal?"

Helena smiled. "Yes, to both questions, Mrs. Laurens."

Aunt Sarah cleared her throat. "I saw another carriage with its servant parked in the drive, Helena. Do you have other guests?"

"Oh, that's a client for Lydia."

Her aunt craned her thin neck toward Helena, frowning. "Clients? And who is Lydia, and why does she have *clients*?" She emphasized the last word in a higher key.

Mrs. Rhett sat forward. "I think I can best answer that. Lydia Lewis is a companion and dear young friend of mine who decided to emigrate from England with me. She's an excellent seamstress, and Helena was so good as to inform her friends who might need sewing done."

The woman stiffened and clapped her thin hands. "Are you making our wonderful Windemere into a place of business, Helena?"

Helena took a deep breath. "No, Aunt Sarah. Gideon and I have decided to help Miss Lewis find employment. She desires a new beginning in America, and she makes no excuses about needing to work." She smiled and patted her aunt's hands. "It's the Christian thing to do, you know. She's a talented, industrious lady. You'll meet her when we dine."

Aunt Sarah huffed and mumbled, "Well, I hope I can still hold my head up in Charleston when this news gets out."

As soon as Gideon and his father-in-law strode down the back steps, Allston stopped and gripped his arm. "Son, my news can't wait another minute. I've decided to go on a trip to the islands to see about my merchant contacts there, and I want you to go with me. Will you?"

Gideon's brow lifted, and a thrill ran up his spine. Even though he would seldom admit it to himself, he did miss the sea and sailing. There was nothing to compare with a sunny day at the helm of a ship, with the fresh, salty air filling the sails and his lungs as the ship cut a foaming path through the waves. "Sir, I'm an old married man now, and Helena will have to help make that decision. Let me talk to her first. I must admit, the idea is tantalizing."

At the meal later, Gideon could hardly concentrate on the conversations flowing around the table. He did take note of the steely stares Miss Sarah gave Lydia. What was bothering the elderly lady?

The thought of sailing the ocean again and seeing the islands on simple merchant business cast worry about Helena's aunt from his mind and filled him with excitement. But could he leave the plantation for the two-week trip and feel peace about it?

Samson...he knew as much or more than he did about the plantation work and its people. And thank God, Gideon had dealt with Kunta and removed the former stableman. Joseph Laurens was doing a wonderful job with the horses.

Then there was Helena. The old ache flooded his heart. Would she ever become the loving wife he so desired? Would his absence, like the old saying, help her heart grow fonder?

Helena interrupted his thoughts. "Gideon, you're scarcely eating anything, and you're so quiet." She turned toward John Allston. "And, Father, you look like a man with a secret. I've lived with you too long not to know something is in the works. Can you share it with the rest of us?"

John Allston laid down his fork, and a grin spread across his face. "I'm going to make a trip to the islands on merchant business, and I've asked Gideon to go with me."

Gideon stiffened in surprise. He'd asked John to let him first talk with Helena.

His father-in-law seemed to notice his discomfort. "Now he's not said yet whether he'll go, Helena. He said you had to be part of the decision, so I've overstepped."

Helena cast a cool look at Gideon, then lifted her chin. "You've not overstepped, Father. My husband can go wherever he wants to go."

Her annoyed voice surprised and embarrassed Gideon.

His mother lowered her eyes to her plate, as did Lydia. Miss Sarah dabbed her thin lips with her napkin, and a gleam came into her eyes. What was the old lady's problem? Was she happy to see Helena's attitude showing in front of their guests?

Gideon covered his annoyance with a grin. "I'm relieved to see my lovely wife has some reservations about my potential absence, at least." Then he reached over and patted her hand. "We will discuss this later, Helena. You know my only plan is to please you, so you have nothing to be uneasy about."

She lowered her eyes, and her cheeks turned pink.

Gideon stood. "Let's withdraw to the parlor with the ladies today." He glanced at Helena, willing her to settle. Would she ever grow up?

John Allston rose and came to his daughter. "Yes, and Helena, would you grace us with a selection on the pianoforte? It's been much too long since I heard you play."

Gideon had never heard her play. "That would be wonderful, Helena."

Mother came over and patted her shoulder. "Yes, please do, my dear. We'd love to hear your music."

Lydia and even Miss Sarah added their voices. Perhaps the affirmation would soothe his wife so that they might have a productive conversation later.

~

*H*elena sat at the pianoforte and tried to still her thudding heart. Why had she said what she did? A bad feeling sat like a rock in her middle. How could she be such a careless hostess? Maybe it had to do with how Lydia Lewis had scarcely taken her eyes off Gideon throughout the meal. And when did Gideon learn to handle her own impishness so skillfully?

After a swift mental inventory of the music she knew by heart, Helena chose a favorite piece. She stretched her fingers and poised her hands above the keyboard, then launched into the music. Melody flowed from within and burst out to fill the room. She lost herself in the music's mood. The parlor, the people, her uneasiness, and confusion all faded away. Even her husband's astonished face vanished from her vision as her exaltation in the music captivated her. When the last note sounded, she sat with her head bowed, spent. A moment of silence followed before boisterous clapping roused her.

Gideon came to her side. "Helena, I had no idea you could play like that."

She smiled, stood, and turned to nod at her audience.

Later that evening, Gideon joined her on the upstairs veranda. Soft twilight with violet and indigo streaks blanketed the trees below and the plantation buildings. She stood looking across the railing. He came to stand beside her, but he didn't touch her. "It used to be called the gloaming by the Scottish."

"What did?"

"The magical time after the sun sets and before night falls."

"Do you believe in magical times?"

She turned to glance at him but turned quickly away. "Just sunsets and sunrises."

"Helena, sitting at the pianoforte tonight, you created a magical moment."

She turned her face farther from him but couldn't keep a smile from stretching her lips. Maybe she did have something unique to offer—like Lydia Lewis.

He placed his hands on her shoulders, turned her toward him, and looked into her eyes. "Tell me plainly, Helena. Do you mind if I sail to the islands with your father? If you say you do, I won't go."

"No, I don't mind...and I'm sorry for the way I acted at dinner."

Surprise and pleasure lit his face in the gathering darkness, and she recognized his intent to kiss her. But she slipped from his grasp and stepped back inside the hall. Her heart drummed in her throat, and she had to force her feet to move swiftly to her room and safety from his mesmerizing presence.

~

Two days later, Gideon stood beside John on deck of the *Victoria*, Allston's largest merchant vessel, a brig with two square-rigged masts and purported great maneuverability. Enjoying the brilliant sunshine and fresh wind filling the sails and his lungs, he couldn't keep from glancing toward the helmsman as they sailed down the southern coast toward the Caribbean. What would it be like to sail a ship again with nothing but decent cargo like lumber, rice, and hides beneath his feet? Despite his effort to suppress it, the memory of moaning, packed slaves on his slaver ship passed through his mind. He'd repented. Why couldn't he forget? Had God not forgiven him?

John must have noticed his attention toward the pilot because he touched Gideon's arm. "Son, how would you like to take a turn at the helm? You've sailed similar ships in the past, I assume?"

John's offer roused Gideon from the pit where his memories had taken him and returned him to the sunshine. "Yes, sir. I have, and I'd be delighted to steer your *Victoria* a while and give your helmsman a break."

Allston smiled. "By all means."

Gideon sailed the brig every other day for the rest of the six-day journey until they reached the Jamaican harbor, where the helmsman took over to pilot the ship through the numerous jetties and buoys.

Things had changed since Gideon had sailed into the British-governed port of Kingston. As the *Victoria* slid into a docking space, familiar sounds, sights, and smells filled the late-afternoon air. Curses of overseers directing sweating slaves unloading sloops, brigs, and other ships darkened the atmosphere. Animals bleating, chickens squawking, and someone playing a flute down the way rounded out the general melee. The stench of rank bodies found a challenge from the barbecuing efforts of dockside native cooks. As the aroma of roasting pork loins and beef ribs floated across the harbor, Gideon's stomach growled.

He and John disembarked and strolled down King Street, the chief thoroughfare, toward an inn at a far corner. Roving crowds of different nationalities thronged the area, and Jamaican women in their colorful red plaid dresses and headpieces paraded past them. Two of them smiled and tried to catch Gideon's eye, but he ignored them.

The sign above the two-story wooden building with red shutters read, *Privateers' Inn*. A tavern occupied the first floor, and John led him from the late hot sun in the street into the cooler shadow of the inn. As they crossed the room to an oaken bar, the odors of unwashed bodies and rum hit Gideon in the face.

John grimaced, then grinned. "Whew, I need something to wet my throat. I'm going to have the British Navy favorite, grog rum. It's good here. How about you?"

Turning his back to the bar, Gideon surveyed the unsavory blokes around the tavern's many tables. Some of them appeared to be pirates, whose cold stares now focused on himself and John. He swung back toward the bartender, a muscular individual whose colorful shirt and bandanna provided a bright contrast to his dark skin. "Can you give me the grog with the citrus and water only, leave off the rum?"

The man's dark eyes flashed at him in disbelief.

John leaned toward Gideon. "Son, you don't want to do that. Water here is unsafe." He turned toward the bartender. "Give him the grog, only go easy on the rum."

The next morning, Gideon met John in the dining room early for their trip to the first sugar plantation, Rosewood. A rented carriage picked them up at the street entrance.

During the hour-long trip to the estate near the Blue Mountains, John filled Gideon in on the plantation's details. "Rosewood's owner is Jacob Owenby, a fine gentleman and longtime friend. I've bought his cured sugar crop for many years. You ever toured a sugar mill and watched sugar made from the cane?"

Gideon shook his head, already feeling the island heat at the early hour they traveled. "No. I look forward to learning about it."

He steeled himself to endure the sight of all the intensive slave labor that produced Jamaica's main export. Britain had abolished the international slave trade in 1807 in all her provinces, including the island, and he thanked God America had followed suit in 1808, but the battle to end slavery and set free the already enslaved masses was far from over. John Newton and the statesman William Wilberforce, whom he knew when he fled England, had worked tirelessly to get Parliament to abolish slavery. Had Wilberforce made any progress in the government?

As their carriage pulled up in front of an elegant Georgian-style great house, the apparent owner of Rosewood sauntered down the many steps of his house to welcome them. Three slaves preceded the short, robust, red-faced gentleman in his white duck tailcoat, pants, and black boots. The servants assisted them from the carriage and then took the horse and conveyance away. The plantation owner gave a brief bow to them. "So good to see you in Jamaica again, sir." The man extended his hand first to John, then to Gideon as John introduced Jacob Owenby.

Mr. Owenby led them up the steps and into a cool, brightly tiled atrium, then into a spacious parlor decorated in orange and beige silk fabrics and shining walnut furniture. The scent of lemon oil floated in the air.

Their host gestured to a silk-covered sofa, then took a seat in a highbacked damask chair himself. "We have quite a harvest coming in, John, and on your next trip, we will have quite a shipment for you."

"That's good, Jacob. So all is well here, weatherwise and with your...slaves?" John took his pipe from his coat pocket and proceeded to fill it. A servant came forward and dipped a thin stick into a candle flame, then held it out to him. After John lit his pipe, the pungent tobacco scent filled the room.

Owenby dismissed the servant with a flick of his hand. When the door closed behind the man, Jacob leaned forward and frowned. "The weather's been fine, no hurricanes, but who knows how long we'll be safe from a slave uprising? There are whispers every week of some rebellion smoldering here and there. I tell my fellow planters, the only hope is to have a strong overseer who can put the fear of God into any wanting to cause trouble, and I've got one of the best."

Gideon's stomach tightened. No doubt the man was handy with the whip.

After the midday meal, they rode horses down the back road of Rosewood past sugarcane fields full of men and women workers who chopped cane and piled it into wagons.

When they halted for a few moments, Gideon removed his hat and wiped the sweat from his forehead. He hated to see even young children helping pick up dropped pieces of cane in the hot sun and throw them up on the wagons. One boy stumbled and fell, and the overseer came and stood over him and yelled at him, brandishing his whip. Gideon clenched his teeth and prepared to jump from his horse and stop the man if he began hitting the child, but the boy scrambled up and away.

The scene so angered Gideon that the rest of Owenby's explanation of the harvesting process fell on deaf ears. His knowledge of slavery's cruelties overrode the information of how the slaves fed the cane into presses so that cane juice flowed into a vat on the other side. The slaves' hurried movements betrayed their fear of the overseer's whip.

Allston turned to Owenby. "Why is that man with the machete standing beside the revolving metal rollers?"

The owner grimaced. "Few planters like to answer that question, but since you asked, I'll tell you harvesting sugar out of cane is a dangerous business. Particularly here at the press. He's standing there in case one of the men gets his arm caught in the rollers. He's there to chop his arm off and save his life."

Gideon's stomach roiled, and he wished only to head back to the great house and forget the rest of the tour.

"But don't worry, that's never happened since my family has owned Rosewood." Jacob Owenby grinned and led them from the presses.

Reluctantly, Gideon followed past the boiling house, where the roaring fires boiled vats of cane juice down to thick molasses, then to the curing building. There the molasses turned into golden-brown muscovado sugar.

Owenby indicated a stack of barrels. "Those are hogsheads of raw sugar we ship to Europe to further refine into the white crystals you put in your tea and cakes."

On their return to the great house, halfway along the road, a dark-skinned figure stepped out of the woods and blocked the lane before them. A red robe draped his skinny frame, and a turban hat topped salt-and-pepper braids that trailed over his shoulders. What appeared to be a mottled snakeskin encircled his neck. Pointing a bony finger at Gideon and John, he muttered in a foreign tongue, though his tone bespoke a warning.

Gideon's gelding snorted and backed a pace.

Jacob shouted, "Out of the way, old man. We don't want to hear any of your dire predictions. What are you doing on Rosewood property? Go back to your mountain hideaway."

The man turned and disappeared into the woods.

Allston looked at Owenby. "Did you understand what he said?"

Jacob swiped the sweat from his upper lip. "Yes, but you don't want to hear it. He never has any good news for anyone. He's an obeah man, a witch doctor."

"But was it to me, to Gideon? How would he even know us?"

Owenby shook his head, and his lips tightened. "It's always something crazy. He said you two better go back where you came from, that evil is at work against your house. It means nothing, John, be assured."

Despite the reassurance, Gideon's sense of unease increased tenfold. Should he have ever left Windemere Plantation?

CHAPTER 11

The night after Gideon and her father left for Jamaica, Helena lay in bed, staring through the darkness at the ceiling. Heat lay like a sticky weight over her, and she kicked the sheet to the bottom of the bed. With a sigh, she rolled onto her side and punched her pillow into a more comfortable shape. The minutes ticked past, measured by the clock on her mantel, but sleep eluded her.

Memories of the times her mother had knelt beside her bed to pray while her father had been away on a sea voyage floated across her mind. How long had it been since she prayed about anything? She took a deep, painful breath and rose. Guilt blanketed her, and a chill crept over her. Now it was not only her father traveling, but Gideon as well. She knelt beside her bed and prayed for their safe travel, struggling for the right words. Little by little, warmth crept back into her body, and she climbed into bed and fell asleep.

The next morning, a banging on the front door interrupted breakfast. Helena exchanged curious glances with Mrs. Rhett and Lydia. Who could be calling at this early hour?

Moments later, their elderly butler appeared. Embarrassment etched his dark features. He cleared his throat and addressed Helena.

"Missus, the minister's wife is here and wonders if there is anyone here what can...what can..." His voice quavered and stopped. He looked unhappy, and his gaze flew to Mrs. Rhett, as if as a last resort. "Help wid a...baby coming."

Gideon's mother stood and glanced at Lydia. "Of course, we can help. Lydia most certainly can."

Lydia laid down her napkin and stood, her eyes brightening. "Yes, I can."

Helena led both into the hall and greeted Mary Wingard.

Worry lines pinched the woman's usually placid face. She looked at the three of them, then turned her attention to Helena. "Did I understand that one of your guests here is a midwife?" She wrung her hands.

"Yes, I am a midwife, ma'am." Lydia stepped forward as she spoke.

"Thank God. Can you come with me right away? We've a young woman who appeared on our doorstep at dawn and is about to give birth. My buggy is outside."

"Let me get my satchel and a wrap, and I'll come." Lydia headed up the stairs, and Mary Wingard waited at the front door.

Helena followed Lydia. "I want to come with you. Do you mind?"

Lydia halted at the door of her room and smiled. "Not a bit. I'd love to have your assistance. Get your cloak, dear. It's no telling how long we'll be gone."

Mrs. Rhett stepped into the doorway and glanced at them both. "You two go without me. I'm...not feeling my best since breakfast. I think I'll lie back down for a spell."

Lydia stopped collecting her things and took Mrs. Rhett's hand. "Are you sure you're going to be all right?"

"Oh, yes. I just didn't sleep well last night. A nap will take care of it."

All the way to the minister's parsonage, Helena wanted to tell Lydia she doubted how much assistance she'd be as she'd never witnessed the birth of anything but a foal or calf.

Mary Wingard led them to an upstairs bedroom while hard groans echoed down the hallway. Lydia turned to the minister's wife.

"Please boil a gallon of water and bring plenty of linens and a half cup of melted butter."

In the bedroom, Helena stood to the side, feeling useless, but quivers of excitement traveled up her spine. Would she get to see, for the first time, the miracle of birth, as her mother had called it when she'd helped women in their slave quarters have babies? But Helena had never been allowed to attend a birthing.

Lydia placed her tapestry medical bag at the foot of the bed and walked to the head. Beneath a thin sheet, a girl who couldn't be more than fifteen years old thrashed about in pain. Her red tresses spread about her on the pillow, and her sweat-soaked bangs clung to her skin. Lydia laid her hand on the young woman's damp forehead. "My dear, what is your name, and is this your first child?"

The patient nodded, and dark-green eyes full of fear looked up into Lydia's calm face. "It's my first, and my name's Zettie, and I'm afeared." The words flew out her thin, dry lips between pains.

"Well, you calm yourself, dear Zettie. Our mighty God loves to help bring a new life into the world He created. And He's sent me to assist."

The young woman's face fell. Then words gushed from her mouth. "I doubts He'll help me, ma'am. I ain't never been married. And this babe's pa is a sailor. When I got with child and wouldn't...agree to... get rid of it...he took off to sea." Her last words ended in a groan as another pain gripped her.

Lydia patted the thin shoulder. "Zettie, God will most certainly help you, and you made the right decision to save this new life." She strode to the washstand on the wall, poured water into the bowl, then scrubbed and dried her hands. After tying a clean white apron around her waist, she spread a folded cloth over the top of a trunk at the foot of the four-poster bed. Then she laid out bandages, scissors, string, needles, nappies, a small baby gown, notepaper, and chamomile tea. She did this quickly, often glancing up at her patient. With a smile, she handed a soft washcloth to Helena. "Take this and wet it at the washstand and dab Zettie's face. She'll appreciate it."

Helena wet the cloth and moved to Zettie's head. Frightened green eyes looked up at her, then the pretty face scrunched in pain.

When the pain subsided, Helena pushed damp red strands of hair from Zettie's brow and dabbed her face with the cool cloth. The girl sighed and whispered her thanks.

Lydia rubbed the warm butter on her hands and examined her patient. She smiled and announced, "This baby is turned the right way, praise the Lord."

During the next two hours, Helena watched as Zettie labored to bring her baby into the world. She couldn't hold back the tears when the young woman writhed about in pain. Lydia amazed her with her loving care and encouragement to the mother.

At last, with one final groan and push, Zettie's tiny son made his entrance into the world. His lusty cries sounded like music to the women who witnessed his mother's struggles.

Helena swallowed a lump in her throat. Indeed, the birth of a child was a miracle.

Lydia's face lit with joy as she took care of the little one, tied the cord, then snipped it. She sponged the small body, then slid the gown over him and wrapped him in a soft blanket. His little fist found his mouth.

Lydia turned to Helena. "Take this fine boy and give him to his mother."

Helena's eyes flew to Lydia's, and an unexpected warmth surged through her. Could she hold a newborn? Her heart rose in delight as she took the little bundle into her arms. The child looked up at her with bright eyes, and she fell in love immediately. He made sucking sounds with his tiny fist, and she kissed his soft forehead before handing him to his mother.

"Did you say it's a boy?" A weak smile followed the mother's hoarse whisper as she took her son.

Lydia continued her ministrations to the young woman. "Yes, you've a fine boy, Zettie. And a big one. My guess is, he's over eight pounds. You did an excellent job. Have you a name in mind?"

"I think Timothy." Her glowing eyes softened. "That was my pa's name."

"You have family here, Zettie?"

"My pa and ma, they done died with the fever when I was twelve."

"I'm sorry to hear it, but now you are a mother and have your own little one to raise. The Lord will help you if you ask Him." Lydia finished her work at the foot of the bed, wrote notes in her little book, and came to look down at her patient and new baby. "Do you have anyone, any other extended family member, maybe an aunt here in Charleston, who might help you?"

Zettie's eyes lowered as she held Timothy to her breast. "I don't have no one, ma'am. That's why I come to the minister's house."

Lydia's brows rose, and she glanced at Helena. Sadness filled Helena thinking of the young mother who was herself an orphan. Thank God for the Wingards who were trying to help the mother. She made up her mind to send a generous gift to assist.

~

The next day, Helena walked to the side porch where Gideon's mother sat with her Bible open on her lap. Birds twittered in the tall oaks shading most of the porch in the late afternoon, but Mrs. Rhett had her chair situated to catch a few rays of July sunshine. Sliding into a shady rocker nearby, Helena looked at her mother-in-law closely. The paleness of her face and how she hadn't seemed her usual self the last few days concerned her. Was she missing Gideon that much? It would still be several days, even a week or more, before they could expect him and her father back from the islands.

Mrs. Rhett smiled and greeted her. "Oh, Helena, how nice of you to join me. I am just catching up with my Bible reading. Do you like to read the Bible?"

Helena's cheeks became warm. "I'm sorry to say, I don't read it much." *Not at all*, a voice inside her head whispered. Her mother had read the Bible every morning that Helena could remember. Why had she never thought to do the same? But was it necessary?

Her mother-in-law laid her folded, veined hands on the open pages. "I highly recommend it. It's where I get help, instructions, and peace."

Helena firmed her lips and took a deep breath. "But isn't that what we have ministers and church services for, Mrs. Rhett?" Her words, laced with stubborn defiance she couldn't resist, landed like lead on the peaceful porch. She hated them the minute they flowed from her lips.

"Helena, please listen carefully to what I'm going to say." Her mother-in-law's voice was lower and more intense than Helena could remember hearing it, and her eyes shone with an unusual brightness. "Reading and knowing the Bible have everything to do with how you make decisions for the rest of your life. People make up the church. Those who preach the word of God are just people too. God anoints and calls many of them to serve Him in that way, but they are still human." She leaned her head back on the rocker as if tired. "People can make mistakes. Even preachers and teachers can form opinions and beliefs based on their own experiences or interpretations instead of the Bible."

Helena's shoulders tightened. "I'm not sure I understand what you mean, Mrs. Rhett." She'd always thought the minister in their Charleston church knew everything of any importance and had the correct interpretation. Her father certainly thought so.

The woman turned her head to gaze into Helena's face and sighed. "In England right now, and I'm sure in places here in America, there are men, good men, in pulpits, but they preach opposite messages about slavery. In England, we had one minister, John Newton, who swayed the nation with his preaching that slavery is wrong, very wrong. Gideon met him. In fact, he was the one who led my son from his old life of slave trading into salvation. Did Gideon tell you about it, Helena?"

She ducked her head. "Yes, he's told me." A shiver traveled up her spine at the memory. Her husband admitted he agreed with people like the Reverend Newton and freeing the slaves. What implications would that have on their lives at Windemere? The South would be against anyone who wanted to free the slaves. Her Charleston minister had even said God ordained slavery and plantation owners like her father to own and take care of them.

The woman's smile relieved the tension. "The main thing I'm trying to share with you, Helena, is to read the Bible for yourself, then ask our Lord and Savior, Jesus Christ, to show you the truth about whatever situation you face or for which you need wisdom."

Helena cocked her chin. "But that takes lots of work, doesn't it?"

"Yes," Mrs. Rhett said in an unapologetic tone, but her eyes shone with kindness. "And unfortunately, that is why many people are merely like sheep led by a person who claims to have the whole truth. It's much easier to be led by a forceful, charismatic person than dig out truths for ourselves from God's word." She reached out and patted Helena's hand. "But I don't think you will do that, my dear. Like Gideon, I believe you will search out the truth for yourself." She took a deep, slow breath. "You know Gideon loves you very much, and so do I."

Helena's heart warmed toward Mrs. Rhett, and when the woman closed her eyes and again leaned her head back onto the tall rocker headpiece as if to nap, Helena rose and went to her room. She changed into her boots and riding skirt, then searched for her mother's Bible in the top of her chifforobe. When she found it, she slipped it into her skirt pocket, then ran to the stable and watched Mr. Laurens saddle her mare. Once Helena was astride, Stormy seemed to sense where to go without Helena's urging and stretched into a gallop to her secret place.

After looping Stormy's reins over a branch, she hurried to a warm rock overlooking the Ashley River. Opening her Bible, she began to read in the book of Psalms. Her mother had several markings at Psalm 91 as if she'd read it many times. Helena could almost hear her mother's voice reciting the verses.

*He who dwells in the secret place of the Most High shall
abide under the shadow of the Almighty.
I will say of the Lord, "He is my refuge and my fortress; My
God, in Him I will trust."
Surely He shall deliver you from the snare of the fowler and
from the perilous pestilence.
He shall cover you with His feathers, and under His wings
you shall take refuge; His truth shall be your shield and
buckler.
You shall not be afraid of the terror by night, nor of the
arrow that flies by day,
Nor of the pestilence that walks in darkness, nor of the
destruction that lays waste at noonday.
A thousand may fall at your side, and ten thousand at your
right hand; But it shall not come near you.
Only with your eyes shall you look, and see the reward of
the wicked.
Because you have made the Lord, who is my refuge, even
the Most High, your dwelling place,
No evil shall befall you, nor shall any plague come near
your dwelling;
For He shall give his angels charge over you, to keep you in
all your ways.
In their hands they shall bear you up, lest you dash your
foot against a stone.
You shall tread upon the lion and the cobra, the young lion
and the serpent you shall trample underfoot.
Because he has set his love upon Me, therefore I will deliver
him; I will set him on high, because he has known My
name.
He shall call upon Me, and I will answer him; I will be with
him in trouble; I will deliver him and honor him.
With long life I will satisfy him, and show him My
salvation.*

The sun sinking over the water finally no longer gave enough light to read, and sleep pressed against Helena's eyelids. Closing the Bible, she leaned back to rest a few moments before heading home. Her mother's sweet face filled her mind, and she sighed. Why didn't God give her a much longer life?

A rough hand pounding her shoulder against the hard rock woke her. Through the twilight, she looked up into the evilest face she'd ever seen. Bold, dark eyes in a hardened, scarred visage leered at her through an unkempt beard. Sheer, black fright swept through her.

"Don't yell, if you want to live." His guttural voice sent shivers up her spine, and a scream strangled in her throat. The odor of his unwashed body and soured alcohol made her gag.

Behind her, Stormy's snort and stamping hoof alerted her that someone else approached.

The assailant jerked her to her feet, bruising her arm as he twisted it behind her.

The pain brought her to her full senses. She regained her voice. "What do you think you're doing? Turn me loose, you—you filthy vulture!" Her angry voice only made her captor laugh.

Another attacker moved from behind him and forced a stinking gag over her mouth and tied it tight behind her head. She kicked, twisted, and struck out with her free arm, but to no avail. The next moment, the man secured a rope around both her hands, then dropped a rough fabric sack, like the burlap used on her father's plantations, over her head and encased her body. The scratchy touch of it on her skin and the grainy smell of it almost suffocated her. She whimpered through her gag.

"You behave, fancy little filly, and you won't get hurt." The man's raucous voice, laced with mockery, sent chills up her spine. He cast a rope around the sack and her legs, preventing all movement on her part. When one of the attackers hoisted her across his hard shoulders like a sack of potatoes, horror gripped her. The blood rushed to her head, and blackness swooped toward her, but she fought it. Reality chilled her to her toes. These horrid men meant to abduct her. But why? Helplessness overpowered her and left weakness in its wake.

"Let's get her to the boat before any other vessel shows up on the river," her captor hissed through the darkness.

Another thick voice responded, "Yeah, we've got us a good 'un this time. Gonna bring lots of gold."

Other words she could not discern passed between the two men, and another voice spoke near where she'd tied Stormy. She clenched her eyes as tears filled them. What would happen to her beloved mare? *Dear God, don't let them leave her tied to that tree to starve or fight any wild animal that might find her.*

The sound of water lapping against the bank reached her ears. Then her captor swung her from his shoulder and tossed her down in a boat swaying with the movement of the river. It jolted and wobbled as two men climbed in, or was it three?

"Boy, what kept you? We wuz about to leave without you." The same angry voice that had first spoken to Helena queried someone who stepped into the vessel.

The subdued response of a younger person reached Helena's ears as blackness threatened to claim her. "The horse, sir, I—" Was that a slave's voice? She missed his last words.

"You what? How stupid can you be, boy? If that horse finds the way back to its barn—" Then a string of curse words echoed over the water. Finally, the only sound in the night became the oars slapping the surface of the river. *Dear God, help me. Where are they taking me?* She gave up and surrendered to the dizzy darkness pressing against her. It sucked her into its murky depths.

CHAPTER 12

Gideon stood at the helm of the sleek *Victoria*. He delighted in the sunset's beauty. Vivid shades of pink, purple, and orange draped across the sky while the golden orb sank into the Atlantic. They'd be home the next day about noon if the current brisk wind held. Right now, the warm breeze billowed the sails out as far as they could go. The ship skipped across the waves as if happy to be returning to Charleston. He frowned. A strange urge to pray for Helena filled his heart. Was she all right? Had something happened at the plantation? If it had, he and John wouldn't learn about it until they docked the next morning. He took a deep breath and whispered a prayer. *Lord Jesus, only You know if something has happened to Helena or at the plantation. Please send your angels to protect and help in whatever way needed.*

"Son, you worried about something?" John Allston walked up on the quarter deck and leaned on the railing. "Or just getting tired? Want me to get my pilot back up here?"

Gideon tried to smooth out his frown and smiled. "No, just ready to get home, I think. And that's going to be soon if this good wind holds."

John took out his pipe, filled it, and lit it. "You know that crazy witch doctor almost put a chill on me wondering if he meant evil was headed to our house. But then last night when Owenby's plantation sugar mill got set on fire, I decided the omen was meant for him. What do you think?"

Gideon shook his head. "Sir, I don't put any store into anything that demented man would say. There are two types of spirits at work in the world, John Newton told me. The Holy Spirit of the Bible and demonic spirits connected to the devil. I know by which spirit the island witch doctor would speak. Who knows what happened at the sugar mill? It could've been some mistake in the process they use to heat the syrup. Or it could've been an enemy of Owenby. In any case, I'm glad they saved the rest of the buildings."

"I agree, but I have to tell you, I wondered if the strange man's warning had anything to do with the diagnosis old Doc Hanks gave me a few weeks ago." He scratched his chin. "I haven't even told Helena."

Gideon turned to look at him. "Your diagnosis?"

"Told me my old ticker was about worn out, that's what he said." Allston smiled. "But I'm not worried about it. When it's my time to go, I'll go and not before." He walked away.

Gripping the helm tighter, Gideon thought about Helena. How would she respond to that upsetting piece of news? But did she have an idea already? Her words during his proposal seemed to drift back on the sea breeze. *Our marriage will make Father happy. He's not well.*

When evening came, the regular pilot took over the helm.

Gideon told John he would turn in early, and he did so right after the evening meal. But he had trouble falling asleep. He rose, lit a candle, and pulled his Bible into his lap. He prayed and then read from Psalm 4 the verse he usually turned to when sleep escaped him. *I will both lay me down in peace, and sleep: for thou, Lord, only makest me dwell in safety.*

The next morning, Gideon steered the *Victoria* into her usual berth at the end of Gadsden Wharf. John gave docking orders to his crew, then motioned for Gideon to follow him down the gangplank.

Gideon grabbed up his sailor bag and strode down the way toward the Windemere carriage and groom waiting for them.

A haggard-faced James Cooper, Allston's office clerk, came hurrying toward them from the harbor building.

"Well, man, go ahead and tell me, whatever has happened." John Allston turned and scanned the docked ships bobbing in the tide behind them. "I don't see the *Maribelle* or the *Lucinda*. Have either had a mishap?"

James shook his head. "No, no, sir. Not your ships." He cast a fearful look at Gideon. "It's your wife, sir, Mistress Helena. She's missing. Been missing since yesterday afternoon."

Gideon stiffened and halted midstride. He dropped his sailor bag on the dock with a thud. "Missing? Whatever do you mean, man?"

"She went riding off on her horse and never came back. They said the horse came back after dark. Mr. Samson, he took men and been looking for her all night." The man's words rushed out in one breath.

An icy blast gripped Gideon's spine, and an iron fist lodged in his middle.

Beside him, Allston's face turned to alabaster, and his hand flew to his heart.

～

Sunlight danced across Helena's face. By slow degrees, she drifted into consciousness. When she pried open her eyes, a beam of light from the porthole blinded her. She turned her head away. The swaying movement of the room confirmed she was on a ship, anchored and bobbing with the tide. Nothing around her seemed familiar, certainly not the thick red satin bedspread or the size of the bed and soft pillow behind her. As she pushed herself upright, last night's terrifying events surged back with stark clarity.

Terrible men who looked and acted like pirates had kidnapped her. Had they brought her to wherever she was?

Curling her legs under her, Helena surveyed her surroundings. A stout door bisected one red satin-covered wall. In the open space between the door and the bed, a Persian rug glowed with jeweled tones of red, yellow, and blue. Another realization rocked her. The instruments of her capture—the sack, gag, and ropes—had been removed, as well as her clothing. Her riding outfit now lay folded on a nearby chair. Her riding boots stood upright near it. The sight of her clothing made Helena drop her gaze to the silk nightgown she wore. Whose gown was this? And her hair—she touched the curly tresses that tumbled across her breast. The braid she wore when riding had been loosened. Who had violated her privacy in this way?

She blinked back wetness welling in her eyes. And what had happened to her beloved horse? Had Stormy made it back home, or was she still tied to a tree limb?

A movement in a corner startled her, and she jerked the colorful spread up to her neck and stared. An olive-skinned young woman sat in a rocking chair across the room. A swath of straight brown hair held back by ivory combs flowed over her shoulders and down her back. The girl made no effort to approach the bed. Another quick scan of the room revealed no other presence. Had the female been stationed here to watch her? She hardly seemed a threat unless she had a weapon. Helena scrutinized the girl's hands and her empty lap.

She kept an eye on the young woman as she eased from the bed and reached for her clothing.

The girl stood and shook her head. Her bright-colored skirt rustled as she moved to a trunk nearby, knelt, and opened it. She drew out a lovely green silk gown and brought it to Helena.

"Hello. What is your name, and where am I?" Helena shook her head when the girl proffered the gown. "I prefer my own clothes."

Tears filled the girl's eyes and started down her cheeks. Very comely cheeks and amber eyes with long lashes. Why was she crying?

"Who are you, and where am I?" Helena repeated.

The girl pointed to her own ears, then her full lips, and shook her head again.

Helena asked the same question in French.

Another shake of the head.

Then Helena used Spanish, and the girl's face lit with pleasure.

"*Si.* Si." She held out the gown again. In her own language, she told Helena her name, Maria, and very politely asked her to please dress in the green gown. That the *jefe pirate,* boss pirate, would be truly angry at them both if she did not.

Helena acquiesced, and in a soft, sad voice, the girl told her story in Spanish as she helped Helena dress.

"These bad mens kidnapped me from my home in Venezuela, South America, over a month ago. My father owns a cacao plantation there. Every year, we go to a harvest festival in our coastal city. The ship of pirates attacked the city, and my best friend and I were captured." Her eyes filled with tears again. "Like me, she was only sixteen." She gulped back a sob. "Magnolia died of fever two weeks ago."

Helena's heart went out to her, and she curved her arm around her companion's slim shoulder. Her eyes fell on a tray of bread and cheese on a small table in the opposite corner. "Come, let us have something to eat. I'm famished." Maria sat with her but didn't touch the food. Helena sipped a cup of lukewarm tea and tried to distract her. "What is cacao that your plantation raises?"

The girl's eyes brightened. "It's from what chocolate is made. It starts from seedpods, or beans, grown on tall evergreen trees." A bit of a smile started on her lips. "My father planted many of these trees. I loved their sweet-smelling scent. We made dishes from the ground chocolate seeds inside the colorful pods after they ripened. My father had many companies awaiting his harvests." Her eyes looked far away. "Will I ever see my father and mother again or our lovely plantation?"

Helena gazed at her plate. Would she ever see her father, or Gideon or Windemere again? She forced the disturbing thought from her mind. "Do you know where we are right now, Maria?"

"I heard them speak of Charleston, but I don't really know. I've been on this ship for about two months and am only allowed on deck when it's sailing." Her soft voice faded with sadness.

As Helena finished the bread and cheese, heavy steps sounded near the door.

Maria jumped to her feet, her eyes wide.

A harsh voice in the corridor mocked. "How are my two golden songbirds this morning?"

The gruff voice of the pirate who had kidnapped her. Fear twisted around Helena's heart, but iron resolve stiffened her spine. A bar shuffled outside the door, then a key jangled in the lock, and the door swung open. The man ducked to enter and stood before them grinning—the same pirate who had awakened her on the rock in her secret place. Was it just last night or days ago? His muscled frame sucked the air from the room. Wearing the same soiled scarlet scarf tied over his braided hair, the pirate sported a different blue shirt which opened to his waist and revealed a hairy chest. Black pantaloons disappeared into knee-high boots, and his hard eyes roamed over Helena, as if unclothing her.

Maria stepped aside and moved toward her rocker. The pirate grabbed her around the waist and kissed her cheek. "What? No sweet greeting, my Spanish prize?" She twisted from his arms, and he let her go.

Helena took a deep breath, squared her shoulders, and looked the man full in the face. "Sir, you will be sorry you stole me from my father's plantation. I demand you return me home immediately."

A callused hand shot out and slapped her cheek so hard, Helena fell back on the bed, tasting blood from her bitten tongue.

A gasp escaped Maria's lips, and her face paled as she shrank back into her chair.

The pirate bent over Helena. "Don't you ever sass me like that again, little dove." Then he burst into a loud guffaw. "I have plans for you, big ones, as soon as the tide turns and that Navy frigate leaves the harbor. I know a Barbary coast, a long sail away, where sultans will fight for the chance to pay gold for a white dove like you and my little Spanish senorita."

He swaggered back to the cabin entrance, then turned. "I'm heading to a tavern for some relief till the tide changes, but you two don't fret. I'm leaving some guards meaner than me. Just make sure you don't aggravate them, and you'll be safe." He slammed the door behind him. The bolts falling into place vibrated through the cabin.

Maria sat in her chair and wept.

Helena laid her palm against her bruised cheek and started praying. She refused to give in to fear or tears. She prayed everything she could think of praying and finally fell into a deep, troubled sleep.

When she awakened, the light coming through the porthole had weakened, but the vessel still rolled with a placid rhythm against its anchor. Maria dozed off in her chair. Helena rose and peeked out the small opening but only saw a deserted coastline. Where was she? How could anyone find her on a ship hidden in a coastal cove? Surely, Gideon, her father, and the entire plantation were searching for her. But could anyone find her before the ship sailed away?

She sat back on her bed, and the pirate's words came back with chilling force. The threat of being sold as a slave to a sultan made her stomach roil. Every strange story her father had told her growing up when he returned from his trips to the Mediterranean rolled back across her mind. His tales of American sailors taken into slavery on the high seas—and sometimes, even entire villages along European coastal provinces—had made her eyes grow wide. But her mother had told her he embellished the tales to shock her. But had he?

Helena dropped to her knees beside the bed and cried out to God. Her whole life paraded before her, and tears blinded her eyes. The privileged life she'd lived as a wealthy planter's daughter seemed frivolous and meaningless. She had never lacked for a thing and had never imagined there could be such people as the pirate who now had her under his control. Would Gideon and her father ever be able to rescue her before the ship sailed away? A chill rose from her heart to her fingertips. *Slavery.* Would she end up in slavery to a sultan?

Why had she never considered the poor slaves who met all their needs on the plantation? Ever since she was a child, slaves had done everything to make her family's life easy and prosperous. Until now, as her thoughts took her back, she'd been blind to all the times Belle had tightened her lips when Helena had behaved in a spoiled, peevish manner. Was she now to find out what it would be like to be a slave and at the mercy of someone else's desires and moods?

And Gideon, who'd only done her good. Would she ever see him again? Have another chance to make their lives happy? She pressed her face into the side of the bed and sobbed until a prayer rose in her spirit.

Lord Jesus, please forgive me for my proud, selfish, unthankful life. If You're real, come into my heart, deliver me, help me come to know Your plan and purpose for me.

A peace unlike anything she'd ever known flowed over her.

~

Gideon helped John into his merchant office and into a chair. The man struggled to breathe. "James, will you go for Doc Hanks? I'll stay until you return."

"Yes, sir. Right away." The clerk flew out the door.

John gasped out a few words. "No, Gideon, don't stay, don't worry about me, son. Leave the carriage groom with me. I'll make it. Find Helena. And may God help you."

While he drove the horse and carriage toward Windemere at a hazardous gallop, Gideon whispered prayers for both John and Helena. He petitioned God for John's healing and Helena's protection. Where could his wife be? Praying for wisdom, he kept returning to something Helena had often mentioned—her secret place. But where was it?

At Windemere's front entrance, he brought the carriage to an abrupt halt, leaped to the ground, and ran up the steps two at a time.

Samson, with Bentley barking beside him, met him at the door. The man's haggard look spoke volumes. "Sir, so glad you're home."

"Make that two of us, man." Gideon entered, pulled off his hat, and wiped his sweating forehead. "Tell me everything you know about Helena's disappearance. John's clerk told us she never returned yesterday afternoon from her ride."

Samson nodded. "That's right. I was down at the stables late in the evening when Stormy came galloping down the drive with her saddle on. Put every one of us at the stables in a fright, I can tell you. Seemed like a replay of before. I formed a search group of all our men, and we saddled up and searched. Sir, I had no idea how big this plantation was, but I do now." He hung his head. "We've spent all night and ain't found a single clue of what has happened to Miss Helena, sir. I sure am sorry."

"Has the sheriff been notified?"

"Yes, sir. I sent one of the servants into Charleston at daylight to notify him. If you're going to search again, I'm coming with you."

Gideon shook his head. "Listen, man, you're all burned out. Get some rest. I'll take it from here. But one question. Did any of your group search down the banks of the Ashley?"

Samson took a deep breath. "Not so much, sir. We never knew Miss Helena to take a boat. She always took Stormy."

Gideon headed out with Bentley at his heels.

Wringing her hands, Mrs. Laurens hurried up the hall and stopped him before he reached the door. "Sir, I'm so sorry our men haven't found Miss Helena. My poor Joseph and even our Daniel's been out all night looking. I've just made them lie down for a spell."

Belle approached from behind the housekeeper. Tears brimmed in her eyes. "Sir, I'll continue praying. May the Lord help you find Helena."

Gideon acknowledged the women's sympathy with a nod, then strode to the barn. When he entered, Daniel scooted down the steps from the family's apartment. "Sir, we be so glad you're back. Are you going to search some more? Can I go with you?"

"No, young man. Your mama told me you've been out all night and need to get some rest."

The boy's face fell. "Well, I can at least fetch your horse." He sped down the corridor, and Gideon followed. When he saw his master, Hero nickered, and he received a firm pat on his thick neck.

In minutes, the boy had the horse ready to go. Gideon mounted, then called over his shoulder, "Thank you, son. Now get some rest as your mama said."

Gideon started down near the dock at the river's edge and followed the riverbank north as best he could through the undergrowth. He vaguely remembered Helena talking about the river being near her secret place. Bentley, often barking with excitement, kept up with him and made a wide sweep into the riverbank bushes and trees, sniffing the ground. As Gideon skirted their cotton fields, one brief happy thought broke through the dark cloud of his concern for Helena. The cotton harvest looked promising. Then he totally forgot it as his search kept turning fruitless. He'd been sure her secret place fronted the river, but what if he passed the plantation boundary without finding it?

An hour later, long past the cotton fields, Gideon wound some way back from the river, due to impassable bushes and undergrowth. He came into an open area with a large rock in the middle. Sunlight filtered down through the trees, and birdsong filled their branches. Tempted to dismount and rest Hero, he paused. Bentley, sniffing around the large rock, started barking with a different, higher sound to it.

"What is it, boy?" Gideon dismounted, swiped the sweat from his brow, and walked to where the dog sniffed something on the ground and scratched at it.

He knelt, pushed away leaves, and discovered a worn Bible. Opening the leather cover, he found the name of Helena's mother on the inside cover. His heart leaped, and he slipped the book into his shirt. Surely, this was Helena's secret place.

He searched around the area and soon found a spot where a horse had been tethered to a tree limb. He recognized the finely shaped tracks of Stormy, whose Arabian hooves were smaller, the shoes thinner, than his own horse. Then he searched all around the area, scanning the ground for tracks. First, he had to separate his own tracks from others blanketing the area. He followed two pairs of heavy boot tracks that led to the water's edge and evidence a rowboat had once been hauled ashore and tied to a bush. Bile rose in his throat. *Dear God, has she been kidnapped and taken away in a boat?* The idea made him dizzy, and he sank on his haunches, staring at the river.

Bentley's frenzied barking and the crunch of leaves underfoot warned Gideon that someone approached. He pushed to his feet and whirled.

Kunta crept into the clearing. How had the young man followed him to Helena's secret place? The man's blue eyes were wide and glittered with fear. His stiff face, paler than its usual cocoa color, gleamed with sweat.

Bentley quit barking and wagged his tail.

With a jerky stride, Kunta drew near, breathing hard, clenching and unclenching his large fists. "Suh, I got to make a confession. I done something bad, terrible bad."

Gideon frowned. "Kunta, surely you know I'm searching for Helena. Whatever this is, can it wait?" He couldn't keep the harshness from his tone.

Kunta shook his head and wrapped his arms around his chest and trembled. "Suh, it has to do with Miss Helena."

Gideon grabbed him by the shoulders, not caring that his fingers clamped on the freedman like a hawk's talons. "What are you talking about, Kunta?"

A sob escaped from the young man. "I done told some terrible peoples about this secret place, and they come and they take Miss Helena away to their ship." Collapsing on the ground, he beat his fists against the soil and sobbed. "I'm sorry, I'm sorry."

A red haze swam before Gideon's vision. With a roar, he jerked Kunta to his feet. Never had he felt more like committing murder.

"I thought they wuz just going to hold her for ransom." Kunta's blue eyes almost bulged from their sockets, and his breath came in great gulps.

When Gideon's vision cleared, he noted the young man's terror and got a grip on his own fury. He kept hold of Kunta but lightened his iron grip. He needed to get this whole story quickly, not drive the fellow to break and run.

Gideon growled. "Tell me all, Kunta, and fast."

The story that came forth from the shaking young man chilled Gideon's heart. Because of his jealousy of being John's illegitimate son and not eligible to inherit his father's wealth, Kunta had joined with some tavern pirate friends to orchestrate Helena's kidnapping. They had planned to demand a ransom, but the boss pirate, who often sailed the Barbary coast, decided they could get a lot more gold selling his precious Helena to a sultan. They were to sail with the morning tide.

Gideon's mouth turned to ashes. The Barbary Coast. He swallowed the horror rising in his raw throat. He was familiar with that coast of pirates, rich sultans, and intrigue. "Where is the ship? And you better tell me the truth, Kunta."

The young man nodded and swiped the tears and sweat from his face. "I can take you there. They got their brig hidden in a cove on the coast. We can row there down the Ashley, and when it runs into the harbor, down the coastline to find the cove. They ain't left yet. I never wanted Miss Helena to be sold...like a slave."

He shook Kunta so hard, the man's teeth rattled. "How do you know they haven't sailed already?"

"I knows it. They waiting for the Navy frigate to move from the harbor. I heard them arguing over it just before I slipped away." He stopped to take a shaky breath. "They left me and two other men to guard the ship while they left for the tavern at Gadsden Wharf. Soon as the other two was busy with their rum, I managed to leave the ship without them knowing. Their plan is to leave with the morning tide tomorrow whether the Navy vessel moves or not."

Gideon took a deep, painful breath. "Was...is Helena hurt?" Visions of his wife being abused by the pirates pummeled his mind. Helena, forcibly kidnapped by ungodly pirates, taken to a waiting ship, beaten into submission and... He forced those thoughts back.

"No, suh. They got her locked up in a special cabin with another girl kidnapped from South America."

With another girl? That information brought Gideon a bit of relief, that Helena was not a woman alone on a ship of pirates, and also concern that another woman was in peril. "We'll go at once from

Windemere's dock as soon as we can get there." But could he trust the young man not to break and run, the first chance he got? He whipped off his bandanna and tied Kunta's hands behind his back, then helped him mount Hero. He got on behind him and galloped from the clearing with Bentley loping behind them.

When they arrived back at the plantation, two strange horses tied to the tethering bar whinnied as Hero approached. Gideon dismounted and jerked Kunta with him up the steps.

Bentley slouched down on the porch, breathing hard and dripping saliva from his tongue.

Mrs. Laurens met Gideon at the door. She raised her brows at Kunta, then addressed Gideon. "Sir, the sheriff and his deputy have arrived. I put them in the parlor, and my husband and Samson have joined them."

"You did fine, Mrs. Laurens." Gideon nodded and strode into the parlor, hauling his prisoner along beside him.

Four men stood in a huddle near the fireplace.

Samson broke from the group and stepped closer. He frowned at the trembling Kunta. "Sir, do you have any news?"

"Yes."

The tall man with the silver badge stepped forward, whipped off his hat, and held out his hand. His brown eyes were all business. "Sheriff Graddy."

Gideon shook his hand. The strong, square jaw and serious demeanor of the sheriff confirmed him to be a man no one messed with if they had any sense.

A shorter man stepped forward.

"My deputy, George. We are so sorry to hear about the disappearance of your wife. We're here to do everything we can to help, Mr. Falconer."

Gideon shook George's hand and laid out the story as fast he could, glancing only at Kunta once as he told his regrettable part in the affair.

Kunta shrunk into himself and lowered his eyes. Tears seeped out.

The sheriff turned to him and pulled a set of handcuffs from his belt. "Mr. Falconer, you think this young man can lead you to the hidden ship?" He removed the bandanna from Kunta's wrists and replaced it with the handcuffs. "Kunta, is that your name?"

Kunta nodded. "Yessuh, I knows I can show him. I's sure sorry for having any part of this foul deed." He sniffed.

"And right you should be." The sheriff glanced back at Gideon. "I know this coast very well, and think I know the cove he's talking about. In years past, it was a known pirate hideout." He turned to Kunta. "Does it have a small stand of cabbage palmetto trees almost hiding the entrance?"

"Yessuh. That's it." Kunta's eyes brightened.

Gideon sucked in a breath. "We must be off, sir. And I ask your permission to take Kunta to show us the way. We've got a skiff at our dock. Samson and Joseph will come with me to help row and anything else needed."

The two men nodded.

As he glanced at Samson and Joseph, the sheriff balled his fist and pushed it into his other open palm. "Sounds like a plan. You and these two men should be able to handle the two guards left on the ship." He glanced at Kunta, then spoke to Gideon. "And I release this man into your keeping for the time being. Also, I know the tavern he referred to down on Gadsden Wharf. George and I will arrest these pirates if they are there. I think I know which ones they are. Have a certain eastern Mediterranean look about them. Almost arrested them a few days ago for fighting and breaking up the place." He rubbed his chin. "And that's not all. I'll alert the Navy frigate to move down the coast and be ready if that ship tries to escape from the cove." He and his deputy left.

In a matter of minutes, Gideon strode onto the Windemere dock and untied the skiff. He held it steady for the others to board, then he stepped in. Gideon and Samson took up the oars, Kunta settled in the bow with Joseph Laurens keeping his eye on him, and the small vessel headed down the Ashley toward Charleston. The sun cast long shadows over the river, but Gideon thanked God that sunset should still be a few hours away.

In an hour, they reached Charleston Harbor, then continued south down the coast. After another half hour, Kunta pointed out the entrance to the cove with its stand of cabbage palmetto trees. Making as little noise as possible, they rowed into the cove. The unusual colored stripes on the sides of the pirate ship anchored out of sight from the coastland water reminded Gideon of the Barbary Coast ships he'd encountered in his earlier sailing days.

He turned to Kunta. "You sure only two pirates are left aboard?"

"Yes, and both will be sleeping off a drunk from their own store of hidden rum. The boss pirate and his crew members won't come back until dark."

Gideon cast off his shirt, then pulled off his boots. He clasped the knife he kept hidden in one of them. Samson followed the same motions.

"Suh, can I go with you?" Kunta whispered.

"No." Gideon was not sure he could ever trust the man again, even after his tearful confession and help in finding the ship. "Samson and I will go." He glanced at Joseph Laurens, who nodded. He would guard Kunta.

Gideon stuck the knife between his teeth and slipped over the side of the skiff into the cool water, and Samson slid in behind him. The only sound in the warm, deceptively lazy afternoon, besides birdsong echoing from the surrounding forest, was the ominous sound of the ship bobbing with the tide against her anchor, the only thing keeping Helena, if she were on board, in Charleston and able to be rescued.

Climbing up the ship's side on the narrow ladder there, Gideon peeked across the deck. He saw no one. Then a slurred voice rippled across the way.

"Jubal, man, you got more of that rum? My bottle's done empty."

Gideon identified the pirate slouched up against a cabin door, next to a pile of rigging. A slight movement across the way revealed another man napping in a hammock. But that pirate didn't respond to the question.

Hoisting himself over the railing, Gideon dropped soundlessly onto the deck in his bare feet. Samson came up behind him. Gideon nodded toward the one sleeping in the hammock, and Samson moved without sound in the man's direction.

When Gideon crept toward the pirate complaining of his empty bottle, he stepped on a plank that creaked. At the sound, the pirate blinked. "Who? What—?" was all that made it out of his mouth before Gideon's hard fist struck his jaw. The man fell back against the cabin door unconscious, and Gideon sliced ropes from the rigging and tied him up like a pig in a poke. This pirate would be quiet and motionless for some time.

He glanced over the deck where a slamming, scuffling noise alerted him Samson was trussing up the other pirate who was dead drunk and offered no resistance. Then they both searched around the deck for any other guards. Could they trust that Kunta had been right about the number?

Hearing and seeing nothing, Gideon moved toward the hatch, opened it, and slipped down into the corridor. Samson stayed with the prisoners.

In the passage, Gideon saw only four closed doors. But one of the doors held a heavy bar of wood across it that could only be lifted from the outside. He strode to it, then hesitated. A heavy locked bolt on the door most certainly required a key. He bit back a word he hadn't used since he became a Christian. Now what?

CHAPTER 13

$\mathcal{H}$elena, roused from an exhausted sleep, sat up and stared at the door. "I think I heard someone in the corridor."

Maria nodded and came to sit on the bed with her. "And there have been bumping sounds from the deck above."

They both quieted as sounds in the corridor confirmed someone at their door.

The loud bump of the bar lifting sounded, and Helena grabbed Maria's arm. Then the rattle of the bolt made them both jump, but the door didn't open.

Maria looked at her with terror-filled eyes.

"Helena!" A familiar voice sounded in the passageway. "Helena, are you in there?"

Gideon! Joy flooded Helena. She uttered a cry and scrambled to the door. "Gideon! Gideon, yes, I'm here. Thank God."

"Yes, thank God, we've found you. Are you all right?"

Happy tears fell down Helena's cheeks. "Yes, and I have a new friend who is here with me, Maria."

Maria wasted no time flying to her side. "Sir, you are an answer to our prayers. Mine for two months." Her Spanish flowed out with strong emotion.

"Helena, it will take me a few more moments to get this bolt off, but gather up anything you and your friend need to bring with you. I'm taking you both out of here."

Helena hugged Maria. "Yes, yes. We will be ready, dearest." It surprised her how easy that endearing word rolled off her tongue. But she was not the same woman who had been brought to this detestable ship.

When the door opened, Helena flew into Gideon's arms. How good her face felt against his hard chest, and his arms around her made her so happy, she felt faint. Why had it taken her so long to realize Gideon Falconer was and would always be someone she could count on?

He examined her bruised cheek. "How I'd love to give a bigger bruise to whoever did that to you, Helena. Is there any other...injury?"

She shook her head. "No, dear. Your being here makes me forget even that hurt."

Clamoring up to the deck with Gideon's aid, Helena reveled in the safe circle of his arm around her waist amid the late-afternoon light. Was this nightmare really over? Gideon's loving glances down at her tripped her heart. His hoarse voice expressing thanks to God showed a depth of emotion she would never forget. She heard him giving orders as if from far away, but his warmth surrounded her as they moved to the ship's railing.

She recognized Samson as he held out his hand to Maria. The two of them disappeared over the ship's railing into a boat below. Stepping into the skiff, her friend exclaimed, as if recognizing a familiar face, "You came back and brought help. ¡*Gracias a Dios!*"

As Gideon guided her over the railing and into the rowboat, Helena barely noticed Joseph Laurens and one of the Windemere slaves waiting for them in the small vessel. The setting sun baptized them in shades of pink, orange, and purple. She sat with Gideon, pressed close to him, with his arm encircling her. Samson and Joseph manned the oars. Long before they arrived at the Windemere dock in the falling darkness, she fell into a dream-like state between wakeful-ness and exhaustion.

Gideon whispered something to Samson about the slave, then carried Helena in his arms up from the dock.

Maria followed into the house, and Gideon asked Mrs. Laurens to show her to a room. He spoke in Spanish to the young woman. "Maria, you are welcome in our home. Mrs. Laurens will take you to a room."

"Thank you, sir. I'll be fine. I pray Helena will be also. Thank you again for rescuing us."

Helena heard their conversation as if in a dream. Gideon carried her up the stairs to her bedroom. She became aware of Belle undressing her and sliding her a gown over her head. Her maid kept whispering, "Thank you, Lord Jesus. Thank you." Tucked into her bed, Helena sighed and soon dropped into a deep sleep, but not before she felt Gideon's presence reenter the room and his lips caress her forehead.

~

The next morning, Gideon rose early and checked on Kunta locked in the extra pantry room off the kitchen. There were no windows from which he could escape, and the door had a strong lock. He wanted to talk to him before Marm Esther came in to start breakfast.

Kunta sat on a pallet next to sacks of flour and rice. He rose when Gideon entered. The morning light shining through the door revealed the worried lines on the young man's face, as if he'd slept little.

"Suh, what's gonna happen to me?" The blue eyes, shadowed with fear, searched Gideon's face.

"That's what we will find out today, Kunta, after I see the sheriff."

"Suh, I'm real sorry. Do you think Miss Helena can forgive me?"

Gideon hardened his jaw. "Even if she can, I'm not sure I can." Not to mention John Allston. How would his father-in-law respond to his secret son's deed? Gideon might as well be perfectly honest with the perpetrator of Helena's abduction. "Do you really understand how criminal your actions were? My precious wife could've ended up taken to the Barbary Coast and sold as a slave." A chill shot up his spine even voicing it.

Tears gathered in Kunta's eyes. "Yessuh, I knows how wrong I wuz. But I thought they wuz just gonna ask for ransom. When I found out different, that's when I decided to break with the pirates and come tell you."

"That was the one good thing you did, Kunta, and I'm so glad you did." He forced back the black thoughts and let the happiness that Helena was safe up in her bedroom, still sleeping off her ordeal, flow back into his spirit.

Marm Esther came in the kitchen door and marched into the room. She pointed a long finger at Kunta. "Young man, I heard from Belle what you done. Nothing but the old devil got ahold of you. What wuz you thinking? After all I done tried to teach you." Her stiff, angry voice filled the morning air.

Kunta hung his head and dropped back onto a bag of flour. He swiped at the tears seeping down his face.

The cook reared back and put her hands on her hips. "You should be wiping them tears. But you best be praying for the good Lord to forgive you." She marched out of the room, and Gideon followed and locked the door.

She turned to Gideon. "Sir, what de law gonna do to him? I done been trying to raise that boy right since his ma passed. But guess I's failed."

"I don't know, Marm Esther, how the law will apply, since he's no longer a Windemere slave but a freedman. I aim to find out. Meanwhile, here's your key to the room. Give him his meals, and Samson will take him outside two or three times a day, until we find out."

He strode back toward the house, and Samson and Bentley caught up with him. The dog barked and begged for a pet, and Gideon rubbed the massive blond head.

"What yo' plans for today, sir?" Samson's eyebrows lifted.

"I'm going into Charleston to check with the sheriff and check on John Allston. He took the good news well last night that we'd rescued Helena, but the shock of it all seems to have weakened him. Will you take care of things here? Keep Kunta confined until we know what the sheriff will do with him."

"I will, and please tell Mr. Allston we pray he's recovering."

Gideon walked into the house and to Helena's bedroom. He opened the door softly and saw Belle sitting nearby. Had she sat there all night?

The maid rose and came out of the room to whisper, "Sir, I thought I'd let her sleep, she's sleeping so peacefully. But do you want me to awaken her?"

"Absolutely not. I just wanted to see if she was all right. If she awakens, tell her I've gone into Charleston to check on some things, and I'll be back by midday, most likely."

Belle smiled. "I sure will, sir."

As Gideon drove the carriage into Charleston, he mulled over the fact that he must find out if John would be willing to tell Helena that Kunta was his son and her half brother. She deserved to know how her abduction had occurred. And if the young man were truly repentant, would John want to send him to prison for the many years the law might require?

He drove up first to the sheriff's headquarters off Bay Street, and an officer led him into Sheriff Graddy's office.

The man stood behind his desk in front of a bay window. The sunlight bounced off the sparkling water behind him and outlined his tough frame. He held out his hand. "Sorry I missed you last night when you came to report that you had rescued your wife, but I got the message. Have a seat."

Gideon sat on a hard but serviceable chair.

Sheriff Graddy dropped into his armchair behind the desk and steepled his strong hands under his chin. "We were busy rounding up that pirate crew. Part of them were at another tavern, but we believe we've got them all, including the two you left bound on the ship. And we've confiscated the ship."

"That's what I wanted to hear, Sheriff. I appreciate the excellent work you and your men have done."

Concern darkened the sheriff's bright amber eyes. "Mrs. Falconer all right?"

"Yes, thank God. Only exhausted by the whole experience, but I left her sleeping soundly at Windemere with her maid keeping watch."

A smile lit Graddy's face. "That's great. These criminals won't be bothering anyone else for a long time. And what about the mulatto boy who had a part in this? You still have him under lock and key?"

Gideon nodded. "He's part of our plantation people, but Allston gave him his free papers a year ago. I believe he's sorry for having ever met up with the pirates. What will happen to him? Do you have to take him into custody?"

"Since he's a freed slave, all you need to do is sign this warrant to bring charges against him, and we'll go from there." He slid a paper across his desk.

Gideon picked it up, skimmed it, then laid it back down. "I'm heading over to check on Helena's father, John Allston. We'll talk about Kunta. Mr. Allston...has thought a lot of the young man, and I'd like to know his feelings on whether to press charges. Do you mind?"

"Not at all. Just drop back by any time and let me know what you decide. Since the young man helped facilitate the ladies' rescue and the pirates' arrest, it may go easier on him in front of a judge, but you never know."

A few minutes later, Gideon hurried up Allston's townhouse steps. John's elderly sister, Sarah, met him at the door. Before Gideon could even greet the thin, impeccably dressed woman, she frowned and confronted him. "I'm here to help look after John. I hope you haven't got anything upsetting to tell him. He doesn't need anything distressing. How's Helena?" That last question came as an afterthought, he was sure.

Gideon removed his hat and entered. "Ma'am, I'm sure John will be glad to see me, and I'm happy to report Helena is doing fine, resting after her ordeal." He moved around her and strode up the steps.

The robed man sat in a chair in front of a large window. A smile lit his pale face when he saw his visitor. "Gideon, come in, come in. What's the latest? Your long ride down here last night set my heart at ease, even if you didn't have time to give me any details. How is my daughter this morning? Was she...harmed in any way?"

Gideon threw his hat on a chair, then took a seat near Allston. "No, thank God, not harmed. Just exhausted. I left her with Belle still sleeping a couple of hours ago."

Allston breathed a sigh of relief.

Was the man strong enough to hear the truth about Kunta's part in the abduction? "How about you, sir? What did the doc have to say?"

John shook his head. "About the same. He bled me, as usual. Told me to take it easy." He gestured to a small bottle on his nightstand. "And he gave me that for any chest pain." He leaned forward. "But don't worry about me. Tell me how you found Helena so fast."

Gideon took a deep breath and told the story, including Kunta's part fueled by jealousy, and the young man's repentance. He shared about rescuing Maria, abducted from Venezuela by the same pirates, and now at Windemere with Helena until they could arrange for her travel home.

Allston frowned, closed his eyes, and leaned his head back on his chair. He looked older than ever before. "With Kunta, my sin comes back to haunt me, though I've repented many times. But how can I allow my son to go to jail for my mistakes, maybe for the rest of his life? He's only sixteen." He sat back up. "Is he already arrested?"

"Not yet. He's at Windemere. I locked him in the old pantry room until I could talk with you and the sheriff." Gideon cleared his throat. "Sheriff Graddy knows the whole story. He knows Kunta facilitated Helena's abduction but also her rescue and the arrest of all the pirates. He says if we want to press charges against him, all I need to do is sign a warrant, and he'll take him off my hands."

"You say without Kunta, you may never have found Helena...in time?"

"Of that, I'm positive. When I detected she'd been abducted from her secret place and taken away on the river which opens onto the Atlantic, I knew how impossible it could be to ever discover where she might be. On that riverbank, I felt like yelling and cursing, but I prayed instead. Then Kunta showed up with his tearful confession and offer to take me to the very ship where the pirates held Helena."

"And you say he's really sorry for what he did?"

"I believe he is."

Allston stared into his face, his blue eyes reminding Gideon of Helena, as well as Kunta. The man sighed. "I know the pirate crew should get the full justice of the law, not only for Helena but for the other young woman as well. But do you think...we could have some mercy on Kunta?"

"Do you mean not sign the warrant?"

"Yes."

Realizing how stiff he'd held his neck during the conversation, Gideon stretched it and his shoulders. Then he returned John's steady gaze. "I'll be glad to do whatever you say, sir, but I believe we must bring Helena into this decision. She needs to know the truth of why and how this happened to her and decide if she can offer forgiveness."

Silence reigned for several seconds. Then Allston drew a deep breath. "I think that would be right. She needs to know the truth of why this happened...and meet her half brother." His face paled even more. "But would you tell her...about it, Gideon? I don't think I have the strength to do so, just now."

Gideon stood, concerned at how weakness overcame the man. "Yes, sir. I'll do it, then I'll take care of...any further steps. You can rest assured."

"Please don't tell Helena about my seeing the doc. It might worry her. I will be fine." He took a long breath. "Will you hand me that bottle over there on the nightstand?"

Gideon moved to grab it and placed it in the man's hand. "Do I need to call the doctor? Will you be all right?"

John gave a weak smile. "I'll be fine. This medicine is a little miracle. Come back when you have more news, son."

Gideon drove back to Windemere in more peace than he'd had in the past twenty-four hours. Helena was home safe and recovering. And John wanted her to have the truth about his family secret. She needed to know, but would she be strong enough to bear it?

His mother met him in the plantation hall. "Gideon, how wonderful you were able to find and rescue Helena. I've been in to see her, and she seems fine and is recovering from the terrible experience."

He gestured to his mother, and she followed him into the parlor. Gideon closed the door, dropped his hat on a table, then took a seat across from her. "What have you been told about Helena's abduction?"

"Well, that Charleston pirates kidnapped her from her secret place on the Ashley River and the sheriff has arrested all of them." A smile lit her face. "I'm so glad it's over, Gideon. Praise God the Lord helped you rescue her and the fine young woman, Maria."

When Gideon didn't respond for a moment, she cast a questioning look at him. "Is there more?"

"Yes, there's more. What I'm going to tell you, you must keep confidential. I'm only sharing it so you can pray."

His mother reached out and touched his hand. "Of course, son."

"One of our young plantation workers told the pirates how to find Helena's secret place. He was a Windemere slave, but is now a free adolescent, named Kunta. John Allston emancipated him about a year ago." Gideon ran his hand through his hair. "He freed Kunta because he is Helena's half brother."

His mother gasped. "Oh."

Gideon almost missed her soft response. "I've just left Allston. I went to ask him what we should do with Kunta. Right now, I have him secured in the old pantry next to the kitchen. He is sorry and repentant for his part in this. The pirates lied to him from the start.

Told him they were just going to hold her for ransom. But their real plan was to sail to the Barbary Coast and sell her and Maria into slavery."

His mother's hand flew to cover her mouth. "How dreadful."

Gideon leaned toward her. "Mother, I'd never have found Helena if Kunta hadn't come to me, confessed, and then showed me the ship where she was being held. John Allston wants to have mercy on the young man and not sign a warrant to have him arrested. He could spend many years in prison like the pirates will undoubtedly do. They were all caught by the sheriff and their ship confiscated." John swallowed to moisten his dry throat. "I told John Helena needs to know the truth about Kunta and be a part of the decision. He agreed. Also, John is seeing a doctor. Had some kind of attack when we learned about his daughter's abduction. But he asked me not to tell Helena about his health right now. Do you see why I need you to pray?"

She sat forward. "Yes, I do. You're going to talk to Helena today?"

Gideon stood. "Do you know if she's been up, had breakfast or the midday meal?"

"Yes, she has had both. Helena came down for the meals and sat with me and Maria. She seemed like her normal self."

Gideon stood. "I'll go up to her now. We need to get this thing settled about Kunta."

"And I'll go to my bedroom to pray, Gideon. I know the Lord will show you how to break this news to Helena and help both of you know what to do about her half brother." She stood and smiled at him. "And I will pray for her father as well."

He found Helena about to leave her room, dressed for horseback riding.

She flew into his arms and buried her face against his throat. "Oh, Gideon. I feel as though I'm back from the dead. If you'd not found me..." Her voice broke.

His heart pounded against his ribs so hard, and delight flowed so deliciously over him, he wasn't sure he could speak. He lifted her chin and claimed her soft lips. When she responded with passion, he pulled her tight and deepened the kiss.

Finally, raising his mouth from hers, he gazed into her eyes. He must come back to his senses and talk to her before he forgot everything he came to do. It took an enormous effort, but he placed his hands on her waist and moved her back an inch or so, then took her hand and led her to the chairs before the window. He pulled his seat up close to her and sat. Her startling blue eyes, brightened by the tears, stared at him as if she saw into his very soul.

He took a deep breath and clasped her small hand in his. "Helena, I need to talk to you about your abduction."

She shook her head. "No, Gideon, I'm trying to forget it. Can't we just thank God and go on about our lives? How thankful I am you rescued me." She lifted one of his hands, pressed it to her cheek, then opened his palm and kissed it.

He almost forgot why he'd come. He clenched his lips, then spoke. "We will most definitely go on about our lives, and I look forward to it with all my heart, but there's something you need to know, dearest." His voice sounded hoarse even to him.

She released his hand and sat back in her chair. "All right. I'm listening."

As gently as he could, he shared the story, only telling her that one of their young former slaves, Kunta, whom her father had freed a year before, had learned of her secret place and told the pirates about it.

Helena frowned and crossed her arms over her bosom. "Why would he do that? And why would my father have freed him if he's such a...a wicked person?"

"That's the hard part I must tell you, Helena. Your father wants me to tell you. Can you receive it?"

She exhaled with apparent exasperation and looked into his eyes. "Gideon, please stop hedging and tell me what this is all about. I'm sure I can receive it. Certainly, if it's from dear Papa."

Gideon whispered a prayer in his heart. "Kunta is your half

brother. He did what he did because he was jealous of you and your inheritance."

Helena stood, her face flaming. She paced across the room, her riding boots making clicking sounds, then she came back to stare at him. "Are you telling me my father...sired a child...by one of our...female slaves?"

He nodded. "The woman died of fever when Kunta was about fourteen."

Helena dropped into her chair, and her nostrils flared. "What my dear, precious mother must have gone through, and I knew nothing about it." She sighed and slumped. Then she raised her head, and a new light came into her eyes. "I want to see this...young man. How old is he?"

"Helena, that's what I hoped you would say. He's sixteen and very repentant about what he did to you. In fact, if he'd not come to me and confessed and taken me to the ship where you were being held..." He shook his head. "I'd probably never been able to find and rescue you in time."

Helena closed her eyes for a moment. "And was he arrested with the rest of the pirates?"

"No, he's here on the plantation. I've secured him until we can decide what's to be done with him. If we sign a warrant, the sheriff will get him and he'll spend many years in prison, most likely."

She bit her lip. "Is that what my father wants?"

"No. He wants to give Kunta mercy. He feels he's partly responsible...because of his own sin when the boy was conceived, which he tells me he's often repented of. I told your father you needed to know the truth and be part of whatever decision we make regarding the young man."

"Where is...Kunta?"

"Come, I'll take you to him."

~

*H*elena swallowed to moisten her dry throat as Gideon led her to the kitchen, then to the spare pantry. He lit a candle and handed it to her.

At the door, he removed a key from his pocket and opened it. They entered.

A dark figure rose from a sitting position on sacks of corn meal and flour, then fell at her feet. "Miss Helena, I's so sorry. Will you please forgive me?" The voice, half child, half man, broke into quiet sobs.

Her own misery, tears, and prayers on the pirate ship when she had little hope of rescue flashed across her mind. She reached down and touched the hot, shaking shoulder. "I forgive you, Kunta. Now please stand up."

Gideon helped him to his feet. When he stood, Helena noted the sturdy body. But when he swiped his tears away with his sleeve and looked at her, she almost dropped the candle. The blue eyes, like the very ones she saw in her mirror every morning and whenever she looked at her father, shocked her to the core. Gideon's arm came around her waist as if he understood.

She took a deep breath and looked up at Gideon. "Can't he come out of this...pantry and sit in the kitchen for a moment?"

Gideon nodded and opened the door wide. Helena followed the two of them to the large kitchen table in the slaves' dining area. Since it was still a while until the evening meal would be prepared, the building was empty except for the three of them.

For the next half hour, Helena got to know her half brother. She asked questions, and he was quick to respond. Peace now reflected from his face, and his wide hands, soon to be the large hands of a grown man, lay open on the table.

"Tell me about your mother, Kunta. I now know...that my father...was your father." Helena could not keep the shock from her voice.

The boy's eyes widened, and he stared at her for a moment, then lowered his glance. "My mama, she helped all the folk while she was alive. Anything that ailed them and when they got sick or when they had babies." He stole a glance at Helena once again, and his face brightened. "Sometimes she let me help with the sick. And I still remember where all her herbs grow in the woods and fields."

"You're interested in helping the sick, Kunta?"

"That's the best thing I like to do, ma'am."

"Where...do you stay, Kunta?"

"Your father done give me a cabin down past the stables, and I ask'd Marm Esther move in with me. She be my housekeeper." He smiled. "And she try to be my boss."

Helena glanced at Gideon. "Well, we must decide about your future, Kunta. Do you understand that you can go to prison for what you did? All those pirates are there now."

The young man gulped and nodded.

"Will you promise to obey Marm Esther and stay out of trouble if we let you stay on the plantation?"

Moisture gathered in his eyes. "Yes, ma'am, I know I done wrong. I ain't never going back to that tavern where I met those bad men." He looked at Gideon. "And I will do my best at whatever job you give me, Mister Gideon. This is my home. I want to stay."

The kitchen door opened, and Marm Esther shuffled in. Her eyes widened, and she stopped all motion when she saw the gathering. "Is I 'rupting somethin'? I kin come later..." She turned back.

Helena stood. "No, Marm Esther. You've come just at the right time. Kunta has promised to turn over a new leaf. He's never going back to the taverns, and he's going to obey you and stay out of trouble. And that's how he won't have to go to jail."

Moisture sparked in the elderly woman's eyes, and a tear slid down her smooth cheek. "That be 'zactly what I been praying for." She trudged over to Kunta. "Boy, I'm going to hold you to that promise. You hear?"

"Yes, ma'am."

She opened her arms, and Kunta pressed into them.

Helena left with Gideon. Outside, she took a deep breath of warm summer air, cooled in the shade of the tall oak trees. The screech of a peacock shattered the quietness. She looked up at Gideon. "I still have time for my ride. What are your plans?"

"I must go back and tell the sheriff what we've decided about Kunta. And I'll drop by your father's afterwards." He touched her arm. "Two things I need to share. First, the doctor has visited your father, but John said to tell you not to worry, that he's fine. Second, would you mind not riding to your secret place, Helena? In fact, limit your riding time to half an hour, please. It's going to take me a bit to adjust and think it safe again."

She smiled up at him, then on impulse stood on her toes and planted a kiss on his lips. "All right. Would it make you feel better if I take Bentley with me?"

Gideon looked around as if to see if anyone watched them. He pulled her into his arms and kissed her soundly. "Yes, Bentley is a clever idea. He's big enough to scare most anyone."

Later, riding down the plantation road astride Stormy, Helena couldn't keep a smile from her lips still warm from Gideon's kiss. She must let nothing stop her from opening her heart to the man who had proven his love and care for her over and over. The question of the gift of Windemere somehow seemed less important.

∼

Gideon asked Joseph to harness up the carriage for the trip to Charleston. He re-entered the house and ran into his mother and Maria heading toward the parlor. Just the two with whom he needed to speak. He greeted them and followed them into the sitting room.

His mother and the young woman sat on the sofa. He stood before them.

Maria's eyes exuded her thankfulness before she spoke in Spanish. "Sir, I truly am so grateful for your rescue. And I need to talk to you about how I might get home to Venezuela. My poor parents, I'm sure, have been prostrated with grief since I was abducted."

Gideon nodded. "You're right. And I plan to do everything in my power to return you home. But give me a bit of time, and I will come up with the best plan to get you there." Hopefully, she could understand his imperfect Spanish.

"Oh, sir, thank you, thank you." She clasped her hands under her chin and blinked back tears.

His mother patted Maria's arm as if she'd understood. "There, I knew my son would take care of this. Be at peace."

Whether the girl comprehended his mother's English or not, she gauged the emotion, swiped at her cheek, and gave a tremulous smile.

When he walked back to the stables, Laurens had the carriage harnessed for him. "Thank you, Joseph, for your help in the rescue."

"You're most welcome, sir, and we're so glad we found the ladies in time...and unharmed."

Gideon swung up into the carriage and reached for the reins. Laurens handed them to him but looked ready to comment again. "Is there something else, Joseph?"

The man lowered his head, then glanced back up at him. "About Kunta. What's gonna happen to him, sir? He's just an overgrown boy...not much older than my boy...and he seemed right sorry."

"He's staying here and not going to jail, Joseph. Helena made that decision. He begged her forgiveness, and she granted it."

The man looked relieved. "I know what he did was wrong, mighty wrong, but I'm glad he's going to get another chance to do right." He tipped his hat and turned back into the barn.

In Charleston, Gideon went by the sheriff's office first and told him to keep the warrant paper. They wouldn't be needing it. Then he moved on to John Allston's townhouse.

The moment he pulled up to the hitching bar, he knew something was wrong. He jumped out of the carriage and tied the horse to the post. Where was the usual slave to take charge of the animal? He hurried up the steps and across the wide front porch and rapped with the horseshoe knocker. No response. He turned the knob and entered the silent hall.

"Hello, anyone here?" His voice echoed down the hall and up the staircase.

The head of the elderly butler appeared at the top of the staircase. "Oh, Mr. Gideon. I'm so glad you're here. It's Mr. Allston. Miz Sarah sent the footman for the doctor, but he's taking a mighty long time getting here."

Gideon took the steps two at a time. In Allston's room, with the curtains drawn, the space seemed dark and sinister. He discerned John in the bed with Sarah bent over him wiping his forehead with a damp cloth. The housekeeper and a young servant girl entered the room behind Gideon with fresh linens and water.

Sarah looked at him, the parchment skin of her face porcelain, her eyes wide. "Sir, I'm so glad you're here. John's not well at all. He's hot and then he's cold. Where could that doctor be?" Her voice ended on an angry note.

She moved away to the window, and Gideon came to the bedside. "John, can you hear me?"

The eyes stayed closed in the man's pale face, paler than Gideon remembered on his earlier visit. "Yes, Gideon. I can hear you, but you sound far away. I'm afraid I'm not much longer for this world."

His weak, slurred voice shocked Gideon. "Don't say that, sir. Miss Sarah has sent for the doctor."

"Lean down, my son. I don't have much time." A shaky hand reached up from the bedcovers, and Gideon folded it into his.

"I'm here, John."

The man's lips started to move, but no sound came out. Gideon leaned down close and finally heard the man's whispered words. "Helena has met Kunta?"

"Yes, and everything is going to be all right, John. She's fine."

"She's not going to send him to prison?"

"No. She's completely forgiven him. So have I. But we will keep an eye on him."

The rigid face relaxed. Then, with earnest effort, John pulled

Gideon closer. "In the safe in my office...at the dock, is my will. You'll find the code...to the safe taped under...the desk...drawer." John's voice grew weaker, and Gideon leaned closer. "Helena...and you will...inherit...what's left of my...estate." A shadow passed over his eyes. "But I would like...the boy to be given...one hundred acres...of his own. Will you see...that he gets it...when he...comes...of age?"

"Yes, I will do that, sir."

John's head and body sank deeper into the bedding as he exhaled one last breath. His pale face changed into marble, and his hand fell from Gideon's.

Moisture gathered in Gideon's eyes. Death was no stranger to him, but he had come to love the man who had just died while holding Gideon's hand.

Crying erupted from Sarah, the housekeeper, and the girl. The elderly butler only stood straighter, but he flicked at something on his wrinkled cheek.

Sarah pressed a handkerchief to her face and left the room.

The housekeeper moved to draw open the drapes and open a window, and the girl assisted and asked why. The woman looked scandalized. "Why, to allow Mr. Allston's spirit to escape to heaven, dear girl."

Sounds of someone entering below floated up the stairs. Soon, the doctor joined them in the bedroom. He took one look at the bed's resident and then stepped back out. Gideon followed him.

The man spoke to Gideon. "Sir, you must be Allston's son-in-law. Am I right?"

"Yes."

"Please accept my condolences. I told John a year ago his heart was getting weak, but he didn't want to believe it."

"Heart trouble is what he died of?"

"Yes, no doubt in my mind. Sorry I couldn't get here sooner, but there wasn't anything I could've done, other than make him comfortable. Was he lucid to the end?"

"Yes. Thank you for coming, anyway, Doc. What do we owe you for your services?"

"Oh, don't worry about that, my good man. John hasn't been able to pay me the past six months, and I won't be looking for anything now."

"What?" Gideon's shock must've shown on his face.

The doctor pursed his lips and shook his head. "You didn't know about Allston's gambling habit?"

CHAPTER 14

After speaking with the grief-stricken sister, Gideon gave the servants instructions to prepare Allston's body and order a coffin. Then he drove the carriage to John's office at the dock. On the way there, he wrestled over the doctor's shocking revelation that he'd not been paid the past six months, and that Allston had a serious gambling habit. Could it be true?

Finding Allston's clerk absent, he searched for the safe's code taped under the desk drawer and obtained it. The safe clicked open. Surprised at how little it held, Gideon found only the will with several legal papers attached to it with a ribbon circling it all. He stuffed the documents inside his shirt and left.

Driving back to Windemere, he searched for the right words to tell Helena her father had passed. He would investigate the doctor's revelation later.

On the plantation house's long front drive, Helena galloped past his carriage with a wave and happy smile. When he drove up to the entrance, she awaited him. Servants took charge of Stormy and the carriage.

"What has you looking so glum, Gideon? I thought I might as well wait for you at the door and sort it out."

He reached for her hand. "Come, I do have some news, my dear. Sad news, I'm sorry to say."

She stiffened, and her blue eyes searched his. "My father. Is it my father?"

He nodded. "Let's sit in the parlor, and I'll tell you about it, dear one."

They entered the parlor, and Gideon closed the door, then sat beside her on the sofa. He took both her hands in his and told how he found her father and how he held his hand in the last moments. He decided not to tell her Allston had collapsed earlier when first hearing of her abduction. That would only stir up more emotion regarding her terrible experience.

Tears streamed down Helena's face, and she could hardly speak. "Gideon, I'm so sad sweet Papa has passed, but I'm happy you were with him." Her voice broke with sorrow. "I've felt for some time he wasn't well, and he was working too hard, always seemed stressed."

He handed her his handkerchief, and she placed it on her face and gulped sobs.

Gideon drew her into his arms. When she finally lifted her head, he kissed her forehead. "We must prepare for his funeral. Can we talk about it now, or do you wish to wait an hour or two to collect yourself?"

Helena blew her nose and took a deep, shaky breath. "Let's talk now. Papa would want to be buried beside my mother at Saint Andrew's Parish Church on the road to Charleston. We can have the service there and have visitation here afterward." She wiped her eyes. "Papa was never a pompous person. and I'm sure he'd prefer a simple service. What do you think, Gideon?"

"I think you're right, dear. Do it as simple as you would like." If the doctor's strange words proved factual, how much cash would be available to pay for a funeral? Less expensive would be best. He'd need to visit the family lawyer as soon as possible. But first, he'd read the will he still had in his shirt.

Helena sniffed and rose. "I will go to my room to make plans. I'll find Mrs. Laurens and Belle." She looked at the large mirror on the opposite wall. "We must cover all the mirrors. And I will need a new black gown."

"Cover the mirrors?"

"Yes, surely you know why. It's to stop any more bad luck coming to our house, and it's to help keep our minds thinking on a higher image than ourselves."

Gideon strode to his office and shut the door. Sitting down at his desk, he pulled the will and legal papers from inside his shirt. The will read simply:

I leave all my earthly goods, any monies, real estate, slaves, and animals, to my daughter, Helena Allston Falconer, and to her husband, Gideon. To be theirs to hold and to keep once my funeral expenses and all debts are paid. With one exception. I direct that one hundred acres of land from one of my plantations be allotted to and given to one of my former slaves, now a freedman, Kunta, upon his obtaining the age of twenty-one.

The will was signed by John Allston and witnessed by two other signatures.

Gideon laid the will aside and took up the other attached documents, one by one.

To his shock, the four documents were property titles with mortgage forms attached. Allston Hall and John's Charleston townhouse in which he now lay, had been mortgaged to the hilt. Two of his three ships had also been mortgaged to their assessed worth. With bated breath, Gideon picked up the last folded document composed of three pages, and his heart fell to his feet when he saw the name of Windemere in the first heading. Was it also mortgaged beyond belief? But John had given, or tried to give him, the title to the plantation the day he married Helena. Could he have taken a mortgage on it since their wedding and when it was no longer in his name?

He scanned the first page, Windemere's property title. The second page was a mortgage for many thousands of dollars. On the third page, John had composed a transfer of the title to Helena. But scanning the front and back of that document, Gideon could find no government stamps or signatures that the transfer had ever taken place or been recorded.

But who or what bank held the mortgages? He scanned back through the documents and found a common entity, Hellams Low Country Bank. But he'd never heard of it. He'd check into everything after the funeral. But his first visit would be to the family lawyer and before he came to read the will.

He dropped the papers on his desk and fell back into his chair. How had he never suspected John Allston of a gambling habit that could—had—depleted his fortune? And Helena's? Would the family lawyer have more updated information? He checked the documents and found the name, Joshua Becket, Esquire, 151 Meeting Street. Something about the name seemed familiar, but he couldn't remember meeting the man. He checked the time and decided to try and catch the man in his office before the day ended. Packing the papers into a satchel, he left Windemere.

Gideon drove the carriage into Charleston to Meeting Street. A modest sign at 151 confirmed he'd found the lawyer's office. Pulling into the empty side drive, he jumped down and tied the horse's reins to the hitching bar, then walked up the five steps of the brick building. He lifted a brass lion-head knocker and released it against the heavy oak door. The sound reverberated on the quiet street. A maid in a white cap with sprigs of red hair escaping opened the door and assessed him through pale green eyes.

"May I see Attorney Becket?"

A smile creased her lips. "Come in, sir. I'm not sure, but his assistant will be glad to check for you." She led him into the blue-tiled hall and to a man sitting at a desk.

The assistant looked up, then stood, smiling. He came around the desk and held out his hand. "Gideon! Gideon Falconer."

"Adam White, how good to see you. I had totally forgotten you decided to pursue law after your great naval career." Gideon walked closer and shook his hand. "How are Hannah and the four little ones? I saw her and Aunt Sophia at our wedding."

"Fine, everybody's fine. Sorry I had to miss your wedding. How is the married life and Helena, your chosen?"

Gideon was happy to have a good report, finally, about married life. The memory of his and Helena's recent kisses warmed him still. She seemed a different person since her abduction. "We're happy, Adam. God has blessed me with a fine wife."

"Glad to hear it." He indicated a red leather chair in front of the desk, and Gideon sat. Adam moved back behind his desk. "What brings you to Becket Law Firm?"

"John Allson, Helena's father, has just passed, and I understand Attorney Becket has handled some of John's business. I came to see him. If I need an appointment, I can certainly come back another day."

Adam White's eyes took on a strong look of sympathy. "Sorry to hear that. Please give my condolences to Helena." He stood. "Let me check with Mr. Becket. His last client left a few minutes ago." He walked down the hall, gave a brief knock at a door, and entered.

Gideon glanced around Adam's desk. Anyone could guess about the man's naval career. A model frigate with its sails spread wide sat in a place of honor with its American flag atop the mast. A solid miniature cannonball with one flat side worked as a paperweight on top of a stack of papers. Another miniature, a shiny anchor, held down files packed on the corner.

Adam reappeared, standing in the door he had entered. "Gideon, come right in. Mr. Becket can see you."

Gideon walked into the spacious office with its tall windows looking out on Meeting Street. Mellow wood dominated the room in the wide oak desk, in the arms of the leather-covered chairs, and in the gleaming floor. A red-and-blue Persian rug sat under the desk and chairs. A smell of lemon oil floated in the air. Joshua Becket stood from behind the desk. The man's lean form boasted a dark coat and white vest with a red cravat. Short salt-and-pepper hair framed his tanned, square face. A trim mustache and beard, also with some gray, gave him a sophisticated look. But the bright intelligent eyes hooked Gideon's attention most.

"Sir, this is Gideon Falconer. He married John Allston's daughter, Helena." He smiled. "And I knew him some years back. A fine fellow. Gideon, please meet Lawyer Joshua Becket."

Joshua held out a strong hand, and Gideon shook it. "Please have a seat, Mr. Falconer."

Adam White excused himself.

Gideon sat and placed his satchel on his lap.

Lawyer Becket moved back into his high-backed red leather chair. "Sorry to hear about John Allston. Please give Helena and your family my condolences. I understood some time ago he was not in the best of health. I assume you're here to talk about his will and estate?"

"Yes." Gideon took the documents from the bag and placed them on Becket's desk.

The man's bright eyes glanced at them. "Did Allston tell you about his...mortgages before he passed?"

"No, he didn't tell me a thing except where to find these papers. You can imagine my shock."

Becket nodded. "I tried my best to talk John out of some of his decisions, but to no avail."

"Do you have any updates or changes to these documents? I was hoping..."

Becket picked them up and looked through them one by one. "No, these are the latest copies as far as I can ascertain. Of course, the originals are in the hands of the mortgage holder." He looked at Gideon with sympathy. "If he never mentioned any of this, I'm sure it was a shock to you and Helena."

"Helena doesn't know yet. I wanted to talk to you first. Can you tell me anything about the bank listed as holding the mortgages?"

"I possibly can tell you the individual who signed and provided the mortgage cash." Becket stood and opened a file behind his desk and withdrew a paper. He scanned it. "Ah, here is the name. I only met him once. George Beauregard."

CHAPTER 15

Disturbing thoughts plagued Gideon as he drove back to Windemere. How could a man as smart as he'd thought John Allston to be get into such debt with a foolish fop like George Beauregard? Had it all been by gambling losses with George, or with others also, and John had applied to George to cover the losses? A shocking idea struck him, and he clenched his teeth. Was debt why Allston was insisting Helena marry the man when she had tried to escape Beauregard by jumping into the Ashley River? He cast that one aside. Surely not. That would be like...bartering one's daughter to pay off one's debts.

When he arrived at Windemere and strode into the house, black fabric covered all the mirrors he passed. He hurried up the steps to Helena's room. His wife stood on a stool while Lydia, kneeling on the floor, pinned the hem of Helena's black dress. His mother sat nearby as well as Maria. All the women greeted him. Even with grief marking her face, Helena was still beautiful and made his heart jump against his ribs.

She dabbed her nose with a handkerchief. "We're getting our mourning gowns ready, Gideon. Thank God everyone has one but me and Maria, and Lydia is going to fix that."

When would he be able to talk privately with her?

"Gideon, I sent a message to the pastor of St. Andrew's Parish Church, and he responded that Friday would be a suitable time for the service. Does that sound good to you?"

He nodded. "Sounds fine."

Helena stared at him. "Did you come to tell me something?"

"It can wait." He turned to go, but his mother called him.

She glanced at Helena, then Maria. "Gideon, dear, with this sad shock, I've mentioned to Maria it might be a couple of weeks or so before you can think about a plan to help her home. I believe she understands."

"Mother, you're right, it will be a while before I can think up a plan. But we won't forget her."

Gideon assumed Maria didn't understand what they'd said, so it surprised him when she responded in her own language. "Sir, in this terrible grief, please do not concern yourself over my need. I'm sure the time will come when it will be right."

He responded in Spanish. "Thank you, young lady. The right time will come. Meanwhile, you are our very welcome guest."

He nodded a farewell and left the women. Their soft voices arose in the room as he closed the door. How would he ever be able to sail Maria home now? Would he and Helena even own a controlling interest in one of John's ships after the estate settlement?

He headed into his study and found the key to the household lockbox. How much cash did they have on hand? He'd balanced the books the past month, but for the life of him couldn't remember the balance. They always had plenty to meet all the bills, and the expected cotton harvest would surely replenish the till. So he never worried about money. He breathed easier when he discovered enough extra savings, beyond the monthly household expenses, to cover John's funeral.

He stood and walked out the back entrance to consult with Samson about the cotton harvest coming a few months away. Their very existence might depend on it being the best one the plantation had ever produced. He whispered a prayer as he walked toward

Samson's cabin. *Lord Jesus, show me exactly what to do in this situation. Comfort Helena. Prepare her for what I must add to her grief about her father's gambling debts which may swallow most of her inheritance.*

~

Helena slipped from her bed and looked out her bedroom window the day of her father's funeral. She bit her lip. Where had the pretty sunshine of the day before gone? Dark clouds obliterated the sun and threatened rain. No birds chirped in the trees, and a mist covered the plantation grounds. The humidity made her face feel clammy. She took a deep breath and forced a smile when Belle knocked and came in to help her dress in her black gown and veiled bonnet.

One relief, for which she was grateful, was she had not had to deal with Aunt Sarah about the funeral plans. Her elderly aunt was prostrate over her brother's death and had left the townhouse and gone back to Allston Hall, where Papa had given her a home when she'd lost her husband years earlier.

After the brief service in the hundred-year-old church, Helena led Mrs. Rhett, Lydia, Maria, and the few neighbors in attendance out of the church. Glancing at the last rows of pews, she gasped and almost dropped the one red rose stem she carried in her black-gloved hand. George Beauregard stood in the shadows in a far corner. She quickly averted her eyes and continued following the coffin carried by Gideon, Samson, and four other men out the door and to the cemetery.

The smell of cut grass and damp, freshly dug earth floated on the humid air. Darker clouds blocked the sun and gave an eerie look to their procession. The minister opened the gate in the wrought-iron fence that surrounded the burial ground with its varied headstones. Some tall, some short, one small for a child rose along the path they traversed to the Allston plot. There one large marble headstone bore her mother's name, and fresh tears gathered in Helena's eyes as they stopped beside it. Some Windemere house servants stood along the fence with sad faces, but Mrs. Laurens, Marm Esther, and the kitchen help would be at the plantation, readying the refreshments for after-funeral visitors.

She looked up at the darkened, glowering sky and whispered a prayer that the rain would hold off. As the men lowered the coffin into the ground, she lifted her veil and dabbed a handkerchief to her eyes, then moved to stand at the head of the grave. After helping place the coffin at the graveside, Gideon came to stand beside her.

The minister took his place at the opposite end of the opening and read the final Scripture and prayed. Helena dropped her rose into the grave, then stooped, grasped a handful of the damp, piled-up earth, and deposited it onto her father's coffin. A sob escaped, and Gideon put his arm around her. Lightning flashed across the sky, and a loud clap of thunder rolled over the cemetery and echoed across the adjoining fields. When a few large raindrops fell, the minister stashed his prayer book inside his robe and darted back toward the church.

Gideon placed his hand on Helena's elbow and helped her, with his mother, Lydia, and Maria following, to their waiting coach he'd cleaned and made ready in case of rain. As the conveyance moved away and up the road, Helena turned back and saw the gravediggers shoveling the dark soil into her father's grave. Her dearest Papa. Tears flowed freely down her cheeks, and Gideon handed her his fresh handkerchief.

At the house, Helena could not force a bite of the scones or sandwiches between her lips, even with Gideon's gentle encouragement. She finally took a few sips of the hot tea he brought her. Except for his strong presence near her, she might never have made it through the tiring time. When the last visitor left, relief flooded her.

One thought kept piercing her sad heart, revving up her angst. Why had George Beauregard come to the funeral after the way her father had sent him packing the day she'd jumped into the Ashley River to escape the man's clutches? If Gideon had seen him, he gave no evidence of it.

She collapsed at the foot of the stairs and welcomed Gideon's strong arms catching her. Feeling protected, safe, she relaxed against him. He carried her upstairs and laid her on her bed. Bending near, he pressed a warm, wonderful kiss on her lips and left. Thunder clapped and lightning flashed over the plantation house, but it didn't disturb her. The sound of heavy rain pelting her bedroom windows lulled her into a grief-exhausted sleep.

~

The next morning Belle, as Gideon had requested, alerted him in his study that Helena had risen and had finished breakfast on the veranda. He must talk to her before Lawyer Becket arrived to read the will. He hurried up the steps and out to the balcony. Lovely morning sunshine, after the storm of the night, blazed across the plantation yard and flowed over Helena sitting at the small glass-topped white wicker table. Birds chirped in the tall oak trees beyond, but Gideon only had eyes for Helena. Dressed in her black gown and even with her eyes and nose still pink from grief, she was a most welcome sight to him. He pulled out a chair and sat.

Helena blotted her lips and greeted him. "Gideon, I've something to share with you that happened to me on the pirate ship."

His heart lurched. Had they harmed her?

She must have seen the concern that stiffened his face. "No, no, nothing bad. Something...good."

He drew in a deep breath. "Thank God. I've not told you how much I prayed even from the night of your abduction when we were sailing home, and I didn't even know anything had happened to you. But I felt led to pray fervently for you."

Helena's eyes widened, and she placed her hand near his resting on the table. "Really?"

"The Lord can and often does let us know when the enemy is attempting harm to a loved one, and we get an urge to pray."

Helena took a deep breath. "That's good to know. I had no idea about things like that. But your prayers did work, dear Gideon. You rescued me, but also the Lord met with me before you got there." She looked up into his eyes. "Because of your prayers."

Gideon's heart pounded, and he pressed Helena's hand. "I'm glad. Tell me about it. Then I've something to share with you."

She lowered her chin, but her eyes lit. "When I realized the horrid boss pirate planned to...sell me to a sultan on the Barbary Coast, I gave up all my pride, and I cried out to God to save and to help me. He answered my plea. A river of peace flowed through me. For the first time in all my life, I knew God was real and that Jesus Christ's death and resurrection meant I could be a new person, forgiven, strengthened, loved. Before, I only had a religious idea of who He was, but no real relationship."

Gideon's heart blossomed with joy, even with the unwelcome news he had yet to share with her lodged in his throat.

She lifted her face and looked into his eyes. Her voice broke. "I came to see how spoiled, unreasonable I'd been all my life. To our servants, whom I'd never appreciated or felt compassion for...and especially to you, who'd done nothing but good for me. I have carried a grudge since our marriage that you only married me to...get Windemere." Moisture brightened her eyes, and she leaned forward. "Oh, Gideon, I'm so sorry I've been such a poor wife to you." She stood. "And I don't care if Father did give you Windemere or any other plantation. I want to be the best wife to you I can be."

Warmth spread over Gideon like oil poured on his head. Did she mean what it sounded like? He rose and pulled her into his arms. He lifted her chin and planted a gentle kiss on her trembling lips, then he deepened the kiss until she was breathless. He finally raised his head and looked into her eyes, deep blue pools. "What you've shared is the best news I've heard in a long time, dear Helena."

Holding her, he released a deep, happy breath. Was their marriage in name only going to become real in every way? That thought sent spirals of excitement up his spine, and his mouth went dry. With heroic effort, he reined it all in. *The mortgages.* He must share about them before the lawyer came.

He swallowed, led her over to the small sofa, and sat beside her.

"There's something we must talk about. I came up here this morning before the family lawyer comes to read the will."

"Lawyer Becket's coming to read the will?"

"Yes. But I need to prepare you for a shock, my dearest." He took her hands into his, and she gazed into his face with her brow raised.

"Did you have any idea that your father...had a gambling habit?"

She grimaced. "I'm afraid so. My poor mother even knew it before she passed. I overheard her and Father talking one day when I was about twelve. I didn't understand all of it, but I heard her begging him to stop gambling."

Gideon relaxed. At least what he had to tell her wouldn't be a complete shock. "Well, dearest, I have to tell you, he apparently didn't quit gambling because...there are mortgages on all his properties, including Windemere."

Helena pulled back to stare at him. "Mortgages? Can't we pay them off?"

"Probably not without...selling some of the properties."

She frowned. "Which ones?"

Gideon cleared his throat. "That's what we will have to find out, decide." As fear darkened her eyes, he added, "I'm believing the cotton harvest here will help save Windemere."

Helena shook her head and stood. She walked to the veranda banister and gazed over it.

But did she see what Gideon saw—the idyllic, fragrant beauty of a summer morning at Windemere after a storm?

She turned back to stare at him. "I can't believe Papa would do this...to me, to us. And to think, all these months since we married, I've fretted that he gave Windemere to you to entice you to marry me. But he'd gambled it into debt and couldn't have." She flicked a tear from her cheek, then turned away.

He stood and went to her. Putting his arms around her waist from behind, he drew her into the crook of his arms. Nothing seemed as important as it had when he'd first learned of the debts. Helena wanted a real marriage. Peace and confidence baptized him. As if feeling his assurance, she relaxed against him and sighed.

Leaning down, he spoke softly into her ear. "There's one more perhaps surprising thing I need to tell you, dear. Promise me you won't let it destroy your happiness—what we're both feeling right now."

"I promise." With her head still pressed against his shoulder, her whispered words relieved him.

He took a deep breath. "George Beauregard holds all the mortgages."

She stiffened and pulled away from him to stare into his face. "George Beauregard?" Her voice rose with raw emotion.

"Yes, but I will deal with him. Don't worry yourself about it."

She moved from him and wrapped her arms around herself. Her lovely face changed to an angry red. "Now I understand. Now I know why he made his hateful comment at our wedding, and why he showed up at Father's funeral."

He put his hands on her shoulders, willing her to calm down. "I didn't see him at the funeral, and what did he say at our wedding?"

"He was in a back corner at Papa's service, and at our wedding, the pompous blackguard whispered to me while we stood at the door after the ceremony, 'Don't assume it's all over between us.'" She mimicked his mocking tone.

Gideon tried to draw her back into his arms, but she was stiff as a board. He lifted her chin. "Helena, now I remember your telling me that comment. But Beauregard was beaten, and he knew it."

She looked into his eyes. "But he's not beaten. He's beaten *us* if he can take the plantations." She pressed her face against his shoulder and groaned.

Gideon could only hold her and pray over her.

Later that day, they sat with Lawyer Joshua Becket in Gideon's study. The man confirmed Beauregard held the mortgages and for how much on Windemere, Allston Hall, the townhouse, and two of the ships.

Helena's face paled as Becket spelled out the amounts, but her jaw hardened into granite, and her blue eyes blazed. Gideon was proud of the calm Helena. No tears, no recriminations, no hints of retaliation. She had one question. "Sir, when do these mortgages have to be paid?"

Lawyer Becket seemed relieved she was not emotional as many women might be learning of such debt. He smiled. "The good news is that if you're a beneficiary of an estate, you do not personally inherit that estate's debts. But the estate cannot be settled by the probate court until all debts against it are paid. That usually takes some time, and the court could make allowances." He hesitated. "And the court usually will when an estate sale becomes necessary."

Helena had another question. "Is a sale what happens if an estate has more debts than assets?"

Gideon took a deep breath. Might as well get all the sad news.

Becket nodded. "Yes, if the estate has more debts than assets, it becomes an insolvent estate, and the assets are sold and used to pay off as much of the debt as possible. Once it's declared insolvent, the court would decide which assets must be sold and which debts paid first." He glanced back down at the legal papers on the table. "But I don't think yours will be judged insolvent." He looked back up at her and Gideon. "You may choose to sell one of the plantations and possibly one boat, and you could very well clear enough to pay off all the other mortgages."

Gideon spoke up. "Is that what you would advise, sir?"

Becket sat back in his chair. "Yes, unless there are other assets available such as cash, stocks, bonds, or jewelry that might add up to enough to pay off one or more of the mortgages." He looked at them questioningly. "I've handled Mr. Allston's business for years, but he never gave me a list of additional assets. Have either of you seen such a list or know of other assets?"

Gideon shook his head. "John never talked to me about any other assets." He glanced at Helena, whose expression became thoughtful.

"I'm...not sure," she finally admitted, and smiled at the lawyer.

Joshua Becket took his leave.

They accompanied him to the front entrance. As soon as he drove off in his carriage, Helena beckoned Gideon to follow her. Secrecy blanketed her attitude.

CHAPTER 16

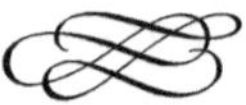

*H*elena led Gideon first to the kitchen, where she secured the housekeeper's extra set of keys from a nail inside a cabinet. Then she hurried up the stairs and across the landing to a narrow door in the far corner of the second-floor hall.

Gideon expressed surprise. "I've never noticed this door before. Where does it go?"

She smiled as she found a key and fitted it into the lock. "Come and see." Opening the door, she proceeded up a set of tall, narrow, winding steps, thankful for the small window along the way that provided the only light. The heat increased as she and Gideon ascended. Perspiration trickled down her back.

Finally, the steps ended at an unpainted door. She pulled another key from the ring and opened it. "This is where it leads, dear Gideon. Our Windemere attic." Turning back, she glanced into his face. "I've not been up here in years, but there's something I want to check on, and I know the heat is oppressive. Are you still with me?"

"I'm still with you, explorer lady." He pulled a handkerchief from his pocket and swiped his forehead.

She entered the attic onto the uncarpeted floorboards, the same wood as the strong overhead exposed cypress girders she remembered when her mother first brought her here. The musty smell of old paraphernalia shut away from sunshine and fresh air permeated the large room. Light streamed through one fair-sized window overhead and revealed dancing dust motes, faded sheets partially covering outdated furniture, old crates with their contents scribbled on their side, rolled-up rugs, picture frames, a dressmaker's dummy, and the inevitable animal scat on the floor.

"Ugh. Watch your step, Gideon," she called behind her. She stopped in the middle of the space and looked around. "Just give me a few moments to remember." Then she saw it. Her mother's large green trunk protruded from behind a tall mirror on a far wall. She hurried to it, grabbed the leather handle on the exposed end, and tried to pull the container toward the window's light. It barely budged.

"Helena, don't strain yourself. Let me help." Gideon caught up with her and pulled the trunk into the beam of light.

Helena tugged a small key on a ribbon from her pocket, then got on her knees in front of the trunk. She inserted the key and turned it until it clicked. Opening the top, she searched inside and pulled out a blue velvet box about the size of a shoebox. Blue was her mother's favorite color. She closed the trunk lid and set the box on top, then opened it. "This was my mother's special savings, as she called it. I'd almost forgotten about it." She pulled a string of pearls from the container and held them toward the light. Then a sapphire necklace. Her mother's favorite pieces made moisture gather in her eyes.

Scooting down on his haunches, Gideon whistled and reached out to touch the jewelry glistening in the beam of sunlight. "This reminds me of the jewels that fell out of your pocket after I rescued you from the river. And I remember a sack of gold coins too." He smiled at her.

She frowned. "But I had Papa put them in his safe when I returned home. Were they not there?"

Gideon's lips tightened "No, only the deeds...and mortgages. Sorry."

Helena bit her lower lip, then shook her head and laid the pearls and sapphire necklace aside. She pulled the smaller box over for Gideon to see inside. "But these papers are what came to my mind when Lawyer Becket mentioned bonds and stocks. Could this be some of that? It looks like certificates of some sort." She lifted one and handed it to Gideon, then lifted another to peruse herself.

She wiped the perspiration from her upper lip. "This says *United States American Revolutionary War Bond,* and it says it's worth seventy-five dollars."

Gideon's eyes widened as he looked at one she'd given him. "Helena, if these bonds are still valid, they could be worth something." He fingered the stack in the box. "Without counting them, I'd say they could be worth a good deal of money, if still good."

Helena gulped back tears. "My mother left me this box, and when we packed up her stuff, it went into the trunk. I never knew what these certificates meant. It's like she is reaching out from the grave to bless us, Gideon. Perhaps she invested in these after finding out about Papa's gambling." She set the blue box aside with the jewelry and closed the trunk.

Gideon reached over and caressed her cheek. "She must have loved you very much, and this was her way of trying to protect your inheritance. The next step we should take is to show these bonds to Becket. He'll know if they're valid and what they might be worth."

He stood and helped Helena to her feet, then drew her close. "But I think you need to keep the jewelry in memory of your mother." He touched her lips with his own, and a silken cocoon wrapped around her and dried her tears.

She looked up into his face and smiled. "Now let's get out of this heat, sir."

～

That afternoon, Lawyer Becket perused the bonds and gave Gideon some good news. "These were issued to pay off the Revolutionary War debt, and they are still valid." He leaned back in his chair and smiled at Gideon. "President Madison is honoring and paying face value for each bond with interest added. I believe you may have enough here to pay off the mortgage on Windemere."

Gideon left the man's office in excellent spirits and drove back to Windemere, with the sunset baptizing him in warm shades of deep pink, purple, and gold. He couldn't stop smiling, thinking about his good news to share about the bonds. And Helena's earlier testimony of God's move in her life filled him with hope. Even Becket reminding him they still had the other two mortgaged properties to deal with didn't diminish his happiness. A prayer kept whispering in his heart. *Thank you, Father God.*

He strode into the plantation, calling Helena's name, but just as quick, doubt assailed him. Would she still be in the same good mood of the past twenty-four hours? Was there hope of a new beginning for them?

His mother came from the parlor. "She retired early and should be in her room, I believe, son. You look as though you might have good news."

He gave her a kiss on her cheek. "I do, Mother. I most certainly do."

She smiled, and her eyes lit with happiness and with some kind of knowledge that had always intrigued him as a boy when he saw it in her face. "Then you best be quick about letting her know. Life is waiting for you two."

What could his mother mean? Had she guessed that he and Helena had never consummated their marriage?

He led her into the parlor and closed the door. "Mother, if you mean what I think you mean, you've guessed...all is not as it should be in our marriage?"

She smiled. "Yes, dear boy. Tell me, do you really love Helena with your whole heart?"

He ran his hand through his hair. "So much it hurts. Even the times she's acted like a spoiled child who distrusts me. My prayer has been that you, my dear mother, might help me know how to win Helena's heart."

His mother smiled her perceptive smile. "There's One I know who can help you win her heart, son, and when you love, you can count on it, He's on your side."

Hope filled the room and Gideon's heart. He opened the parlor door, strode up the stairs two at a time, and lifted his hand to knock at her bedroom door, but it opened for him.

Helena, radiant and more beautiful than he'd ever seen her in a lavender gown and robe, welcomed him. "I knew it would be you. I saw you ride up from my window." She opened the door wider, and he entered.

When he told her the good news about the bonds, she laughed and fell into his arms.

His first kiss on her tender lips kindled the fire in his heart into flame. And if the expression on Helena's face meant anything, she felt it too.

Gideon closed and locked the bedroom door.

~

Helena awoke happier than she could ever remember. She reached over to touch Gideon and found his side of the bed empty. She sat up, stretched, and whispered a prayer of thanksgiving. This thing called married life was going to be wonderful.

A knock sounded at the door. She called, "Enter."

Belle strode in, suppressing a smile. "Your husband said to tell you he's gone to check the cotton fields with Samson. I also need to tell you a visitor has just arrived asking to see you."

Helena frowned. "A visitor this time of morning?"

Belle gestured to the clock on the dresser. "This late time of morning."

Helena rose and walked barefoot to her washstand. "Who is it?"

"Mr. George Beauregard."

Helena dropped the cloth she was holding and bent to pick it up, glad Belle could not see the expression on her face. What could the man want? Did he come to gloat over the financial power he held over them?

She took her time dressing, hoping Gideon would return to face George. When she could no longer delay, she left her room and walked slowly down the stairs. As luck would have it, the man strolled out of the parlor when she was halfway down, looked up at her, and smiled. He was, as usual, dressed to the hilt in silks and satins, his favorite colors of blue and white, with black boots that his servant had likely spent hours polishing.

He held out both hands. "Hello, dear. I was beginning to wonder if you would see me, but I assured myself you were the too-proper little planation mistress to hold a grudge or leave a visitor waiting too long."

His smooth voice she'd never forgotten irritated her. Ignoring his outstretched hands, she strode past him and into the empty parlor.

He followed.

She walked to the mantel, turned, and looked at him, not offering to sit or asking him to take a seat. "Why have you come, George?"

He drew a step closer, and she backed up two. "Why do you think I've come? I was so sorry about your father's passing and..."

She interrupted him. "You came to gloat. How dare you cause my father to...lose so much gambling with you. I really wonder if you tricked him, used marked cards, or some such thing I've heard about."

His smile faded. "That, my dear, is a dangerous accusation. I've had duels fought in my name for just such talk. Men have died for words like those." Then he flicked a soft, thin hand heavy with rings across the lace at his wrist. "But I will ignore your accusation, my dear." A brittle smile creased his bearded face again. "I've come, as I said, to express my condolences. And to say I've always wanted only what is good for you." His face turned serious. "Helena, my dear..." He advanced toward her.

She stiffened and threw out her uplifted hand to stop him. "You've expressed your condolences. You can leave now." Helena scarcely recognized her own voice. Never had she spoken such harsh words to a visitor. A movement beyond George attracted her attention. Gideon's mother stood in the doorway.

Helena lowered her arm, smiled, and welcomed her. "Hello, Mother Falconer. This is an old family...friend, Mr. George Beauregard. He came to express his condolences but was just preparing to leave."

Gideon's mother came forward and greeted the man. "Pleased to make your acquaintance." She cast a glance at Helena. "And thank you for coming. I'm sorry my son, Gideon, is out on the plantation this morning, I believe."

George bowed. "That is my loss, ma'am, but I'm sorry to say, I cannot stay." He reached inside his coat and pulled out a thick, folded letter, which he offered to Helena. "Please accept my...thoughts I've taken the time to jot down."

With reluctance, Helena took the missive and pushed it into her skirt pocket. Anything to get him to leave.

Beauregard bowed again, picked up his hat and silver cane at the side table, and prepared to depart. At the door, he turned and gave one last, piercing look at Helena before stepping outside.

Shaken by that strange last gaze from him, she thanked God when he left.

Mother Falconer came to pat her hand. "My dear, I'm sorry, but I couldn't help but overhear your...other comment to the gentleman. The man is not a family friend, is he?"

Helena swallowed. "No, Mother Falconer, he is not, and he's not a gentleman, but I tried to be as...cordial as I could." She blinked, and heat rose in her face. Had Gideon told his mother any of her history with George Beauregard or about the mortgages? If not, Helena would not do so today. Not when she'd known such happiness when she awoke earlier. The memory of the night before in Gideon's arms sent a delicious tingle up her spine. She would not let George Beauregard's visit steal an ounce of her happiness. No matter what threat he might have written in the missive in her pocket. She'd burn it in her fireplace upstairs.

"Well, all these things do finally work out for our good, dear. Isn't that what the Bible promises us?"

Helena forced her tight face into a relaxed mode and smiled. "Yes, and I'm going to believe it."

Mother Falconer settled on the sofa with her embroidery, and Helena left. She stopped by the dining room for a cold scone and tea, then walked back to her room.

She threw George's letter into the fireplace and added kindling. But Belle would need to bring some tinder from the kitchen to ignite it in the bedroom this time of year. She moved to the bell rope and pulled it.

~

As Gideon rode up the farm road from the cotton fields with Samson beside him and Bentley loping along, he noticed a fancy carriage driving away at a fast clip up the front drive. He didn't recognize the conveyance. Who had visited this morning?

Dropping his horse off at the stable, he bid Samson good day and strode into the house and up the stairs. Was his lovely wife awake yet? His heart rejoiced at last night's memory of their love coming to full expression. He whispered a prayer thanking God for their blessed union.

Near her door, he ran into Belle just leaving Helena's room. She shook her head. "Why would anyone want to start a fire this time of year?"

Gideon only glanced at her and knocked at Helena's door.

"Enter."

He came in, and Helena flew into his arms. Gideon chuckled. How wonderful his life had become overnight. Lifting her chin, he kissed her soundly but discerned something was wrong. "Has something happened, my love? As we came up from the fields, I saw a carriage flying up the front drive. And are you cold?" At that moment, something crackled and spit on the hearth, and the pungent smell of smoke flowed into the room.

Helena pulled away from him and dropped down into one of the chairs in front of her bedroom window. When she gestured for him to join her, he sat next to her. Something had upset her. He was learning her moods fast.

"George Beauregard came to visit, he said to express his condolences, but of course, he came to gloat." Her voice was dry, her face shadowed.

"Is that all? The man doesn't know when he's beaten, does he? Don't let one thought about him distress you, dear wife."

"That's exactly how I feel. He gave me a letter, and I decided to burn it unread." She nodded toward the fireplace.

"What?" Gideon jumped up and dashed to the fireplace.

CHAPTER 17

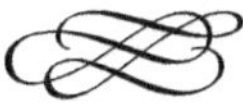

Gideon toasted his fingers before grabbing the poker to push the thick missive away from the spreading flame. He reached down, grabbed it, and blew on the smoking edge.

Helena spoke from behind him. "Dearest, what are you doing? I thought you said we mustn't let a thought of George steal our happiness. I'm sure he's gloating or making more threats."

Gideon came back to sit next to Helena, shaking the letter in the air. "All the more reason to see what the man has on his mind." He reached into his pocket for his small knife and slit the missive open, avoiding the hot, melted wax sealing it. He opened the folded sheets, read through them quickly, and whooped. "Helena, these are the original mortgages—all marked *paid*."

She leaned forward. "I don't believe it."

He handed the sheets to her.

She glanced through them. Her mouth dropped open, and her eyes widened. "What does it mean, Gideon?"

What could it mean? Did the hardened gambler Beauregard— who'd undoubtedly ruined quite a few folks' fortunes, if the gambling tales about him were true—have a complete change of heart? "Legally, I believe it means we are free from all the debts, but I have no idea why the man would do this." He looked closely at Helena. "Do you have any idea?"

She sniffed and lowered her face. "I have no idea. I've never given George Beauregard any kind of encouragement, even before I met you, Gideon." She swallowed and looked into his eyes. "Much less, after we...married."

"Well, tomorrow morning I'm off to Lawyer Becket just to make sure these documents are valid." He stood and pulled Helena into his arms. "But today let's relax and be thankful that it appears that God has delivered us. Windemere is safe as well as Allston Hall, your father's townhouse, and all the ships—if these documents prove it. And I think they will."

She looked up into his face. "Why are you so confident, my husband?"

He grinned. "It's not too hard for me to imagine that Beauregard would fall so in love with you he would take this bold kind of action to show it. You are incredibly special, you know." He kissed her forehead, then the top of her nose.

~

Helena harrumphed. But the memory of George's burning gaze at her before he'd left attempted to dissipate some of her denial. Shaking that thought away, she smiled at Gideon. "Hardly. I'm unaware that he's ever had a heart for anything or for anyone except gambling and taking advantage of foolish people who gamble with him."

He stopped her words with a deep kiss, then lifted his head. "Let's keep all this to ourselves for the time being, my dear, the mortgages and the hopeful cancellation. Do you agree?"

She answered by standing on her tiptoes and placing a warm kiss on his lips.

At the midday meal, Helena recognized sadness flitting over Maria's face during the conversations, and she took a deep breath. "Gideon, dear, have you any update on how we might help Maria get back to her home in Venezuela?" She spoke in Spanish and smiled at Maria.

Gideon swiped his lips with his napkin and nodded, then responded in the young woman's language. "I'm sure we'll be able to work out something in a few weeks, Maria. I have sailed in the Caribbean waters quite a few times in the past and look forward to a new trip there."

Maria's eyes brightened.

Gideon repeated his words in English for his mother and Lydia.

"That's wonderful, son." Mother Falconer smiled and patted Maria's hand beside her.

Lydia cleared her throat. "I have some personal news to share."

Helena turned toward her as did every other person at the table.

"I have a seamstress position offered to me at the Berkeley Fabric Emporium in Charleston, where we've traded since we came from England." Lydia swallowed and her face turned pink. "And I've prayed about it and believe it's the next step for me. I'll have my own private rooms above the shop." She smiled around the table.

"Lydia, that's wonderful," Helena exclaimed. "But we will miss you here." She glanced at Mother Falconer, who would feel the loss of her friend's companionship the most.

Gideon's mother smiled. "No one will miss her more than I will, but I, too, think it's a great opportunity she shouldn't pass up."

Lydia's eyes gleamed with moisture, and she ducked her head.

Gideon leaned back in his chair. "Of course, she shouldn't pass it up. Not if she feels it is in God's plan." He looked at her. "Congratulations, Lydia. I pray everything works out well. And remember, you still have a home here if you ever need it."

Helena smiled at her. "Yes, you certainly do, Lydia. And you'll always get my orders for any new clothing I might need."

The woman flicked a tear that escaped down her cheek. "Now look at that. You are making me cry, and I was determined not to. But thank you, all of you, for making me feel so welcome here." She stood. "Please excuse me, but I am in the process of packing. Mrs. Berkeley's son Robert will be picking me up in the morning."

Helena frowned. "So soon?"

Lydia nodded and left the dining room.

Mother Falconer laid down her napkin. "She told me about this last week, so I'm more prepared. She's been a best friend and helper to me. But this, I believe, is the new life she has been praying for."

The following morning, Helena sat in the parlor with Gideon's mother while they both worked on a piece of embroidery. "Have you seen Maria this morning?" Helena asked.

"Actually, she told me she wanted to visit in the kitchen with Marm Esther. Seems she likes Southern cooking and wants to learn how to cook certain dishes before she returns home. But I wonder if there might not be another attraction there."

"Another attraction?"

"She's told me she made friends with Kunta when he first arrived on the pirate ship and that he helped her in several ways. And I believe they're about the same age."

Before Helena could respond, Mrs. Laurens came to the door and announced a visitor at the front entrance.

Helena nodded at the woman. "It must be Lydia's Robert."

A tall, handsome man soon appeared in the doorway with the housekeeper. He bowed when he saw them and walked forward.

First, he held out his hand to Gideon's mother. "You must be Mrs. Rhett? Robert Berkeley."

She nodded and shook his hand.

Then he turned to Helena. "And, Helena Falconer, I believe? Lydia has told us a lot about you two. I feel I know you."

Helena shook the firm hand and found the man's brown eyes intelligent and steady.

Footsteps sounded down the stairs, and Lydia appeared in the doorway. Two servants held her bags. When her eyes met those of Robert Berkeley, the woman's cheeks turned a bright pink. And the man stood straighter and fidgeted with his cravat.

So that is how it is between these two. Delighted, Helena smiled and came forward.

"Lydia, we've just met Mr. Berkeley, and I'm glad to say, we are releasing you into capable hands. Is that not so, Mother Falconer?"

She stood as well. "Yes, that is." She hugged Lydia and probably would've hugged Robert Berkeley, but he turned and lifted all three bags as if they were featherweights.

With just as much ease, it seemed God was looking out for all of them.

~

The following day, Gideon assured a skeptical Helena that the mortgages were truly marked paid on their properties. She stood at her bedroom window. "I do believe that is the sheriff riding up."

Coming to stand beside her, Gideon nodded. "Wonder what he wants. Let's go down."

Gideon greeted the sheriff, and he and Helena led him into the parlor. The big man in his gray uniform with its shiny silver badge made the room seem smaller, especially when Bentley lumbered in behind him.

The lawman patted the big blond head of the dog begging for a touch, then removed his hat. He looked up at Gideon and Helena. "Good to see you two again. I've got some news which may surprise you."

"Won't you have a seat, sir?" Helena gestured to a chair.

He shook his head and fingered his hat. "No, no, I don't have that much time, but I did want to tell you the latest development."

Gideon cocked his chin and folded his arms across his chest. "We're all ears."

"One of the younger pirates we arrested made an interesting confession late yesterday evening after we separated him from the others to question him. We told him if he told the whole truth, it might go easier on him. He said that a man by the name of George Beauregard paid the boss pirate to abduct you, Mrs. Falconer." His steady gaze remained on Helena. "Do you know the man?"

Helena gasped. "Yes, sheriff, we do." She sank onto the sofa. "And you say he paid the pirates to...?"

Gideon came to stand beside her. "He was once a family friend but had ceased to be. George came to see us the day before yesterday, he said to express his sympathy for the passing of Mr. Allston. I was out on the plantation, but Helena did meet with him briefly."

"The day before yesterday? He came here?" The sheriff's eyes flew from Gideon to Helena.

Helena sighed. "Yes, he did, much to my discomfort." She lowered her head and fingered her skirt.

The sheriff balled a fist and slammed it into his other palm. "That's interesting. You might have been the last one to see him."

Gideon laid his hand on Helena's shoulder. "What do you mean?"

"I did some investigating and went out this morning to arrest him at his Cooper River estate. It's completely abandoned, not a single servant on the place or even a chicken scratching in the barnyard. His sloop was also gone. That vessel was a seaworthy vessel from all accounts of those who knew him. It's our opinion he has escaped to heaven knows where."

Helena took a deep breath. "But...the pirate boss told me he was...going to sell me to a Mediterranean sultan on the Barbary Coast."

The sheriff nodded. "Yes, the boss pirate took Beauregard's money to abduct you, and all the time, the pirate planned to deceive the man and do just that."

Helena turned to glance at Gideon, her face stiff and pale. Gideon's blood boiled to think that George had stood right in this room two days ago. Had his plan been to get Helena to go with him by choice or by force? But he ended up giving her the letter after his mother came into the parlor. Thank God his mother had entered when she did.

Helena glanced at him with an appeal in her eyes, and Gideon understood. She would not want to reveal the information about John Allston's debt and mortgages Beauregard had held. What good could it do now? Let her father's good name stay as clean as possible.

"Sir, thank you for sharing this further news with us." He glanced down at Helena. "We are shocked to learn that George Beauregard instigated the abduction...but very thankful it failed. And thank you for all the help you and your men have been."

Sheriff Graddy set his hat neatly back on. "You're most welcome. We'll keep an eye out for that sloop if it ever returns to Charleston. I have to say, I doubt we'll see the man again. He knows we'll arrest him if he shows up here. The bank in town confirmed that Beauregard had withdrawn all his funds and closed his accounts. And we're locking up his plantation estate till a judge decides what to do with it." He took his leave. "Good day to both of you."

After the man left, Gideon took Helena's hand and pulled her to her feet and into his arms. He gave her a warm hug. "I think we've seen the last of Beauregard, dear. We can enjoy our lives in peace." He sat his chin on her head and delighted in her clean, womanly scent with a sprinkle of lavender.

Helena pulled back and looked up into his face. "Why do you think Geoge paid off the mortgages before he escaped in his sloop?"

Gideon took a deep breath. "I don't know. Perhaps the man retained one drop of goodness in his character, and he wanted to make some kind of restitution. Especially when he realized the pirates would eventually talk and implicate him to gain legal favor. He knew he had to sail away." He looked deep into her lovely eyes. "Now we are going to get busy planning the trip for Maria to travel home. If we are going to sail her to Venezuela, we need to get it done before our cotton comes into harvest."

Helena's brow knit. "We?"

"Of course, *we*. Do you think I'd sail off into the lovely warm southern trade winds without the love of my life? We'll have a grand time." He hugged her tighter. "A real honeymoon." His heart lurched at her continued hesitation. "You're not reluctant to sail with me, are you?"

She circled her arms around his strong neck. "No, every reluctant thought in my heart has been eradicated by love." Then she lifted her lips for his passionate kiss.

EPILOGUE

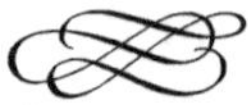

Six weeks later—The Caribbean

Gideon stood on the quarterdeck holding the *Victoria* firm as it sailed over the capping Caribbean Sea. The brisk trade winds filled the sails, helping them make excellent time since leaving the coast of Venezuela, heading home to Charleston.

Helena came to stand beside him. "How soon will we be home, dear one?"

"About two weeks, if these good winds hold."

"I've loved every minute of this trip, Gideon. You're an excellent captain."

With one arm, he drew her to him. "I've enjoyed it, too, my love. But home is calling. I know Samson is hoping we make it back before the cotton harvest begins."

"Will we?"

"We should." He looked down into her face. Concern flickered over him. After all their time sailing in the Caribbean to take Maria home, his wife seemed paler than the day they had left Charleston weeks earlier.

Helena gazed out to sea. "We shouldn't have let Maria's parents talk us into staying a week, but she has such a precious family. And what do you think about Kunta coming with us, then asking to stay in Venezuela? Do you think he'll ever come back to Windemere?"

Gideon laughed. "That's the biggest surprise of all. Him and Maria. But they are young. Too young, I think, to know their minds."

"Well, her family really liked him. He just glowed around them. Could it be God's plan for him to stay? Kunta may find more lasting acceptance with them than with some in Charleston." Helena turned back to glance at Gideon. "At least he and I had some good talks on the way down. I feel as if I know my half brother better. But I do wonder how Marm Esther will take his leaving Windemere."

Gideon chuckled. "Oh, that dear woman might think of it as a relief. She's worked hard trying to steer Kunta right. Besides, your father left him one hundred acres when he comes of age, so we will see him back one day."

Belle appeared on deck and moved to the quarterdeck steps. "My lady, has it occurred to you this is napping time in this southern clime? Most of the crew are snoring in their hammocks."

Gideon cast a loving look at Helena. "Dear, you are most welcome to go below and take a nap, if you feel like it. I've heard you up early several mornings."

Helena lowered her chin. "Yes, I've not been feeling well some mornings, but I feel fine now." She smiled. "However, a little lie down might be good because after dinner I want to watch the sunset with you steering the ship."

She left with Belle.

Left alone in the bright sunlight, capping waves, and cooling ocean breeze, Gideon's dream of freeing the Windemere slaves took hold of him. With the expected funds from the cotton harvest, he might be able to free them and offer wages. With the terrible mortgage threat over, everything good seemed possible. He began to whistle.

~

*L*ying on her bed with the porthole open bringing in the fresh sea breeze, Helena yawned and smiled. Tomorrow she would tell Gideon her news. Or should she wait until they arrived home? Who was she kidding? Every morning now, she had to rise and hang over the boat railing a few minutes until the nausea passed. Gideon would soon guess her news. Some of the crew must know already. Belle had guessed right away.

She touched her abdomen and smiled. If it were a boy, would Gideon agree to name him after her father? And if a girl? Maybe after his mother, Merle? Filled with awe at the new life growing within her, the future seemed hopeful and blessed. How could it not be with a God-fearing man like Gideon beside her? In her heart, she knew that their relationship with Jesus Christ brought assurance that He held their future in His hands.

She turned on her side and soon fell asleep.

ABOUT THE AUTHOR

Elva Cobb Martin is a retired school teacher, a mother, and grandmother who lives in South Carolina with her husband and high school sweetheart, Dwayne. She grew up on a farm in South Carolina and spends many vacations on the Carolina Coast. Her southern roots run deep.

A life-long student of history, her favorite city, Charleston, inspires her stories of romance and adventure. Her love of writing grew out of a desire to share exciting love stories of courageous characters and communicate truths of the Christian faith to bring hope and encouragement. She always pauses for historic houses, gardens, chocolate, and babies of any kind.

If you'd like to keep up with Elva's escapades, find her and a newsletter sign up at http://www.elvamartin.com or stalk her on

Facebook, Twitter, and Pinterest. She'll be glad to alert you when future books are available.

And guess what? She loves to hear from readers! Feel free to drop her a note at elvacmartin@gmail.com

In addition to the Charleston Brides Series, Elva Cobb Martin is author of:

The Barretts of Charleston Series
Book 1: In a Pirate's Debt
Book 2: Summer of Deception

Non-fiction
Power Over Satan: A Bible study on the believer's authority

AUTHOR'S NOTE

With this story, I planned to develop a heroine like Helena who had everything she wanted, including religion, but who had no real relationship with Jesus Christ. Isn't that like many in America today with all our many blessings but no active love for Christ, His written Word, or His love for our fellow man, including the precious unborn and His plan for biblical marriage and gender? Yet our name may be on some church roll and we call ourselves a Christian. I believe our Mighty God is calling America back to Him in faith and obedience to the Bible. I believe He is calling forth new leaders who will stand for truth and righteousness, but we must go to the polls and help raise them up. America has a mighty history, some of it disheartening, but focusing our hearts and minds on Christ gives us courage and confidence, and we can look to the future with hope in our hearts.

And, like Helena, we can cry out to God in humble repentance and return with our whole heart, and He will always answer. Here is a simple prayer I invite you to pray:

Father God, I believe Jesus Christ is Your Son You sent to save me from my sins. I repent and turn from them to You and Your Word. Come into my heart, be not only my Savior, but my Lord and director of my decisions.

Help me find a Bible-preaching church family and do my part in bringing America back to You. I believe You are working mightily in my life, family, and nation, and I give You praise. Amen

Book 1: The Pirate's Purchase

Book 2: The Sultan's Captive

Book 3: The Petticoat Spy

Book 4: The Sugar Baron's Governess

Book 5: The Lieutenant's Secret Love

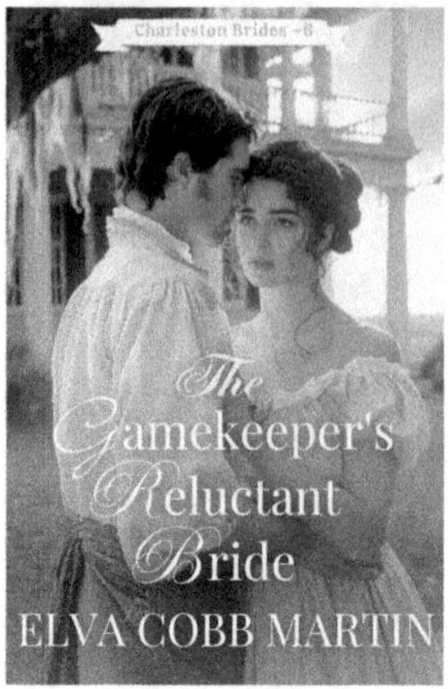

Book 6: The Gamekeeper's Reluctant Bride

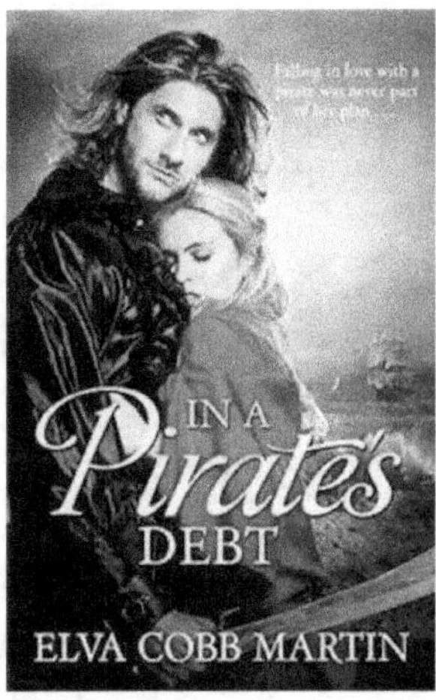

Chapter One

Jamaica, 1720

Marry Sir Roger Poole? Never! Travay Allston rushed up the staircase and into her bedroom. She eased the door shut and sank against it, hoping the men downstairs had not heard her flight. She wrapped her arms around her middle to prevent loud sobs from escaping. Tears ran down her cheeks onto her dinner gown. How could her stepfather, Karston Reed, gamble away the plantation *and her hand in marriage* in a game of cards? Lighting a small candle, she sprang into action. How much time did she have?

Travay snatched the men's clothing she'd stashed under a floorboard after her mother's untimely death. Somehow she had known the day would come when she would have to leave secretly. She quickly donned breeches, shirt, and knee boots. The oversized top required a belt, and she contrived one from a scrap of cloth. She flattened her curls tighter to her head with extra pins and struggled to stuff the mass under a cap. Her fingers brushed against her mother's locket. *Oh, Mama, I miss you!*

From the back of a drawer, she retrieved a leather coin purse filled with her savings from seventeen birthdays and stuffed it into her pocket.

Swallowing the huge lump in her throat, Travay swung her mother's dark cloak over her shoulders. Her reflection in the candlelit mirror caught her attention. A slender young man stared back at her with troubled blue eyes and a stray auburn ringlet springing from under a sailor's cap.

Travay tucked in the curl and lifted her chin. Somehow she would make it to Kingston. She would secure passage on a ship to Charles Town to her aunt, her only living relative. She pushed a small knife into the top of her boot like she'd seen her stepfather's overseer do, and darted from the room.

Could she make it to Kingston parish and to her mother's old minister friend before her stepfather and Sir Roger discovered she was missing?

A gusty wind with the threat of rain whipped across her hot face as she hastened down the servants' steps at the back of the house. The moon sailed in and out of clouds like a ghostly galleon, and she sought the shadows while running across the lawn to the barn. The slaves would be in their cabins at this late hour, including Ruby Grace, her personal maid. A sob escaped Travay's lips. The young African girl, Travay's only friend, might bear the brunt of this night's decision. Her stepfather would assume the slave knew of her mistress's plan to run away, and he would order the girl beaten.

A horse's soft nicker met Travay as she entered the shadowy stable. She slipped the bridle over Arundel's head, tossed the saddle onto the silky black back, and tightened the cinch. Opening the stable door, she led the filly out and mounted. At the touch of Travay's knee and the sound of her whisper, the horse paced across the stable yard toward the main entrance.

A high-pitched neigh trumpeted across the front lawn as they neared the house. Travay stiffened. The two men inside could not miss hearing Sir Roger's stallion, which was tied at the steps. Arundel tossed her head, and Travay urged her to a gallop.

Twisting in the saddle as they passed the front of the plantation house, Travay saw a lantern move across the front window toward the staircase. Her stepfather and Sir Roger would be calling up to her. How long would it take them to realize she had run away?

She leaned forward and urged the surefooted Arundel down the ribbon of road and onward, past wind-blown acres of sugarcane that weaved and stretched toward her like sentinels guarding her escape. A crack of lightning split the sky, followed by a deafening boom of thunder. Travay trembled but did not slacken the pace.

Before they reached the crossroads, hoofbeats pounded behind them. Travay bit the side of her lip and tasted blood. It could only be Roger Poole on the mount he'd ridden to Allston Hall, reputedly the fastest horse on the island.

She turned Arundel left at the crossroads, hoping she could make it past the field worker huts and onto the open road toward Kingston before Sir Roger caught up with her. Surely the minister and his wife would shelter her until she could secure passage to Charles Town. The moon disappeared behind turbulent clouds, enveloping her and Arundel in the safety of darkness. "Thank you, God—if you're up there," she whispered.

Half a mile down the road, the salty scent of the wind jerked Travay's head up. She clenched her teeth. How could she have taken the fork to the ocean instead of the road to Kingston? Confusion fogged her brain as her pursuer grew closer.

Arundel came to a bone-jolting halt at the edge of the cliff over-looking the Caribbean. The filly snorted and reared. Travay gripped the reins and moved the horse as far back as possible into a shadowy grove. What should she do? Sir Roger would soon be upon them. Gripped with indecision, she leaned across Arundel's hot neck and patted her, trying to calm the animal, while a cold sweat dotted her own brow.

Roger Poole reined in and headed for the thicket. The moon

sailed from behind a cloud and revealed his sickening smirk. "I know you're in there, Travay. Come out, my dear."

His lustful laugh, the odor of stale tobacco, and his heavy perfume carried on the wind. Shivers of revulsion drew Travay's stomach into a knot, as had all the man's advances since her mother's death. Arundel pawed the soft earth.

"I'll never marry you, Sir Roger. I don't care what my stepfather promised. Why don't you leave me alone?" She ground the words out between her teeth.

"You want to have a little rendezvous now, right here at Lovers' Leap? Then you'd marry me for sure, dear girl. Yes?" His voice was hoarse with rum and anticipation.

Travay froze and clutched the reins tighter. Would he dare? And in this deserted area of the coast, who would hear even her loudest scream? The saliva dried in her mouth. Then a memory, an old story, swept across her chaotic mind. Was the legend true about the girl who jumped from the cliff into the bay below and lived to tell about it?

Sir Roger dismounted and tied the stallion's reins to a small tree. Now his threatening form blocked her escape up the road. He stood with his fists propped on his hips. "Why do you think I came to Jamaica? I watched you growing up in Charles Town and knew one day I'd make you mine, whether I won your hand gambling or by some other method."

The moon cast an evil glow on his handsome, falcon-sharp features. Approaching his mid-thirties, he was still as strong and wiry as younger men—and attractive to most women, if the servants' tales were true. Tonight his silk cloak swirled around him in the wind like the ebony wings of a bird of prey. His arrogant voice did not move her, but the way he accented the words *by some other method* chilled her.

Travay tried to swallow, but her throat was bone dry. Taking a deep breath that ended with a sob, she turned Arundel and coaxed her out of the copse. She leaned close to the horse's wet neck and whispered, "Forgive me, my sweet friend. Jump high and wide. If we die tonight, we die together." *Please God, don't let us get caught on the rocks.*

Arundel blew air through her nose, arched her neck, and side-stepped toward the figure blocking their way up the road.

"That's my girl." Sir Roger sauntered closer and reached for the bridle.

With a gut-wrenching cry, Travay wheeled her mount around toward the sea and swung her riding crop down on the powerful rump. Arundel reared with a high-pitched squeal and shot forward.

Behind her, curses exploded from Sir Roger's mouth.

Travay screamed as she and Arundel hurtled over the cliff's edge. The mare's body slammed into the water. Travay's forehead collided with the horse's neck as the sea sucked them both into its shadowy depths.

Captain Lucas "Bloodstone" Barrett rowed up the bay at twilight with Sydney, his cabin boy, to fish for sea trout. When they reached the cove close to a cliff's rock wall, Lucas brought up his oar and set the anchor. He removed his leather baldric, which held his rapier and pistols, and launched a hook into the deep water. The boy cast his line on the other side of the boat.

For several days, Barrett had kept his brigantine hidden in an inlet on the backside of the island until the careening of the ship's hull could be completed. His raucous, sweating, and bare-chested crew had labored in the southern sun all day. Scraping the barnacles that had attached to the underside of the ship and patching places that had begun to rot had taken three days. Tonight, in celebration that the difficult, dangerous job was done, he knew his men would drink themselves into a rum stupor. They would pick quarrels and fight amidst the cursing and vulgarities Bloodstone no longer enjoyed.

As pirates went, they were as tough as any. And he had to command their respect at all times, or he'd find a mutiny on his hands. Fishing, when he got a chance, provided a little diversion from their offensive behaviors.

"Sydney, you be sure and watch that line. These waters used to be full of sea trout. I am expecting to take a catch back to the ship."

"Sure, Cap'n. I got me eyeballs peeled for the lit'lest quiver in this here string." The thirteen-year-old leaned over the side of the yawl.

Lucas's line jerked and grew taut, then slackened as the fish slipped away. He bit back a word he'd been trying to eliminate from his vocabulary since meeting Reverend Wentworth.

A terrible scream from the rock cliff above riveted his attention upward. A horse and rider flew over the longboat and plunged into the bay a stone's throw away from Lucas' boat. Waves rocked and scraped their small craft against the rock wall.

"Blimey!" Sydney dropped his short pole. "Cap'n, you see that?"

Lucas dropped his fishing line and searched the churning water where the two had disappeared. Iron bands tightened across his chest. "Yes. May God have mercy on them."

"I trove it was just a boy in that saddle! What we gonna do?"

Pebbles slid down the rock embankment above them. Lucas motioned for Sydney to be quiet. A man's angry voice above them loaded the evening air with curses. Next, the sound of galloping hooves confirmed someone leaving the top of the cliff.

The captain peeled off his shirt, stuck a knife between his teeth, and dove into the bay. The moon sailed from behind a cloud and revealed the dark forms of the horse and rider plunging about in the deep water below the surface. Lucas swam down toward them, praying he would be in time. He reached the limp form of the rider, whose long hair floated up into his face. He brushed the strands from his vision and loosened the boot caught in a stirrup. The horse, struggling to rise, had its reins caught between two rocks. Lucas hacked them loose, then pulled the rider to the surface. The horse surfaced beyond them and swam toward the opposite shore, emerged, shook, and trotted away.

Lucas swam back to the boat with the rider in tow. He pushed the cold body with its deathly pale face into the boat and then climbed in himself. He slung the person and his dripping mane of hair over his lap and pounded on the undersized back. As the soft curve of a bosom pressed onto his knees, Lucas' hand stopped in midair.

The person coughed and spewed vomit on Lucas' boots. "Stop it, you're killing me." The irate, feminine voice left no doubt about gender.

The captain glanced at Sydney.

The boy's mouth dropped open. "Swounds! Cap'n Bloodstone, it's a milady."

The girl issued another sharp command. "Let me up!" She kicked and squirmed.

"Yes, ma'am." Lucas placed his hands about the small waist, hidden among layers of a soaked shirt, and lifted her from his lap.

He set her on the rower's bench and held her steady a moment. She pushed his hands away, bent forward, and retched again. He moved his feet just in time.

Travay wiped her mouth and clawed dripping strands of hair from her face. She peered through the mist at her rescuers, a man and a boy. Both wore bandanas tied around their heads and bright sashes around their waists. The man's wet, bare chest and muscular arms glistened in the moonlight. Something about his untamed look and scent of sea and spice caused her heart to hammer against her ribs. Captain Bloodstone—that was what the boy had called him.

Above them, a rock dislodged and tumbled down the cliff. Travay looked up. Fear struck her heart. She jumped back into the captain's lap.

"If you are worried about your pursuer, ma'am, he is gone."

His deep, confident voice sounded like that of a gentleman, and the strong arms he placed around Travay comforted her but did nothing to clear the confusion in her mind. *What pursuer?*

The captain's heart beat against Travay's shoulder, and the welcome warmth from his body enveloped her, reminding her of when she sat on her father's lap as a child. She twisted to glance at his face. He smiled, and she could not help admiring his square jaw, slim mustache, and white teeth. His breath feathered her cheek, but a mischievous glint emanated from bright eyes. Who was he really? And fie! What was she doing jumping onto his lap?

Travay pushed away from him and crawled back onto the rower's bench. Shivers shook her whole body, and dizziness flowed over her in waves. She touched a bump on her forehead and clasped her arms. She tried to focus on her rescuers and to recall what had happened to bring her into their longboat. The young man's gold hoop earrings twinkled as the boat rocked with the tide. A gleaming silver sword and a carved leather baldric lay on the floor of the boat. She glanced across the bay. The moon sailed from behind a cloud and illuminated a sleek brigantine bobbing with the tide. A black flag waved from its masthead.

Pirates. Murdering, thieving pirates.

Darkness crept over Travay, and she slumped forward.

If you love historical romance, check out our other Wild Heart books!

The Heir's Predicament by Lorri Dudley

He controls the answers to her past and future, but she threatens his inheritance and his heart.

Maggie Prescott may not know her real name, the circumstances of her birth, or her father's identity, but based on a song her shipwrecked birthmother taught her before she died, Maggie's certain the answers lie on the island of Antigua. Unbeknownst to her beloved adopted family, she sends her maid to finishing school in her stead and convinces her uncle, Captain Anthony Middleton, to sail her to the Leeward Islands. Time is of the essence to discover her heritage before the next family gathering exposes her duplicity.

Lord Samuel Fredrick Harcourt Granville was groomed to inherit the Cardon title and lands, but the possession of his father's temper has put Samuel's future in jeopardy. After discovering his fiancée cavorting with his so-called friend, the ensuing altercation lands Samuel in court before the House of Lords. As an example, for all aristocratic sons to quell their hedonistic living, the House of Lords banishes Samuel to the island of Antigua until he can prove he's worthy of his privileged birth.

On the island, Samuel works to rein in his temper and revive a dying sugar plantation. Still, his return to England and all his efforts are threatened when a mysterious woman breaks into his island home, claiming to be the true heiress of the sugar plantation. Guilt, resentment, and fresh yearnings sizzle under the island sun as Maggie's search uncovers a much greater treasure than either of them expected.

Revealing the Truth by Lorri Dudley

His suspect holds a secret, but can he uncover the truth before she steals his heart?

When Katherine Jenkins is rescued from the side of the road, half-frozen and left for dead, her only option is to stay silent about her identity or risk being shipped back to her ruthless guardian, who will kill to get his hands on her inheritance and the famous Jenkins Lipizzaner horses. But even under the pretense of amnesia, she cannot shake the memory of her sister and Katherine's need to reach her before their guardian, or his marauding bandits, finish her off. Will she be safe in the earl's manor, or will the assailant climbing through her window be the death of her?

British spy, Stephen Hartington's assignment to uncover an underground horse-thieving ring brings him home to his family's manor, and the last thing he expected was to be struck with a candlestick upon climbing through the guest chamber window. The manor's feisty and intriguing new house guest throws Stephen's best-laid plans into turmoil and raises questions about the timing of her appearance, the convenience of her memory loss, and her impeccable riding skills. Could he be housing the horse thief he'd been ordered to capture—or worse, falling in love with her?

❧

A Heart's Forever Home by Lena Nelson Dooley

A single lawyer whose clients think he needs a wife.

A woman who needs a forever home...or a forever family...or a forever love.

Although Traesa Killdare is a grown woman now, the discovery that her adoption wasn't finalized sends her reeling. Especially when her beloved grandmother dies and the only siblings she's ever known exile her from the family property without a penny to her name.

Wilson Pollard works hard for the best interest of his law clients, even those who think a marriage would make him more "suitable" in his career. And when the beloved granddaughter of a recently deceased client comes to him for help, he knows he must do whatever necessary to make her situation better.

As each of their circumstances worsen, a marriage of convenience seems the only answer for both. Traesa can't help but fall for her new husband—the man who's given her both his home and his name. But what will it take for Wilson to realize he loves her? Will a not-so-natural disaster open his eyes and heart?